Praise for *A Study in Honor*

"A gritty, fast-paced investigation with a memorable and compelling duo of main characters. I can't wait to see what Janet and Sara get up to next."

—Aliette de Bodard, Nebula Award–winning author of
The House of Binding Thorns and *The Tea Master and the Detective*

"*A Study in Honor* is a fast-moving, diverse science-fictional Holmes and Watson reinterpretation set in near-future Washington, DC. As a deliciously intersectional makeover of a famous literary duo it's enormously satisfying. Clean, clear, and vastly enjoyable."

—Nicola Griffith, Lambda Literary
Award–winning author of *So Lucky*

"An entertaining and empathetic dystopian procedural that navigates the capital of an America at war with itself, tracking the path to recovery from personal and national trauma."

—Christopher Brown, author of *Tropic of Kansas*

"O'Dell's prose is sharp and clean, rising at times to the poetic, and her near-future Washington, DC, feels like a real city. The USA of *A Study in Honor* is a place with deep political divisions, and some of that comes into play in this story. It feels appropriately complicated as a future, and not a simplistic future vision of now."

—*Locus*

"Readers who pick this up for the novelty of Watson and Holmes as black women will be impressed by how well O'Dell realizes them as full, rich characters. This is a real treat for fans of Conan Doyle and SF mysteries."

—*Publishers Weekly*

A
Study
in Honor

A
Study
in Honor

Claire
O'Dell

HARPER Voyager
An Imprint of HarperCollins *Publishers*

HarperCollins books may be purchased for educational, business, or sales promotional use. For information, please email the Special Markets Department at SPsales@harpercollins.com.

Harper Voyager and design are trademarks of HarperCollins Publishers LLC.

FIRST EDITION

Designed by Paula Russell Szafranski

Frontispiece © thongyhod/Shutterstock

Library of Congress Cataloging-in-Publication Data has been applied for.

ISBN 978-0-06-269930-5

18 19 20 21 22   LSC   10 9 8 7 6 5 4 3 2 1

To my son, Matt—

For your poetry and your persistence

1

AUGUST 20. *Almost home. Well, for some definition of* almost *and* home. *No thanks to the U.S. Army or Amtrak. We were already six hours behind schedule when we transferred from the military line in Pittsburgh. No sooner did we board the new train than Amtrak announced its own delay. Something about repairs to the switch. Why was I surprised? It was the same as when I shipped out, except the train heading west wasn't nearly as crowded as this one. Thirty of us from Alton, Illinois, all medical discharges, not to mention the civilians we collected along the way. I'm not the only one missing pieces of myself. I sometimes think . . .*

The train rattled around a curve. My pen skipped over the journal page, leaving a blurry green trail. I muttered a curse, softer because of those same civilians, and was about to continue writing when the digital screen at the head of the car switched on and the loudspeaker crackled. "Union Station. Next stop, Union Station. Passengers bound for Raleigh and Charlotte, transfer here."

The woman next to me, a grandmother returning from a family visit in Baltimore, immediately gathered up her bags from the floor. Others—civilians as well—crowded toward the exit doors, even though we had at least fifteen minutes before the station. Mitchell, a sergeant ending his fourth tour of duty, offered me a wry grin. *Civs. No discipline.* I shrugged and occupied myself with finishing off my journal entry.

---

we have five or six wounded coming home from our so-called War in Oklahoma for every one who's whole and sound. Again, why the surprise? No one ever believed the rebellion would stay put in one state. And I wasn't the only one who doubted we'd see peace within two years. Or four. These past twelve months, though

---

I had to pause, to swallow the panic that boiled up whenever I thought about the war, especially anything to do with this past and most disastrous year. *Stop whining,* I told myself. I had volunteered all on my lonesome. I knew what I was getting into. Same as Mitchell over there. Or the hundreds of patients I had operated on. We all had different reasons, some of them honorable, some of them damned practical. Some of us had left because life left us few choices.

Angela had said I only wanted the glory of war.

My sister had stared at me in disbelieving silence when I told her I wanted to make a difference, in the only way I could.

My parents had said nothing. Perhaps they understood they could not change my mind.

Whatever our reasons, none of us had bargained for the shame called Alton, Illinois. *I* had not bargained that I would face the enemy myself. Stupid belief, really. As if a civil war would draw neat and permanent boundaries between our enemies and theirs. My hand still trembling with that remembered fear, I took up my pen and continued to write.

. . . have been the worst. The ordinary citizen rants about our failed economy. (And you won't get no argument from me about that.) Congress yammers how we should have conquered these rebels five, six years ago. Oh, yes, and those New Confederacy rebels are angrier than ever, their guns are bigger and badder and scarier than ever before.

Another jolt sent my pen point stabbing through the paper.

I gave up and shut my journal. I could finish that entry later, once I settled into my hotel. Once I had adjusted to the idea of coming home at last, if only for a few days.

The train jumped onto another set of rails, then settled into a glide as we passed over Florida Avenue. The gas stations and cinder-block storefronts of Northeast DC, even older and more desolate than before, abruptly gave way to the high-rise office buildings of downtown. The last words on the digital sign slid past, to be replaced by a clock counting down the minutes and seconds to arrival.

Three years ago, I had boarded a train much like this one. My possessions had included several intangibles as weighty as the duffel bag I carried: a medical degree from Howard University, three years' residency at Georgetown University Hospital, the belief that I ought to serve my country. Now? Now my mother and father were dead, killed in a terrorist attack in the Atlanta airport. My sister had sold our family home in Suitland, Maryland, and used her half of the inheritance to move to the opposite side of the country. The woman I had loved had written to tell me of her engagement to someone else. The loss of my arm was simply the last and most visible manifestation of time's passage.

As if the thing could translate emotions as well as electrical impulses, my left arm twitched, sending a ripple along the metallic mesh that covered its mechanics. The prosthetic had been retrofitted from a more heavily muscled soldier, one of the many casualties in the latest assault, and its electronics were less than reliable.

The edge of the platform flashed past my window. The digital sign clicked off. Almost there. My pulse gave an uncomfortable leap. Was there anything left here for me, other than old memories and a chance for the future?

I told my pulse to behave itself and stowed my journal and pen in my duffel bag, then extracted myself from my seat to head after Mitchell, who was already stumping down the aisle with the other veterans. Mitchell had served in Syria and the second Iraq occupation, before the uprising inside our own borders forced President Sanches to withdraw our troops. He would have served a fifth tour on the Illinois front, except for the IED that had taken off his leg.

"Captain Watson," he said when we reached the exit doors. "Good luck."

"And to you, Sergeant," I replied.

A final salute, though we no longer merited one. Then we were each taking turns climbing down the metal steps to the concrete platform.

The dense summer heat poured over me. I sucked down a breath filled with the reek of oil and the hot metallic smell from the tracks. August in DC. No wonder Congress went into recess. I swung my duffel bag over my shoulder, checked my grip on its strap, and let the flood tide of passengers carry me toward the station building. Once inside, I fought toward the nearest wall. I wanted a moment to catch my bearings.

Before I could reach my goal, a blow struck me between my shoulders. I swore and spun around to grapple with my attacker—

I froze. The stranger was a thickset white man in a drab blue suit. Not a rebel soldier, an ordinary citizen. He glared at me—a woman, and a black woman at that, who dared to lay hands on him.

"I'm sorry," I said. "I thought—"

I thought you were the enemy, come with assault rifles and grenade launchers and knives.

Before I could finish my sentence, the man had yanked his shirt free and plunged into the crowd. I gained the wall and a niche between two pillars, where I could recover my breath. I was trembling. *I am not a soldier,* I told myself. *I never was. No matter if the war tried to make me one, I left that war behind.*

I dropped my duffel bag between my feet and rubbed my hand cautiously over my left arm, where metal and plastic joined flesh. In spite of the padded sock, the device chafed against my still-tender stump, and my arm ached from hours upon hours in the jolting train. When I flexed my fingers, I felt the ghost of my old hand, as though one overlaid the other, but imperfectly, with my new fingers trailing behind my old and absent ones.

A surgeon needed two reliable hands. Not one of flesh and one of metal and false memories.

I am a surgeon, I told myself. Or I would be again.

The station had emptied out in the past few moments. Several drones passed overhead, very much like the drones that endlessly spied upon the border. Nearby an engine huffed and hissed. Through the grand archway I could see the train that had brought me from Pittsburgh to DC. Two men in canvas overalls lingered next to it, one passing a cigarette to the other. Workmen for the train, or perhaps more discharged soldiers, waiting to depart for home. Half a dozen guards patrolled the platform, with guns at their belts. These days any weapons the police carried would be low-wattage Tasers, but their presence was sobering.

One of the guards glanced in my direction. He whispered into the microphone that looped around his jaw. I saw myself in his eyes—a black woman dressed in baggy trousers and a dusty, sweat-stained T-shirt. A suspicious character, clearly nervous and loitering without cause. I hoisted my duffel bag over my shoulder and headed toward the exit doors.

🔍

The lobby of the District Hotel reminded me of videos from a hundred years ago—the worn carpets, the rose-patterned wallpaper fading to an uncertain gray. I remembered how my parents had wanted to spend a weekend here to celebrate their anniversary. I remembered how they could never get a reservation.

The clerk wanted a credit card or a cash deposit of eight hundred dollars before he would rent me a room. "It's the rules," he said with an uneasy glance at my left hand and how it twitched on the counter.

"I understand." I had expected the price to be high. I took out the pouch from underneath my T-shirt and laid out eight hundred dollars in twenties. The bills were damp and curling from my sweat. "How many nights does this buy me?"

"Two," the young man said. "I wish—"

He was young and white and anxious not to offend.

"It's all right. Rules are rules." I pressed my thumb against the biometric pad. The device was an older model, more for show than to actually verify my identity, I suspected. My guess was confirmed when the clerk presented me with a paper registration form and a ballpoint pen. I filled out the

registration form with my full name and rank. For my home
address, I gave my sister's in San Diego. If the hotel bothered
with a security check, I could count on Grace to give them all
the right answers, even if she complained to me later.

I signed my name and handed the pen back to the clerk.
"May I have my key? I only need the one."

He slid the card key over the counter. His gaze flickered
toward my arm again. Suppressing a sigh, I picked up the
card with my ordinary hand and tucked the other one out of
sight. There would be more days like today, I suspected. More
stares. I would just have to get used to it.

But getting used to it would take a while. As the antique
elevator shuddered and squealed its way to the second floor,
I fingered the card key in my pocket. My nerves, which had
carried me through two long days of buses and trains and
too many strangers, were shredding into invisible bits. *It's not
a cage. I'm just tired.* No matter what I told myself, my breath
came short before the elevator reached the third floor. The
doors jerked open at last and I hurried down the corridor.

The old-fashioned card reader proved to be fickle. It took
me four tries before my door clicked open. By then I had used
up all my courage. I flung my duffel bag inside, and myself
after it, and slammed the door shut. When I turned around,
I tripped over my bag and onto the bed. My fingers dug into
the thin bedspread and I breathed in its musty fragrance,
counting slowly until my heartbeat steadied.

*Damn you, Martínez. Damn you for telling me this would be
so easy.*

Saúl Martínez was the senior surgeon in the medical unit
where I had served. He had operated on me himself, after
the rescue unit brought me in. It was not his fault a bullet
shattered my arm while he had escaped the conflict entirely.
The surgeons reported weekly to headquarters on rotation.

Thursday, April 17, Martínez had driven off in a jeep for Decatur. Friday, the eighteenth, the Oklahoma and Missouri forces had attacked, overrunning the Illinois border and leaving acres of dead and wounded behind.

He had used any number of favors to locate a replacement arm, then to convince another medical unit to lend him their best technician to retrofit the device. He kept watch as I suffered through a day and night of dangerous fever.

"You will live, Captain," he insisted. When the fever broke, and I cursed and swore against the unremitting agony, against the loss of my arm, he repeated, "You will live. You can do this. You can do anything. Go home and demand a new device. They can't refuse you."

Oh, but they could. We made a handy scapegoat, those of us, the living and dead, connected to Alton, Illinois. Ten thousand soldiers of the New Confederacy had overrun the Illinois border, in spite of the land mines, in spite of the armed drones. Ten thousand rebels had left a bloody trail of their own dead to take outpost after Federal outpost. *Inexplicable*, the intelligence reports said. *The Shame of Alton* is what the newsfeeds called it. The news squirts, those evershifting, underground operations in the dark net, had a ruder name. No matter what victories came later, we had failed our country.

People want a name and face to blame, I told Saúl. Couldn't argue with that. Much. Truth be told, I wanted a name and face to blame myself.

And yet, I had worked too hard—and let's be honest, I owed too much money—to throw away my career as a surgeon. So I had returned to DC, to the city where I had lived as a child and later as a student, to exact a more useful reward for my services to my country. I couldn't hope for an entirely new device, not with the war and its needs outpacing the factories, but surely the VA might supply me with one better fitted to my body and my profession. If not . . .

If not, I would need to relocate to the outlying regions of the country. Places like Vermont, New Hampshire, or the smaller towns in Michigan, where rent and groceries cost less. Wherever I landed, there were still jobs I could do with only one reliable hand and some training. GP, for one thing. Medical technician, if it came to that. I could save my money and buy a new device myself.

And I had the example of my mother and father before me. They had laid out their lives in strict straight lines, saving dimes and dollars to leave that goddamned dirt farm in Georgia, moving their family to the outskirts of Washington, DC, and giving their daughters the education they never had. Surely I could do as much.

I unlocked my fingers from the bedspread and levered myself upright. Thick curtains blocked the windows, and it took another moment for my eyes to adjust to the room's half-light. An air conditioner hummed and rattled as it labored to cool the air, which smelled of ozone and my own sweat. I flicked my hand, but nothing happened. Either the automatic lights were broken, or their motion sensors were calibrated for paler skin.

I felt my way to the wall and opened the curtains. Sunlight poured through the window, catching on a cloud of whirling dust specks. The paint on the window frames was peeling, and chicken wire stretched over the outside. Less than ten feet away, another hotel blocked the view. The room itself was tiny, with just enough space for the double bed, a chest of drawers, and a rickety bedside table with an alarm clock. Nothing I hadn't known already from the website reviews, but still faintly depressing.

The alarm clock read six P.M. My appointment with the VA

caseworker was for eight thirty the next morning. Fourteen-plus hours to fill. Back in medical school, I might have taken the Metro around the city, stopped at a diner, then hopped over to a bar for a scotch or two, where I could argue with my fellow interns about hospital politics. After that, Angela and I would have flipped a coin to decide where we spent the night, her place or mine.

That was the old Janet Watson. One day, that would be the new one, too.

Except for Angela, I reminded myself.

Luckily, I would not encounter Angela here. She and her beloved had taken jobs with a private practice in Toronto. Within a few days, I would be gone myself.

I set the alarm for six thirty A.M., then started my preparations for the night.

Dinner was an Italian sub and a can of Diet Coke, bought on the walk from Union Station. I set those items on my bedside table, along with a used paperback with a broken spine. Sustenance for the one-handed, both mental and physical. Then I switched on the overhead light and closed the curtains. I skinned out of my sweat-drenched clothes and changed into a clean loose T-shirt. I also laid out my clothing for the next day. Medical school had trained me to be methodical. War had reinforced those lessons.

Already I felt exhausted.

I'm just tired. I spent three days on buses and trains. I'm just . . . Afraid.

I flicked open the tab on the soda can. Opened my paperback and laid it flat on the bed, cracking the spine even harder. A mystery, one by Nicola Griffith, guaranteed to unwind the hours with impeccable prose and complicated emotions, even if those emotions turned out to be uncomfortable. Or at least, that was my plan. Once again my momentum ground to a halt, and I found myself staring out the window at the brick wall opposite the hotel.

I should make that phone call to Saúl. I promised.

As if I had any choice. Saúl had come to Decatur that last morning, as I was about to board the bus. He had insisted I call him as soon as I got to my hotel room—even better, as soon as I got off the train. Perhaps he had predicted this bout of inertia. Or perhaps he just liked ordering people around. Wouldn't be the first time.

I dug out my cell phone from my duffel bag and swiped my thumb over the bio-reader lock. Before my brain could derail me, I scrolled to Saúl's number on my contacts list and pressed *Connect.*

A predictable pause followed, as my call cycled from the local system to the military lines. The phone clicked, rang once, then clicked again.

"You're late." Saúl's voice came over the line a faint whisper, with a noticeable delay between words. Bad connection? Or possibly the military line had built in a delay so they could monitor conversations.

"Hi, and hello to you too," I said back at him. "And according to Amtrak, I am blessedly on time. For some definition of *blessed.*" I flopped onto the bed, more relieved than I had expected. If the rebels had picked today for another attack, he might've been tied up in surgery for hours. A respite for him, and for the men and women on the front.

Saúl's response was a wheezing laugh. "Goddamned Amtrak. Though I'm not sure I can blame them. I heard the New Confederacy has taken to sabotaging the rail lines. At least you got to DC in one piece. Speaking of pieces, how is that arm of yours? You've been following my instructions about proper care and all that?"

Oh. Sure. Now his voice came through clear and unbroken.

You bossy old man, I thought. I'd called him that more than once, back in Alton. He had laughed every time. To be fair, he only wanted the best for me, just as I had wanted the best for my own patients, so I let my breath trickle out, and with it, any irritation.

"I will," I said. "Just as soon as I get off the phone. I promise."

"That wasn't exactly the question, Dr. Watson."

I closed my eyes and thought of a hundred different answers, none of them productive. Saúl waited me out. He was better at this than I was.

"How are you?" I said eventually.

"Fine. Same as usual. A couple of new surgeons transferred in last week. Typical Ivy League medicos, with too many degrees and not enough humility. I'll have to teach them proper respect for an old man like me."

I laughed. "You mean you plan to terrorize them, the same way you terrorized me."

There was a pause, then a crackling that might have been Saúl laughing back, or the signal dropping momentarily. But the next part came through crisp and clear. "Funny," he said. "I remember things a bit differently. You came marching into my tent that first day, all young and brash and full of self-righteousness. Before I could even say hello, you snapped out, 'Don't you talk down to me, old man, don't you give me none of your New York bullshit, and don't you ever, ever touch my hair.'"

I had said all that. Lord help me, I had. Maybe my sister, Grace, was right, and I thought too much about myself. But the memory eased the sense of strangeness that had grown upon me ever since I had embarked upon the bus in Decatur.

"At least you left my hair alone," I said.

We both lapsed into quiet for a few moments. If I closed my eyes, I could imagine myself back in that miserable tent in

Alton, Illinois, both of us limp and exhausted after a ten-hour stretch of surgery. Or maybe sharing a glass of whiskey while we speculated about our future after the war. I tugged at my pillows, trying to get more comfortable. Over at Saúl's end of the line, an engine coughed and sputtered, then someone called out a laughing insult to the driver. Life in Mobile Unit #2076 had continued without me.

"So how are you really?" I asked.

Saúl didn't answer at first. When he did, his words came out slow and measured, as though he was already calculating what could make it past the government censors. "I'm tired," he said. "All the usual reasons and then some. You could say I'm tired of this damned war, but aren't we all. Our commander was throwing a fit today . . . orders came down . . . inspection . . ."

Static garbled his answer. Either we had triggered the government censors, or the signal in the District Hotel really was that terrible.

"I didn't catch that last part," I said. "What kind of inspection?"

More crackling, then, ". . . VIP from a pharma company making the rounds. Rumor says they have a . . . PTSD but . . ."

I filled in the missing pieces. Visits from pharmaceutical companies weren't all that rare, but ones from a VIP were. Our commander was likely having a fit, making the unit ready for inspection. As for the mention of PTSD . . .

They're afraid. Especially after Alton.

I didn't say anything. Saúl knew this. Maybe the censors hadn't picked up on this conversation before, but I bet they were listening closely now.

"I have that interview early tomorrow," I said at last.

"You should get some sleep," he replied. "Don't forget about that arm."

"I won't."

Another pause, then, "You can do this, Captain."

And don't we both wish that.

But I said all the proper good-byes, and promised to call him back with a civilian email address and a progress report before the week was out. I thumbed the phone to standby, then tucked it back into my duffel bag. Time to continue my preparations for the night.

The bathroom proved to be tiny as well, but at least it was clean and equipped with instant hot water. Even better, the bathtub had a broad flat rim that I could use as my operating table. I dug out my medical supplies from my duffel bag, then surveyed what other articles I could use. The hotel had supplied me with one large bath towel—an unexpected luxury— two smaller ones, and a washrag. I folded one smaller towel into thirds and laid that over the back of the toilet. I disinfected the bathtub rim with the washcloth, then arranged everything I would need: a fresh sock for my stump, swabs, a bottle of antiseptic, and talcum powder. I soaked two of the swabs in antiseptic and set those on my makeshift operating table.

Next came the difficult part. Over the last month the hospital staff had drilled me in the procedure, but I had never liked it. The newest models used biometric panels to control how and when and who could detach a device, not to mention a dozen other adjustments. Mine was not so elegant. Using my fingernails, I pried open the panel on the underside of my device's socket. I knew what came next. My teeth bit hard in anticipation as I tapped the sequence of controls to release the socket from my stump. The suction mechanism hissed. I had just enough time to recover from the swooping sensation and to catch the arm before it clattered onto the floor.

I leaned back against the tiled wall and breathed through

my nose until my stomach settled. My stump ached fiercely, as though releasing it from the socket had freed the pain, and I distinctly felt a throbbing in an elbow that no longer existed. As a test, I pretended to flex my fingers. My ghost hand, the one that only existed in memory, responded. The metal hand in my lap remained inert.

The stump, real enough, was red and swollen from two days of neglect. I washed it first with soap, then wiped it down with one of the swabs. The phantom pain made me hiss. The most genuine pain of my wounded arm made me almost dizzy. But I did not give up, nor did I faint.

Practice, the physical therapist had said. You must practice until you can complete your drill, no matter what.

So practice I did. By the time I had finished, I was sweating in spite of the artificially cool air. Hand shaking, I rubbed the second towel over my face and over my scalp. The stump I let dry on its own while I examined the prosthetic.

Not as bad as I feared. Sweat stained the plastic interior, and one contact had corroded from the salt. It wasn't enough to account for the tics and tremors, however, which had plagued me since they first fitted me with the device. If the VA could not supply me with a new prosthetic, I would need to consult with a technician to fix the problem.

I shut off that train of thought. I could spend the night constructing ifs and maybes. The routine of caring for my stump helped, as it had over the past four months. With the second swab, I cleaned out the interior of the socket, then set the arm on its towel atop the toilet tank. Now for the last step.

I gripped the bottle of talcum powder with my fingers and flipped it upside down. This was the awkward part. No matter how I practiced, the powder ended up everywhere. I shook a small heap onto my palm. By this time, an unnatural cold drenched my skin. I gritted my teeth and hurried through powdering my stump, then fell back against the wall once more.

Shock. I knew the symptoms. It would pass.

It did not pass. Not for many long moments.

When at last the roar in my ears subsided, I fumbled through my supply case until I found the bottle of painkillers. Working with only one hand was damn hard, but I managed to unscrew the cap without spilling any tablets. Next time, I swore, I would open the bottle first.

I peered inside. Twenty more pills. Enough to last ten more days—longer, if I was economical.

I decided I was not so very economical after all. I gulped down two pills, then headed back into the bedroom for my solitary dinner.

2

"Captain Watson. Captain Janet Idara Watson."

I nodded.

The caseworker regarded me with a watery stare. He was a pale man, his blond hair almost invisible against his equally pale skull. His nameplate read TERRENCE ALEXANDER SMITH. Several certificates and employee recognition awards decorated the plain gray walls of his cubicle.

"Do you have your papers?" he asked.

Silently, I handed over the packet I had guarded along with the cash and vouchers throughout the journey from Decatur to Pittsburgh and then to DC. First, the DD Form 214 with all the details of my military record, from the day I volunteered to my medical discharge. Next, the commendation from my commanding officer on my actions during the assault. Third and last, the official report of my injuries with an addendum from Captain Martínez, explaining the inadequacies of my current prosthetic and how that prevented me from resuming my work as a surgeon in civilian life.

Smith examined them with a noncommittal expression. Once or twice, he glanced at me and back to the collection of papers he had spread over his desk. His face was difficult to read. Contempt? Irritation? If the man had been my commanding officer, the signals would have been clear enough—I would have expected a reminder of certain military regulations or an unofficial rebuke for neglecting paperwork, nothing more—but I had lost the knack of dealing with civilians.

"Enlisted October first, three years ago," Smith said. "Assigned to Mobile Medical Unit #2076, stationed in Alton, Illinois. Volunteered for a second tour."

I suppressed a sigh and resigned myself to a pointless review of my career.

"Wounded in action, April twenty-first," he continued. "Discharged August seventeenth with honors."

I didn't bother with a nod. The man droned on in that same slow voice, his accent a carefully rendered Middle Atlantic, with shades of Caroline County or farther south. My attention slipped away, and I could almost hear Martínez's sharper, brusquer voice, a New York City voice, from that last morning in Decatur, before they shipped me home.

They should have given you a Silver Star. Or better.

Well, they didn't, I had told him. *You know why. They can't reward failure, Saúl, and that's what everyone calls it. Everyone who matters, anyway. Besides, I'd rather have the new arm.*

A sudden movement caught my attention. I flinched, hard. It was only by sheer bloody determination that I did not fling myself to the floor. A heartbeat later, I could recognize the movement for what it was—a harmless office worker passing by Smith's cubicle. Even so, my blood thrummed in my ears, and my throat felt raw, as though I had screamed.

The caseworker's gaze flicked up and back down to the papers. This time the contempt was obvious. He should have been used to us by now, dammit. The ones who came back from the wars wounded beyond a surgeon's skills. Evidently not. My Afro was neat enough, but my linen suit hung loosely, and I'd had to unstitch the left sleeve of my jacket to fit my new arm. To this man, undoubtedly used to military precision and the glossy perfection of high-ranking politicians, I must have appeared shabby and lopsided.

What did he expect? I wondered. I had left everything behind three years ago. All my possessions. My offers at Georgetown, Howard, and the University of Maryland. My parents, dead with so many others in that goddamned bombing. My sister, with her unexpected decision to move across the country so she might escape the war. That too was part of my record.

"You have a device already," he said at last.

So that was the problem.

"I do," I said. "As you can see from the medical report, the retrofit was not entirely successful—"

"Do you wish to file a formal complaint?"

I hesitated. A formal complaint meant a demerit for Saúl Martínez, inserted into his military record, to remain there for all time.

"I have no complaints about my treatment," I said carefully. "I'm a surgeon myself. One works with the available supplies, and the invasion left us with shortages, as you can imagine. So rather than leave me without any arm, Dr. Martínez fitted me with the only device available. He did so believing I would receive a more suitable one after my discharge."

"The action in April was classified as a temporary breach of security, not an invasion," Smith said quickly.

Temporary. Four bloody days of temporary. I had to fight back the urge to rage at his quibbling over words—goddamned words—when so many had died. However, I knew better than to raise my voice. I sucked down a breath and willed myself to speak softly, reasonably, politely. "Does that make a difference?"

"Possibly. The department has reclassified certain benefits in the past year and . . ."

And between protests against new taxes and the factions who secretly supported the rebels, the bureaucracy had decided on economy rather than justice.

So much for being polite and reasonable. I stood up and gathered my forms and papers from his desk. To my relief, my left arm did not fail me, though I was trembling with anger. "Thank you. I accept you are not authorized to say more. Now, tell your administrator I wish to speak with her. Today."

♀

I had frightened the man. Oh, his expression never faltered, but I could tell by the rapidity of his movements and the almost formal tone of his voice as he relayed my request to his administrator. "Don't be making trouble," my father and mother had told me. "You might win today, but you'll pay tomorrow."

I've already paid, I told myself.

To my surprise, Terrence Smith's administrator granted me an almost immediate interview with her and her director. Smith had said nothing beyond my name and former rank, and that I requested a reevaluation of my case. They must have accessed my records when I applied for my initial appointment.

An escort brought me up an elevator that required an electronic key and her thumbprint. We left behind the region of cubicles occupied by lower-level bureaucrats, such as Smith, and entered a far more rarefied atmosphere, one populated with tinted glass walls and expansive waiting rooms outside the executive offices.

Immediate could be a relative term, however. My escort brought me to a small air-conditioned cube. There were no windows, only four beige walls hung with the requisite portraits of President Sanches and Vice President Donnovan, now presidential candidate Donnovan.

Sanches . . . I had such mixed feelings about the woman. I admired her intellect. Her ambition left me breathless. Her politics . . . I could understand them well enough. It was like the choices a surgeon had when they were confronted by a difficult case. How often had my teachers and my medical director advised me to take the least disruptive route? Perhaps her conciliations to the moderate and centrist factions were simply another legacy of the war.

But dammit, I had expected so much more from her. The woman won that first election by doing what so many other Democrats could not or would not do when she forged an alliance with the progressive third parties. The Democratic Progressive Party they called it, though it included members of the centrist faction as well. And those first few years, she *had* fulfilled her promises. She had rolled back the evils from that dark period earlier in the century. She had restored civil rights. She had enacted real gun control. And more.

But then came the outrage from the NRA. The Christian fundamentalists. Angry white men—and quite a few women—who wanted the federalists to shut up and go home. They were the ones who believed those dark times had made America great. They were the ones who had made those dark times even darker.

Alida Sanches had not invented gun control or equal rights, but she sure made a handy target to blame when the terrorists took over Federal buildings in Oklahoma and Missouri and declared themselves the New Confederacy. When Kansas, Iowa, and western Arkansas joined them with riots and guns, a new era, a new civil war, had begun.

So for her second term, Sanches had quietly set aside her principles and her sitting vice president, and picked Donnovan as her running mate. A Pennsylvania man, a man from the center and not the left, a man with a blue-collar background. His grandfather had worked in the coal mines. His father had picked up the pieces when that industry crumbled to dust. I could get behind that, sure enough, me being born on a dirt farm in Georgia. It was for those same reasons Donnovan had picked a Harvard lawyer, now a junior senator from Washington State, for his own running mate. East Coast, West Coast. Big city and small town. Senator Jeb Foley from Texas had used the same calculations for his own run for the White House, when he chose Joe Stevens from Iowa.

(And isn't it funny how those calculations always end up picking the white man?)

I had plenty of time to consider Donnovan and Foley and their running mates. At regular intervals, an administrative assistant appeared to ask if I wished for coffee or tea. I accepted the coffee gladly and savored the taste, since there was little else to savor in this barren place. The rage had passed, leaving behind a heaviness and a stillness, which some might have called patience.

Ten o'clock passed without comment. Eleven o'clock as well.

At noon precisely, the assistant returned to escort me through several corridors and into a sunlit office overlooking Vermont Avenue. There, two women introduced themselves as the administrator and director for the Division of Oklahoma Affairs. Ellen Moskowitz and Dr. Lydia Greene were their names, both appointed by President Sanches in her second term, when it became clear the war would not end in two years, or four, or possibly longer. Both were obviously well trained in the necessary diplomacy for their positions. They explained to me the difficulties with funding and the politics involved with medical benefits.

"You mean, I'm left without recourse," I said, interrupting them.

The administrator grimaced. The director was more polished.

"You have your benefits," Greene said. "Pension and medical care."

"As well as our rehabilitation programs," Moskowitz added.

"But no chance for a new device."

I held up my left arm—so quickly that both women recoiled. Sunlight glittered off the brassy mesh that covered the mechanics, accentuating the darker patches where the protective coating had worn away. It was an ugly thing, made uglier by the all-too-obvious difference between its dimensions and what remained of my arm.

I made a fist of my hand. Or rather, I imagined my hand making one. My ghost hand responded as swiftly as my thoughts. My hand of metal shuddered, then the mesh rippled down my arm to my hand, where the fingers at last curled into a knot.

"You see?" I said.

No need to explain what I meant. They saw, these two women with arms and hands untouched by war.

"There's a waiting list," the director said at last.

I nodded. I understood wartime shortages.

"We can't accommodate you ahead of others," the administrator said.

Of course. I was too much a doctor to let others go wanting.

"Where do you intend to relocate?" was their next question.

"I don't," I said.

"But—"

"I intend to find a job here, in DC. And I'll wait, however long I must."

"A year?" the administrator said. "We can't promise anything sooner."

We can't promise anything at all, said the tone of her voice.

Martínez would say they should have promised. My father would have muttered how there were no guarantees for people like us. We had to slide around those obstacles, he told me and Grace. My mother . . . My mother would remind us we had to make and keep our own promises. Both of them stubborn people, but in different ways.

"I'll wait as long as necessary," I repeated.

And to myself, I added, *I will not give up.*

☙

Dr. Greene left her administrator to discuss the details. Cleanup operation, the civilian edition. Moskowitz herself was conscientious enough, but I recognized all the signs of someone wanting to finish off a case, close up the incision, and have me shipped off to a recovery ward far, far away.

"We've entered your data into the system," she said. "Once you have a permanent address, update your records through our portal site. You have a tablet? No? Not a problem. We have facilities here. My assistant can give you an overview. Today, if you wish."

What I wished more than anything was to retreat into my hotel room, where I could turn the shower to its hottest setting and scrub away the indignities of the morning. I also wanted a painkiller, though I hardly needed one. But the craving for a pill frightened me.

"Yes," I said. "I do wish. Thank you."

The assistant escorted me back to the ground floor, then into an open wing with printers and faxes off to one side, and rows of tables equipped with secondhand tablets. There were even a few laptops that surely dated from the previous decade. The Veterans Center had once housed this equipment, the assistant told me. It was only in the last year that the center had closed and merged its operations with the headquarters.

Several workstations had cardboard signs reading OUT OF ORDER taped to the wall or on top of their keyboards. A technician wearing a uniform labeled *tekSolutionsEtc* knelt next to one such station. He had a laptop hooked up to a diagnostic machine on the floor and was fiddling with the controls. As we passed by, Moskowitz's assistant murmured something about the rising cost of repairs.

A warning? A hint about my own not-so-reliable device?

Just because you're paranoid doesn't mean they aren't out to get you.

A few stations beyond the technician and his equipment, we came to an open workstation near the windows overlooking Sixteenth Street. I settled into the chair and followed the instructions for logging in to the portal. I would have access to all the sites for the VA's rehabilitation programs, the assistant explained to me. Job search. Training. Loans and other financial assistance. A link to the nearby VA Medical Center for appointments. The system also permitted limited access to the internet. She walked me through the steps for each feature before she left.

So. First the permanent address. A web search brought up two dozen inexpensive hostels inside the city limits. I located one within walking distance of the VA headquarters. With a few clicks, I reserved a room starting the next day, then set up a local bank account using the hostel's address. More clicks sent a deposit to the hostel to make the reservation binding.

That achieved, I updated my VA records with the new address and account number. Even as I worked, the VA system had transferred any held sums over to my new account.

The total . . . was more encouraging than I had feared, less than I needed.

I rubbed my left shoulder absentmindedly as I studied the numbers. My pension was two thousand a month, including bonuses calculated for bravery under fire. The hostel cost $750 for two weeks, plus the usual local taxes and fees. Even though I still had a few thousand from the sale of our parents' house, I needed money for food, medication, renewed payments on student loans . . .

The tide of hopelessness rolled in. Why bother? Why did I ever bother with university and medical school? I might have taken a degree in business and started earning a salary at twenty-two. But no, I had chosen a career that left me with a debt of several hundred thousand dollars, and that was after the scholarships.

I logged out of the bank portal and rested my head on my hands. One felt soft and warm against my forehead. The other was hard and slick with accumulated damp. Around me, other computers hummed, and I heard another assistant running through the same explanation of log-in, password, and menu structures with yet another veteran. My arm ached from flesh to ghostly hand, and my gut cramped from hunger. The meager continental breakfast at the District Hotel had been six or seven hours ago. Since then, I'd consumed only black coffee and water.

I need money. For money I need work. But for work, I need a new hand and arm. And for that . . .

For that I needed money—an endless Escher sketch of this for that for this.

I felt a dangerous lassitude settling over me. *Move,* I told myself.

Each cubicle was supplied with pens and paper. I scribbled down the addresses for the hostel and my new bank. Tomorrow, I could pick up my e-card before checking out of the hotel. If possible, I could use the card to pay my bill, then take the refund of my deposit in cash. There were certain items beyond the electronic network that I might require. Next step . . .

Next step was to get a job. I brought up the job services site. My cursor hovered over the bright green button labeled *Open New Account.* Right next to that button was a photo of two soldiers, a young man and an even younger woman, their uniforms clean and crisp, both of them smiling, both of them whole. It was that photo that stopped me.

Almost done, Watson. You can do this.

But I couldn't. Not today.

With a sigh I closed the window for the job portal. *Take each step one at a time,* I told myself. *Dinner. Sleep. Conquer the Andes one rock at a time.* I stuffed the paper into my pocket and stood up. Tomorrow there would be time enough for the next rock.

3

A shrill buzz jerked me awake. I lunged out of bed, reaching for the trousers I kept handy, while the noise pulsated inside my skull. *Incoming wounded. Move, move, goddamn it. Move, Captain.*

I grabbed for the frame of my bed. My ghost hand closed over air, and I landed with a thump on the floor, breathless and scared and angry, while the alarm clock rattled and buzzed. I finally located the damned alarm button and stabbed it with my thumb. Even so, it took two tries before the clock gave one last gulp and died.

There's nothing to be afraid of, I told myself. *It's only a dream. I'm safe, safe, safe.*

But my heart was still beating far too fast as I pushed myself up to sitting. Sunlight leaked around the edges of the curtains. From outside came the trill of an all-too-optimistic sparrow. The air conditioner, less optimistic, had died overnight and the air was close and stale. I flipped the clock over and stared blearily at its face.

Six A.M.

God. Too early. Far, far too early.

I rubbed my hand over my face, which was sticky with sweat. Fragments of old bad dreams floated through my thoughts. The horizon erupting into flames. Men and women screaming. The rattle of gunfire. The stink of burnt flesh and blood, including mine. The blank eyes of the rebels as they killed and killed and killed.

But I was alive. I had lost an arm, yes, but I had survived—no matter how much the VA wanted me and my demands to vanish.

By the time the clock chimed seven A.M., I had showered, reattached my arm, and dressed in a fresh T-shirt and trousers. A cursory inspection told me I had no more clean underwear. Laundry, another task, another expense, noted for the ever-longer list of items to track. I fought another bout of lethargy and could almost believe it had vanished as I dutifully visited the bank, checked out of the District Hotel, and carried my duffel bag three miles to the hostel.

The hostel was an ugly squat building tucked between a barbershop and an Ethiopian takeaway. Farther down the block I saw a liquor store with an ATM outside, a couple pawnshops, and a small pickup truck with a sign advertising cheap electronics. It wasn't the worst neighborhood, but it wasn't the best either. The hostel's concrete-brick façade was crumbling and water stained, and I could tell the street would only get noisier at night. Still, the rooms didn't cost much, compared to the District Hotel, and I could walk to the VA from there.

I climbed the front steps and got myself buzzed into what passed for the hostel's lobby. Ugly linoleum floors. Ugly plaster walls made uglier by gouges and peeling paint. The clerk behind his bulletproof glass window roused himself enough to check me in and hand me a programmed card key for the room and the front door. My room was number 217 on the second floor, he told me. The elevator was currently out of service. Stairs at the end of the hallway.

The walls were so thin I could hear every word of an argument between a man and his girlfriend, every gasp from another couple having sex, as I traversed the corridor. The stairs were concrete and blessedly quiet. The second floor was a repeat of the first. I hurried to number 217, unlocked the door of the closet-sized room that would serve as my home for the next year, and collapsed onto the bed.

A long interval passed, during which I registered the *tick, tick* from an old mechanical clock, the absence of ventilation, and the strong aroma of soap and disinfectant.

Footsteps in the corridor roused me long enough to shut the door and draw the bolt. I had little to steal except my cell, my bankcard, and my vanishing stock of painkillers, but these would be riches to some. That brief surge of energy lasted only a few moments. I kicked off my shoes and stowed my duffel bag underneath my cot. The hostel had no air conditioning, but the room did have a fan bolted to the ceiling. I turned the knob to high and sank back into bed.

The mattress was thin and hard, the pillow even harder. In spite of all that, I fell at once into a deep slumber.

Eight days passed.

Mostly I daydreamed. From time to time, I wrote an entry in my journal, but these were little more than fragmented complaints. My appetite had vanished as well. Only the routine demanded by the army medical technicians ensured I ate at least one meal every day and cared for my stump, which I left free of its device unless absolutely necessary. Very little seemed necessary, to tell the truth. My lethargy troubled me, the way the distant hum of gnats might trouble a person's restless sleep. Annoying, but nothing that roused me enough to do anything about it.

So I ate. I slept. I ventured forth now and then to acquire a meal, a new box of swabs, and so on. My cell phone went missing—lost? Stolen? It didn't seem to matter. My favorite pen ran out of ink. I did not bother to replace it.

Then came the morning I woke to discover my bottle of painkillers empty.

At first I did not comprehend the situation. A thin tight band circled my forehead, and my eyes were unfocused. One ill-considered glance at the alarm clock sent my head spinning, and I lifted my ghost hand to my forehead. For one strange moment, I felt the warmth of human skin brush my face. Then came the cascade of memory of the previous day—an inadequate lunch, consisting mostly of coffee. The retreat into my hostel room, where I had shed all my clothes in the sweltering heat. I had retained enough discipline to remove my prosthetic and clean my stump, but then I'd abandoned the cursed device in the bathroom.

They warned you about this stage.

The second assault, the physical therapists called it. I knew it from observing my own patients. A soldier survived the battle, the shock of surgery, disease, and infection. But then came the point when they had used up their strength and courage and were left drowning in despair.

We lose so many then, Saúl Martínez had reminded me. *To drink and drugs, or simply indifference.*

I stood—swayed as my vision blurred—and breathed slowly and steadily until the nausea passed. My scalp and skin itched. An acrid stink filled the room, an amalgam of sweat and stale air and the antiseptic I used. I glanced around at the clothes scattered over the bare floor. Saturday, it was. Labor Day weekend. I nearly succumbed to the desire to fall back asleep until Tuesday. No, I told myself. I would shower and dress and go to the VA. The computers were available until noon.

My newly recovered resolve carried me through the next few hours. I scrubbed myself hurriedly in the communal showers. I reattached my prosthetic and sorted through my duffel bag. The search yielded a set of clothes that did not reek, and the prescription to refill my painkillers. I paused, the paper pinched between the fingers of my clumsy left hand. The ink had faded from the heat and sweat and one of those brief summer downpours.

Drugs and despair. Soon enough I would have to wean myself from these pills. But not yet. Not quite yet. I folded the paper in half and slid it into a pocket.

The trash I piled into a corner to take care of later. I carried the rest of my dirty clothes to the front desk, where I paid the hostel clerk an exorbitant fee to have them laundered and delivered to my room.

Still driven by this unnatural surge of energy, I bought a bottle of aspirin and a can of Diet Coke at the corner 7-Eleven. I downed two aspirin and a falafel from a street truck, then made the long trek to the VA headquarters. By the time I passed through the front doors, the aspirin had blunted the headache, and my blood sugar had caught up with my fading adrenaline.

The air was delightfully, amazingly cool, lifting the sweat from my skin. I wanted to do nothing more than sit there and take deep breaths of air that wasn't clogged by humidity and air pollution. The place was quiet, too. The room was nearly empty this holiday weekend, with only three other veterans in the cubicles, and one uniformed repair technician busy with her cables and wires and tools. Why had I avoided this place?

I knew why. I knew as well that questioning myself was unproductive.

I logged in to the job services site and opened an account. A few clicks later, the VA had transferred the details of my education and medical background. For location, I chose DC. Radius, *20 miles*. Salary range, *N/A*. Availability, *Immediate*. There were no options for *I need work as soon as possible*. Or perhaps that was a given these days.

The site requested a personal email address. Failing that, it would notify me of any matches to my skill set and experience through the portal, which required me to log in periodically. Fine. Yes. I checked the boxes agreeing to the conditions, then switched over to the internet portal to access my new bank account.

Oh. Not good. Not good at all.

The VA had deposited $9,000 from the holding account, which included my last paycheck for active duty. The District Hotel had subtracted $800, the hostel nearly $1,100, a sum that included the security deposit, plus various extra charges such as today's laundry. The bank itself had taken small bites for each transfer. The remainder seemed extravagantly large, even so, until I calculated I would not receive the first deposit for my pension until September 30.

I need money. I need work.

As if in response, the screen chimed and a lightning-bolt icon appeared in the lower left corner. Before I knew it, I was hovering my mouse over the icon, which immediately changed to a pop-up balloon that said, You have seven new openings. Click to view details.

Impossible, I thought even as I clicked. *Nothing is that easy.*

The pop-up spun around to display seven job titles with icons next to each. I was still so surprised it took me a moment to decipher that first entry . . .

Cold washed over my skin as I read the description.

The entry was for a surgeon at Georgetown University Hospital. Entry level, with promises of advancement and training. This could almost have been the same position I had rejected three years ago when I volunteered for the army. There was even that throwaway reference to diversity, which I knew translated to their need for government funding. It was also a position I no longer qualified for.

With a quick, jerky movement, I deleted the entry from the list.

The next two were ads for pyramid schemes. *Delete, delete.*

The fourth and fifth were much better. Suburban Hospital in Montgomery County wanted a doctor for its ER unit. An inner-city walk-in clinic wanted a GP for its night shift. The ER job might require extra training, and the walk-in clinic did not pay well, but this was no time to be picky. I clicked *Apply* for both.

The last two jobs . . . were less than I had hoped for. One was for a lab technician out in the suburbs of Alexandria. The pay rate was better than expected, the hours less so. Half days throughout the regular workweek, with ten-hour shifts on Saturday and Sunday.

Better than a dirt farm, I reminded myself. *Better than starving.*

I clicked *Apply* before I could second-guess myself, but by now I felt emptied out and longed for my hostel room. *One more,* I told myself. Then I would visit the pharmacy to refill the painkillers and eat a proper meal for lunch.

Job number seven was for a medical technician at the VA Medical Center in DC.

No time to stop, to reconsider. I clicked the icon and a bubble appeared midscreen.

Assistant's primary responsibilities are to prescreen patients in regards to their medical condition and forward reports to

the physicians and surgeons on staff. Additional duties might include follow-up review and monitoring patient recovery. Must have good communication skills and practical medical experience. Opportunities for training and advancement.

Two-thirds the pay rate of the lab technician's post, more than twice the responsibilities. Funding had dropped along with the rest of the economy, while costs for material goods were higher than ever before. And what if I could not get my new device by winter? Or spring? I would need adequate savings to establish myself anew.

I just have to get that ER job, don't I?

I clicked *Apply*. Then, before I could change my mind, I logged out of the job portal and shut down my browser session. My hands, both of them, were trembling.

"Go to the pharmacy," I whispered to myself. "Get lunch. And you'll need better interview clothes. If not for these jobs, then for something, someday."

The litany continued on its own. A cell phone to replace the one lost or stolen. One of those convertible tablets with a keyboard and memory sticks so I wouldn't have to rely on the VA computers. A monthly Metro card. Better shoes, for when DC's transportation system failed me. Hair oil from the neighborhood store. The to-do list was nearly enough to send me pelting back to my hostel room. I had to grip the chair while I ran through the breathing exercises the therapists had taught me, before the roaring in my ears faded and I could walk with some semblance of normality toward the exit.

I had my hand on the door when someone called out my name.

"Captain? Dr. Watson? Is that you?"

A lean and knobby black man limped toward me and reached out a hand. I flinched back, still tangled up in my earlier panic.

His smile flickered upward and then faded at my silence. "Do you remember me?" he said.

His face was a study in brown, crisscrossed with old scars. His hair was a grizzled gray and covered his skull in patches. It was the combination of the limp and the scars that reminded me who he was. Jacob. Corporal Jacob Bell. He had transferred to our medical unit and served as my assistant before taking a disability discharge.

"I remember," I said. "I'm sorry—"

"It doesn't matter, Captain. I understand."

To be sure, he would. He had been captured by the enemy and tortured. He had escaped on his own, but some things you could never leave behind.

"How you doing these days?" I said.

"Good enough, Captain. Busy. Not nearly as busy as I was in the service, though." He paused, and I could see the many, many questions he wanted to ask.

"I know a tasty diner," he said at last. "I'm hungry. Are you?"

To my surprise, I was.

I nodded. "Lead on, Corporal."

His tasty diner was a restaurant in the U Street corridor that specialized in Greek dishes. We ordered an enormous plate of feta cheese and hot peppers to share, then a second one of baked phyllo stuffed with roasted lamb and spinach. There were hot tea, cold water, and an abundance of food of the kind and quality I had dreamed about in Illinois. For a while I could do nothing but eat. Jacob did not trouble me. He understood the need to devour food when we had the opportunity. Eventually, however, we both slowed and I could take in my surroundings and my companion. I refilled my water glass. Jacob poured tea for us both.

"You surprised me," I told him. "Popping up like a rabbit the way you did. What happened to going back home to Maine?"

His hesitation was brief but said a lot. "Times be hard, Captain. You know how it goes. The job they were holding for me went to someone else. And . . . other things were harder. Anyway, I ended up in DC. The VA found me a job in the medical center. Orderly. It's not my first choice, but they added a student loan for a local tech college to sweeten things. I go to classes there afternoons and evenings. You?"

"I do well enough," I said. "It's early days, but . . ." With an effort, I expelled a breath and found I could almost smile. "I need money. I want to stay in the city a few months or so. They said they might find me a new arm."

Jacob simply nodded. "Might be. Could be."

Neither of us mentioned the waiting lists, or the cuts in funding that made those waiting lists even longer.

We fell silent over the remains of our lunchtime feast. The waitress brought us a second pot of tea and our bill, with the murmured addendum that we need not rush. We didn't. I was grateful for this chance meeting with an old friend. Jacob too seemed glad for the unhurried meal and the conversation that followed.

"You want a job," he said eventually. "And a better place than that hostel."

I had described my room to him—a bit too vividly, no doubt.

"The problem is money," I said.

"It always is. But maybe I can help. I know someone . . ." He glanced around. "Not sure if she's right for you, though."

"She?"

He shrugged. "A friend of mine. She's not service, but she's not so bad."

I waited, knowing there was more.

"She's . . . particular about things," he went on. "Some might call her difficult, but she has her good points, too. I happen to know she's looking for a partner to split rent on some rooms."

My throat went dry with a sudden and all-too-familiar panic. A stranger. Someone to witness my nightmares, to stare at my missing arm while pretending not to. It was difficult enough in the hostel.

Jacob was watching me with that same kindly smile I remembered from our time in the service, on the days when blood and death became too much for me to bear. A smile that spoke of understanding and not pity.

"You can always say no," he said.

"That I could." My voice came out shakier than I liked. "When do you think I could meet her?"

"Today, if you like. I know where to find her on Saturdays."

No, no, that was much too soon. I needed time—

The panic rushed back, stronger than before. I shut my eyes and gripped the edge of my seat. Usually I could pinpoint the cause. The bang of a car engine that recalled the explosions of war. The touch of a stranger, which yanked me back to that struggle with enemy soldiers as I tried to save my patients. This . . . this was less easy to identify. So I breathed deeply and steadily until the panic subsided.

When I opened my eyes, Jacob appeared to be studying the bill.

"Let's go," I whispered.

He paid the bill over my protests. I retaliated with a generous tip.

"You say you know where to find her?" I asked once we had exited the diner.

"Always. Or, always when she's in the city."

"Then she has rooms now. What happened? Did she secretly murder her former roommate?"

Jacob laughed softly and shook his head. "Not that I've ever heard. No, she lived with friends who had a house in Alexandria. A temporary thing, she said. But then her friends took jobs on the West Coast, and Sara wanted to stay in DC. She found a new set of rooms. They cost more than she likes to pay, but she's decided she has to have this apartment and no other. As I said, she's particular."

"Sara." I repeated the name to myself. "Sara what?"

"Holmes. We met last year. In a movie theater, if you can believe that. She kept cursing up and down about the soundtrack. Which I can tell you was awful, but still. Making that kind of ruckus does no good. I told her to take her noisy self to see the manager, or if she couldn't do that, she ought to buy me a drink. She bought me a drink, then argued with me the whole time."

I laughed. "But you like her."

He smiled back, somewhat ruefully. "As much as she lets me, yes. We talk now and then. Now and then, she buys me a drink. For old times' sake, she says. She knows a fair bit about the service, for all that she's never served." He indicated the crosswalk, where the pedestrian signal blinked green. "Let's turn here. Less traffic this way."

"Where are we going?"

"National Gallery. She likes to spend her Saturdays there, when she can."

We followed R Street east a few blocks, then turned south again onto Ninth, avoiding the tide of Labor Day weekend tourists and the high-security zone around the White House. Drones passed by overhead, marking the outlying borders of that zone. They were thicker in the air than before—a precaution against those latest threats from the New Confederates? Or more of the same from those days when ISIS and al-Qaeda sent their suicide bombers to our shores, when right-wing protesters from within our own country turned violent and presidents could not rely on their own security details?

On the ground, the telephone poles carried signs for the upcoming election. Posters for Jeb Foley and Roy Donnovan were plastered over those of their old opponents from the primaries. Another businessman turned politician, running on the Independent ticket. There were even a few digital signs for the Communist Party, which some prankster had rewired to read Ellison, Obama, and Booker.

Two months and a couple days until the vote. I had hardly thought about the elections before now. War and surgery had consumed all my thoughts. Then came the invasion and my own personal combat to regain myself. Foley and his conservative friends were easy to reject. They hated me and mine, and only a couple of steps separated them from the New Confederacy, as far as I could see. Donnovan . . . was a more difficult pill to swallow. A white man, a straight white man with a history of voting the Centrist Party line, with one or two progressive causes he favored. I understood why Sanches had taken him for her VP, but as president?

At Constitution, we turned back east to the main entrance to the National Gallery. Every spring my teachers had organized a trip to the Mall to see the cherry blossoms. Every autumn, my parents had insisted on a visit to the Museum of Natural History or the Museum of African Art. If Grace and I were extra well behaved, they added the Air and Space Museum to the list.

I miss them. I wish . . .

I wished I'd had the prescience to take a break after the all-consuming years of medical school and my subsequent residency. But there were so few doctors and so many casualties. As the war continued into Sanches's second term and Congress debated whether to undo civil rights for all those people who'd been told they were less than equal because of the color of their skin or gender they loved, just to placate the New Confederacy, I told myself that it was my duty to serve. There would be time enough after my tour of duty ended.

Then came a letter from the State Department, informing me of what I already knew from the newsfeeds—that my parents had died along with hundreds of others when terrorists from the New Confederacy bombed the Atlanta airport. Then a letter from my grandmother, insisting I quit the military, as if she could rule the government as she had once ruled our family. The even more formal letter from my sister's lawyer, dividing our inheritance.

And then, and then . . .

And then came the bloody dawn, with thousands of rebel soldiers overrunning the front lines. The frantic broadcasts from the camp radio tower, broken off with the first explosion, and the even more frantic hours that followed as I and the other surgeons attempted to carry our patients to safety.

We climbed the broad steps to the National Gallery's marble portico and into the rotunda with its black tiled floor and the fountain of silver-veined stone. Cool air fell over me like rainwater as we passed through wide corridors to a staircase leading down to the lower level. After that came a series of smaller rooms with paintings from the twentieth century, then a longer gallery dedicated to works by French and Belgian masters. At last we arrived in a small chamber anchored by two marble statues in opposite corners, and a grand sweep of canvas against the far wall.

Dalí's *Sacrament of the Last Supper*.

I was no Christian, not these days. But, oh, those luminous colors. The images upon images. The small trickeries my teachers had pointed out that added layers of story to the most obvious and outermost one. It almost didn't matter that the Son of Man, a child of Israel and the King of the Jews, was portrayed as a pale-skinned man with yellow hair.

Fuck it, I'm lying. It *did* matter, the same way it rankled when people—mostly white people—stared when I said I was a doctor, a surgeon, and a veteran of the wars. But I could still look beyond the unthinking bigotry of this particular artist, and the assumptions of his age, to the moment he portrayed, when Christ drank the wine and spoke of his body and his blood.

I shivered and passed a hand over my eyes.

Only then did I notice a woman standing in the corner.

She was tall and lean. Her complexion was the darkest brown I had ever seen, the angles of her face were sharp enough to cut, and she wore her hair in locs, arranged in a careless, complicated fashion wound around her head, then plaited and pinned, so they fell in a thick cascade down her back. The cant of her cheekbones, the almost imperceptible folds next to her eyes, spoke of East Asia, or certain nations in Africa. Of a world outside my own.

And she was wealthy. I could tell by the clothes she wore. Loose trousers cut in the latest fashion, and a thin sleeveless shirt made from an ivory cloth, gleaming bright as sunlight and shot through with gold threads. A few pearls were visible among her locs.

Holmes's expression was contained, but I had the distinct impression she was amused. "Bell," she said, her voice rough and low. "What have you brought me?"

"A friend," Jacob said. "Sara Holmes, my friend Dr. Janet Watson. Shake hands, Sara. I know you can."

Sara laughed, a laugh that matched her voice. We closed the distance between us, then both of us hesitated. I sensed a Rubicon before me, an array of choices wise or foolish. Gaius Julius Caesar had made his own choice in that matter and died. Or perhaps I was being fanciful.

Then Holmes reached out to me with a hand covered in lace. "You've come from the war in Oklahoma," she said, and clasped my hand in hers.

My pulse jumped. Of course, I told myself, she would see my metal arm and recognize that I was a wounded vet.

"Hardly a difficult guess," I said. "Unless you stopped reading the newsfeeds."

Sill holding my hand, she regarded me with an amused expression. "True. I don't need this"—here she lifted her other hand, also gloved, and twisted it around—"to make that deduction."

Light glittered off the metallic lace, changing the pale gold to threads of silver. Even in the muddy fields of Alton, we'd heard about this newest offering in network connectivity. I spotted the tiny earbuds that confirmed my guess, and just behind them, the small black discs that implied permanent implants. If she could afford this kind of advanced technology, why did she need someone to share the rent?

"You like my toys?" Holmes said.

My stomach lurched. Not so much at her words, but the attitude behind them. I knew the likes of her from medical school—rich and privileged and mocking those beneath them.

"No," I replied evenly. "I do not like them."

Now she was smiling. "I'm not surprised, Dr. Watson. But my toys tell me you graduated second in your class at Howard University. You finished your residency with honors. And you had three offers within the week, all very good positions as a surgeon. You even had a lover, with lucrative offers of her own in the city. Yet you decided to enlist in the army."

I was sweating, but I knew the cause this time.

"I joined because I wished to," I said. "And I am not afraid of your toys."

She regarded me with wide bright eyes, eyes the color of a midnight sky, flecked with molten copper. "Maybe not. But you are afraid, nevertheless. You have been, since long before the New Civil War and the Shame of Alton. That missing arm terrifies you, Dr. Watson. But not as much as the terror you felt that you could never truly succeed, even with the best arm in the world."

I tried to draw a breath and found no air to fill my lungs. Dimly, I heard Jacob Bell scolding Holmes, but I could not get my throat and tongue to cooperate. A hand clasped my arm. I felt something brush against my leg. Abruptly I broke away and ran back through the corridor. Someone—Jacob—called after me. I rounded a corner into a nest of smaller exhibit rooms, then went to the stairs leading up.

But I could not face the city streets and all those strangers. Not yet. I ducked through to another hall and found a marble bench where I could sit and gather my shreds of courage. To my relief, the hall was empty. I bent over double, arms clasped around my knees, waiting for the thundering in my skull to die down. From a distance came the echo of voices—tourists arguing over their next stop. Then a set of footsteps, as sharp as nails on the tiled floor, approached the nearby entryway. I waited, sick and apprehensive, but no one entered. No one spoke to me.

The footsteps retreated. Gradually the quiet returned. Much more gradually, my pulse slowed and I found my breath again.

God. Dear goddamned God with your so-called love that does not include me or mine. What the everlasting fuck were you thinking to bring me and her together?

God was a trickster, my father used to say. If so, then Sara Holmes could be its manifestation, cruel and capricious.

The image of Holmes as God's trickster called up laughter, however weak. I rubbed my hand over my face. Poor Jacob, the unwilling witness to that scene. I would have to track him down later and apologize. Not here in the museum, though. Not where Sara Holmes might still be lurking. Best to leave now before I encountered her again.

As I pushed myself to my feet, an unfamiliar weight bumped against my leg. What the hell? I scrambled away, but the thing bumped me again, dragging at one of my pockets. Then I remembered that scuffle, the hand clasping my arm, the brush against my trousers. *Holmes, goddamn it.*

As if it could hear my thoughts, the thing burst into a loud staccato buzz. Swearing under my breath, I fumbled inside the pocket. My hand closed over a small flat rectangle that vibrated angrily. A cell phone?

I extracted the device, which immediately stopped vibrating. The thing was the size of an old-fashioned playing card and almost as thin. Made from some kind of silvery metal that felt warm to my touch. It continued to buzz, but more quietly. I ran my thumb over its surface, then along the edges. No buttons, recessed or otherwise. Then I remembered reading about the new voice-activated screens. "Holmes," I said. "Is that you?"

The buzzing stopped. The center of the object transformed from silver to black. Amber text flowed over its surface.

I am sorry. I have the bad habit of showing off, as Jacob will confirm. However, my tendencies do not excuse the hurt I've caused.

The address is 2809 Q Street NW. Your better judgment will no doubt send you back to your hostel room, there to seek quarters less troubling. If by chance you decide to meet the challenge, however, I've instructed the rental agency to send a representative to meet us at 3 p.m. Whatever you choose, I would suggest you take the job with the VA Medical Center.

Regards and Regrets, Sara Holmes

I choked back a laugh, then rubbed my hand over my face, which felt numb from the lingering rage. Difficult, Jacob had called her. Impossible was more like it. However genuine the apology, I could foresee more episodes like this one if we lived in the same apartment.

The text dissolved into a new message: Are you afraid?

"Damn you," I whispered. "Damn you to hell, Sara Holmes."

The screen went blank, as if declining to respond.

Three years ago, I might have tossed the device into the trash and gone away, untouched by that accusation. Back in those days, I'd been as arrogant as Sara Holmes. All the doctors were, the surgeons more than anyone else. I had lost that arrogance, somewhere between my residency and Alton, Illinois.

And what if you went to that apartment? You could prove her wrong. You can prove yourself wrong. And then, Jacob's earlier words. *You can always say no.*

♀

Three o'clock was twenty minutes away.

I hesitated only a moment, then flagged down a taxi. All the taxis in DC had human drivers, either in spite of the new driverless technology or because of it. Two sped past me, flags clicking over to OCCUPIED. A third slowed. I brandished a handful of bills, and the driver pulled over to the curb. "Q Street Northwest," I said. "Number 2809. I have a three o'clock appointment."

The cab's trip display showed 2:57 when we arrived. I handed over two twenties and waved away the change. I would regret the expense later. But here I stood on the sidewalk, with a strange flutter of excitement in my chest as I gazed upward at the apartment building.

It was a modest redbrick structure, only three stories high and with very few flourishes of design. Two sets of stairs wound up through a narrow ivy-covered lawn. More ivy crept up the walls, its pattern echoed by the wrought iron grates covering all the windows. I suspected the ironwork disguised even more effective security—electronic sensors, perhaps. Underneath the windows hung planters filled with Black-eyed Susans, Queen Anne's lace, and other wildflowers that called up memories of the pocket field behind my parents' house, before the local mall overran it.

I do not belong here.

I quashed my doubts and mounted the dozen steps to the entry. There were no doorbells, nor the usual list of names for the residents. Here was a place where the residents clearly valued privacy. In spite of my resolve, I felt a second ping of warning that said my kind was not welcome.

The door swung open and a young woman smiled at me. "Dr. Watson?"

She wore a close-fitting suit of navy silk, with an ivory shirt that billowed over the almost invisible lapels. Her blond hair was clipped short, framing her narrow face in wisps and curls. Whatever she thought of my appearance—my gray T-shirt and baggy trousers, the badly fitted prosthetic arm, the color of my skin—her bland expression gave nothing away.

"I'm Jenna Hudson," she said. "I'm from the rental agency. Ms. Holmes told me to expect you. Please come in."

She gestured to one side. I passed through the door into a cool entryway, floored in dark gray marble, with freshly painted ivory walls. Several tall vases held ferns or English ivy, and a modest staircase coiled upward to the next floor. I could see a hallway extending toward the rear of the building but no sign of any apartments.

"For this particular building, our accommodations are second- and third-floor only," Jenna Hudson was saying to me. "Our clients prefer the added privacy. I hope that's not a difficulty for you."

I couldn't tell if she thought the stairs posed an obstacle for me, with my missing arm, or whether I might simply dislike the idea of a second-floor apartment. "Has Sara Holmes arrived?" I asked instead.

"Ms. Holmes telephoned to say she was delayed, but she would arrive within the hour. I can show you the apartment while we wait. Please follow me."

We climbed the elegant staircase to the second floor. Here there was no other corridor, only four doors that opened onto the wide landing, while the stairs continued upward. Jenna Hudson unlocked the door labeled 2B and stood off to one side.

The sense of not belonging had increased with every step inside this building. As I passed Jenna Hudson into the apartment's entryway, I had to fight against the urge to turn and flee. Only the reminder that I could say no, that I had promised nothing, helped.

But oh, oh, this lovely set of rooms.

It was so perfectly designed, as if God herself had read my desires and transmitted them to the architect two hundred years ago. First a vestibule with its spacious closet to one side, and a niche perfectly fitted for an umbrella stand. The tiles matched those of the landing and the entryway below—dark gray with threads of silver and gold—and the archway into the parlor was edged with more marble of a lighter hue.

Perhaps I made a hum of contentment, because Jenna Hudson smiled with obvious satisfaction. "There are two bedrooms," she said. "Each with access to the main bathroom. There is also a second half bath off the parlor for guests. The kitchen has been updated with new appliances, though if you prefer, you may order meals through our concierge service. The same applies to laundry and other services. Cleaning is part of the rental fee, as are the furnishings themselves."

I could never afford such rooms, with or without extra fees. Who was Sara Holmes that she insisted on an apartment like this? Why did she need a stranger to share it?

Still wondering, I continued through the archway into the parlor.

A vast bay window faced me, with the ubiquitous ironwork and a bank of wildflowers below. Bookcases lined the walls to either side, with another set of shelves beneath. There were even a few books. Austen and Eliot. Woolf and Russ and Lorde. A comfortable couch and two chairs occupied the space in front of the window. I noted an old-fashioned telephone in one corner, the discreet security cameras, and a small cabinet equipped with electronic devices. The whole room had the air of something from the late nineteenth century, but with grace notes of the twenty-first.

I turned through the doorway on my right to find myself in a short hallway. Doors led into a kitchen and a half bath. The kitchen was little more than a galley, but outfitted with granite counters and stainless steel appliances. There was a small alcove next to it that served as a dining nook. I glanced into the bathroom, which matched the rest of the apartment, then noticed the corridor angled around to yet another open area, this one with doorways for the two bedrooms. There were closets everywhere. Exquisite, practical, artistic closets, the kind my mother would have wept for.

This, this was far too much for a retired captain from the army. Especially one who had no prospects for a job.

I returned to the parlor with its bay window overlooking Q Street. Off in the distance, the Washington Monument and Lincoln Memorial were visible above the skyline. I remembered, as a kid, staring up at Lincoln's implacable stone face, hating and loving him all at the same time.

"It's not as expensive as you think."

Sara Holmes leaned against the entry to the parlor, arms folded and her mouth quirked into a smile. The lace gloves on her hands were just visible, though their color had faded to a pale gray.

"How did you—?"

"Deduction. And a certain empathy born of like experience."

She came into the room to stand beside me at the window. I stared at her, trying to unravel what experiences she'd had that could possibly overlap mine.

"I have no job," I said softly.

"Not yet," she agreed.

A bluff. And yet . . .

"Why?" I said next. "You don't need help with the rent. You certainly don't need *me*."

She shrugged. "Then perhaps I simply don't wish to live alone. And you seem restful."

Restful? I almost laughed.

"And you?" I asked. "Are you restful?"

"Not at all. Think of me as a challenge."

Oh, yes. She liked to give challenges.

"Ladies."

Holmes spun around. Her left hand went to one pocket, the other brushed over her forehead. I swallowed down the rush of panic, the same as I felt when I heard the thundering of helicopters approaching camp.

But this was no helicopter, no enemy soldier, only Jenna Hudson. She approached from the vestibule, where she had no doubt listened to our conversation. Had she overheard my comment about having no job?

"Have you decided?" she asked.

Holmes glanced in my direction. "I like it. Very much. But . . ." She tilted a hand toward me. "The decision is yours, Dr. Watson."

No job. Not even an interview yet, though I had not forgotten Sara's mysterious recommendation to take one job over the other.

"How much is the rent?" I asked.

"Your share would be twelve hundred dollars a month, taxes and fees included."

That was . . . far lower than I expected.

Yet not so low that I could immediately disbelieve her. It was possibly—barely—that Hudson Realty needed to keep these apartments occupied. Subsidized rents were not uncommon.

An all-too-vivid image of my hostel room came back to me. The trash in the corridors, the sheets with their ghostlike stains, the walls that did nothing to shut out the noise. The sense of isolation, even amidst the crowds.

My gaze met Sara Holmes's laughing one. I felt the itch of excitement, as I had not for two or three years.

"We'll take it," I said.

4

SEPTEMBER 6. *One week exactly since I met Sara Holmes
in front of Dalí's grand and gaudy painting. One week that
felt much longer than seven days. Longer and stranger,
as though Holmes had grabbed a handful of time, shaking
the days inside out, simply to see what happened. I could
imagine her doing that.*

*So. Let me tell you about this past week, Dear Journal.
Immediately after I agreed to the apartment, Holmes
announced we would meet with Jenna Hudson the following
Friday to sign the lease. Hudson made soft murmuring noises
about Tuesday, not Friday, and really, the company did not
wish to leave the apartment vacant another week. Holmes
ignored her. Friday, she repeated.*

And Friday it was.

*But first came a series of impossibilities, to make Friday
possible.*

*I can't remember anything about Sunday or Monday
except panic and second-guessing. And a quantity of Johnnie*

Walker Red. Thank god for Jacob. Poor Jacob. At one point
I'm certain he wished me back in Alton and himself in Maine.
Tuesday morning, I visited the VA center the moment it
opened. Three emails waited for me in my job search inbox.
Suburban Hospital had filled its position from an internal
review, but they would put me on their waiting list for future
openings. BioStar Laboratories, in Silver Spring, wanted to
interview me three P.M. Wednesday. The VA Medical Center
had an open slot Thursday morning at nine A.M. Please click
Confirm *or* Cancel *to reply.*

I paused. How to describe those interviews? No, not just the
interviews, but the sense of coincidence that permeated the
entire week? Sitting there on my cot in the hostel, I had the impression that Sara Holmes had orchestrated the entire production, from the moment I encountered Jacob Bell, to his mention
of a friend, to that meeting with Sara herself in the National
Gallery.

Half a page remained in the journal, and my pen was running dry. I wrote:

The interviews themselves were ordinary enough.
Questions about my medical training. My plans for the
next five years. How would I rate my ability to cope with
a demanding work environment? They did not ask about
my lost arm, though they clearly wanted to. Government
regulations protecting the rights of the disabled and all
that. Brief polite glances, however—at me, at my device—
were obvious enough. In spite of my anxiety, the thing
behaved throughout. (NB: Does this mean I think of my
device as a dog, somewhat given to mischief? No, my
feelings are hardly that affectionate.)

Six more lines to this page and book. The ink is fading. So.

Two interviews, two offers delivered Thursday afternoon to my VA email. Both required a voice reply. Inside half an hour, I bought a cheap voice-only cell phone from the electronics truck around the corner. By end of day, I had my job. Too fast, too easily, oh yes, but I needed the money. Friday, paperwork and keys and the two months' security deposit. And now this journal is truly finished.

I set the dying pen aside and flexed my right hand. There was much more I had meant to record. The moment of awkwardness when the technician reached for my left arm to record my fingerprints for the security lock. The glance Jenna Hudson exchanged with Sara Holmes when she stated the terms of our lease. How Sara wore no lace gloves that day, and yet I could make out faint lines, like a second set of veins, running over the surface of her skin. The whiff of sandalwood perfume that reminded me of Angela, when we bent over the paperwork to write our signatures. And Sara's sardonic expression when I tried to hand back her texting gadget.

Just as well, I thought. The alarm clock I'd bought last Saturday was ticking fast toward ten A.M. I wanted to check out before the hostel charged me another day's fee. Between the security deposit for the apartment, the cell phone, and a dozen other items I'd bought over the past week, my bank account had dipped alarmingly.

One of those items—a new leather suitcase—lay on the floor next to me, packed with all my possessions, including my old duffel bag. An oversized convertible tablet, bought from the neighborhood pawnshop, leaned against the wall in its vinyl case. I packed my last few items—the alarm clock, my journal, a few other odds and ends that had somehow escaped my attention before—then closed and latched the suitcase.

I glanced around the hostel room one last time. It looked—
if that was possible—even shabbier and emptier than when I
first arrived. Even the bed was stripped, the sheets and blankets returned to the front desk. How had I lived here fifteen
days and left no trace of myself?

It's safer this way, I thought. Then I slung the tablet's bag
over one shoulder and angled the suitcase onto its wheels.
Time to go.

The taxi pulled over to the curb in front of 2809 Q Street.

Common sense had told me to walk the two miles from
the hostel, but apparently I wasn't on good terms with common sense these days. No, I just had to arrive in style, didn't
I, with my expensive luggage and my silk suit bought from
the vintage store, one that disguised any number of defects
except confidence and color.

Girl, you are some fool.

A fool willing to be fooled, as my mother would have
put it.

I had not fooled the driver, however. He was as black as
me, but back at the hostel, when I gave him my destination,
he had demanded a cash deposit—forty dollars—before he
would load my suitcase into his trunk. Even now, as I handed
him a tip, he scowled at me, then at the brick building behind
its winding steps and iron-grated windows.

He didn't need to say what he was thinking. I'd heard it
often enough from the neighbors back in Suitland. Doctor or
surgeon, that was for white people, and though they always
said what a fine thing it was to aim so high, I could tell they
wondered if I thought myself better than them.

Maybe I did. Maybe I was riding for a fall.

I could hear those selfsame words in my grandmother's

voice, back when I was seven and my parents announced they would move north.

The cab drove off. I swung my suitcase onto its wheels and stared up at my new home. It was a hot September day, the wildflowers in riotous bloom, but a faint breeze carried with it a whiff of autumn, of seasons in change, of possibilities I could not yet imagine.

My device shivered, an electronic echo of my nerves. The neighbors would be watching, of course. Black woman. White neighborhood. What was she doing here, and did she mean trouble? The times, they had changed since the 1960s, and those times had changed even more since 2008, when the country elected a black man as their president, but I knew what my parents always said was the truth. *We've changed, but not enough. Otherwise 2016 would never have happened. Otherwise, we'd never have to fight a second civil war.*

I hauled my new suitcase up the dozen stone steps to the portico. Here was the real test. Would my thumbprint work to open the lock?

I do belong here. I do, I told myself.

But my hand was slick with sweat as I studied the discreet gray panel next to the door. The ordinary metal keys were a backup system, Jenna Hudson had explained to us. The older residents preferred them. Our best security, however, lay in the biometric keys, provided by our own fingerprints. I wiped my hand over my trousers and pressed my thumb against the pad. There was a long and doubtful moment of silence, then a soft buzzer sounded and the door clicked open.

The breath escaped my lungs. Yes, for now, I did belong.

I dragged my suitcase inside and shut the door. At our meeting the day before, Hudson had described where to find the service elevator, which was tucked in between the staircase and the rear corridor. It took me swiftly and quietly to the second floor, where I once more faced my doubts.

But my thumbprint unlocked apartment 2B without any fuss.

As I walked through the door, Sara Holmes's texting gadget hummed.

I have some last-minute errands. Expect me at 5 p.m. Can you cook?

For a moment, I was too outraged to think. So many assumptions were built into that short message. Did she ever realize how she sounded? Did she care?

Luckily for someone, the gadget had no reply function. I stuffed it into my pocket and continued into the vestibule, where I propped my suitcase and tablet bag against the wall, so I could make a proper survey unencumbered by baggage.

The living room was exactly as I remembered it, with the enormous padded couch and two wingback chairs facing the window and its view of central DC, where Lincoln and Washington and Jefferson sat in silent self-satisfaction. A faint aroma of wood polish hung in the air, with an even fainter scent I could not identify. Roses? Incense?

In the kitchen, I discovered the cabinets filled to overflowing. Plates and serving dishes. Pots and pans. Glasses of every kind and color. And a truly astonishing array of machinery. Sara's? I doubted that, after her text message, but then I spied a double row of herbs in pots underneath the window. I leaned close to sniff the sharp clean scent of the rosemary, the pungent thyme, the whiff of damp soil.

There were clues here. Ordinary ones. Intriguing ones.

Or perhaps they were simply ingredients for that night's dinner.

I padded down the hall toward the bedrooms. The closets

and the bathroom were empty, except for a prim stack of toilet paper rolls. No towels. Another item I had forgotten about, dammit. After the kitchen, I had expected to find her belongings stored away or stacked throughout the corridor.

The only matter we had left undecided on Friday was the choice of bedrooms. The one to my left was the largest, I remembered. It overlooked the garden along the rear of the building. I tested the latch—it was unlocked—and pushed the door open.

Just as last weekend, the room was empty except for the king-size bed, which sprawled over the gleaming hardwood floor. Unlike last weekend, a miniature grand piano occupied the nook by the window. But my attention was snagged by a square of paper directly in front of me.

I cautiously plucked the note from the floor and opened it. *Mine,* it said.

My breath puffed out in silent laughter.

Oh, yes, this was Sara, so completely Sara.

I ran my fingers over the paper—no, it was parchment. I recalled the texture from college, when we studied calligraphy and illuminated manuscripts in art history class. Holmes had used an ordinary pen, but the strong lines and especially the flourish after the final *e* reminded me of those older scripts. The thickness of the sheet was unusual, even for parchment. In the upper left corner, a curious pattern of bumps caught my eye. I tilted the sheet this way and that. Sunlight gleamed off the thin metallic threads half-buried in the material. A tracking device? Delivery confirmation, translated to paper?

I returned the note precisely to where I'd found it. Stared at it a moment, then laughed again. *Dear Jacob. Do you know what your friend is like? Of course you do. You tried to warn me from the start.*

The second bedroom was smaller, but like everything else in the apartment, its dimensions seemed perfectly proportioned— a bright, sunlit sanctuary with a high patterned ceiling, made even more lovely by the humming air conditioner. Two narrow windows overlooked a second garden that ran along the right-hand side of the building. The garden, well tended as one might expect, was filled to overflowing with more wildflowers, roses, and a cluster of crabapple trees that were already dropping their leaves. Beyond the low brick wall that divided number 2809 from the next property, I saw the angled tower that made one corner of the neighboring house. Was that a shadow I saw behind the curtains? One of the neighbors, watching?

Abruptly, I was exhausted. *No, dammit. I will not run away. Not this time.*

I fetched the suitcase and computer bag from the vestibule and hauled them onto my bed. Clothes were the first and easiest items to dispose of. The bedroom had a series of built-in drawers along one wall. Underwear went into one, T-shirts in the next, then socks and trousers and all the rest, rolled tightly in military fashion.

The room included three narrow closets as well. My few dress suits, remnants from my life before the war, did not even fill half of one. If I wanted, I could transfer the boxes of leftover childhood mementos, which my parents had lovingly preserved, from the storage unit in Suitland.

Another dangerous pause overtook me, another moment wishing for a past I could never recover.

I threw myself into motion once more. Within a few moments, I had unpacked the tablet and its accessories, and arranged them on the desk by the window. The apartment provided us with Wi-Fi as part of our rent, but I would need to research options for email accounts and privacy keys. I didn't want to depend on the VA, or the honor of Hudson Realty.

The tablet booted. I brought up a browser to test the connection. All good. Later I would check the portal for any communication from my new employer. For now, I continued with the present and mundane. The paperbacks I had brought from Alton, or acquired in the past two weeks, fitted into one set of shelves underneath the window. My medical supplies went into a smaller cabinet next to my bed. I automatically counted the bottles and boxes. I would need a new supply of swabs before the week ended. More antiseptic. Not to mention blankets and sheets.

And towels, dammit.

I sank to my knees next to the bed and pressed my fists against my eyes. *Oh, Saúl. You were wrong. I can't do this.*

You can. I could almost hear his voice. *One small bite at a time.*

I had many, many small bites ahead of me. All of them dry and unseasoned.

Stop whining, I told myself. *You have a job. And a life better than the one your parents had on that dirt farm.*

A week from Monday, it was. I would report to the VA Medical Center at eight A.M. for orientation and training for my new position as a medical technician. Twenty-five dollars an hour, thirty hours a week guaranteed. No benefits, but the opportunity to advance through training. BioStar's offer had been for $35 an hour, but they could not promise me a start date earlier than October 13. It was the start date, not any recommendation from Holmes, that had decided me.

Sara Holmes. I tilted my head back and stared at the ceiling as I tried to untangle her character. How had she known about the jobs I had applied for? Why did she claim to need a partner to share the rent? Or perhaps none of that mattered.

After all, I didn't need a friend or companion. I only wanted a refuge from that dreadful hostel. If her agenda provided me with a refuge both lovely and private, who was I to argue?

From far off, a door crashed open.

At once, I dropped to the floor, reaching automatically for a weapon, a club, anything to beat away the enemy. There were six patients in the critical ward, a dozen more in recovery. I had to get them away . . .

The loud *tap, tap, tap* of heels over the tiled entryway broke through my panic. I recognized that pattern. I'd heard it seven days ago, in the National Gallery of Art, and again, outside Jenna Hudson's office.

I released a shuddering breath. I was in DC, not Alton. The intruder was Sara Holmes, not a troop of enemy soldiers. A very angry Sara, however, judging from that slammed door. Was that any less dangerous?

The *tap, tap, tap* vanished around the corner. Moments later, the other bedroom door slammed shut. I waited, my breath held tight as I listened for more clues about Sara and what had broken that seemingly unbreakable façade of arrogance.

Jacob himself had warned me. *Some might call her difficult,* he'd said. I had taken his words for a challenge. How soon before I regretted doing so?

Now. Yesterday. I wanted to laugh. Instead I choked down a sob.

Gradually my heartbeat slowed. Quiet settled over the apartment, drifting through the rooms like winter snow. I still could not bring myself to move. I lay with my cheek against that cool and polished floor, taking deep and steady breaths. Eventually I would stand up. Eventually I would continue to unpack my suitcase, arrange my new life. It would have to be soon, or I risked drowning in lethargy. But not yet. Not . . . quite yet.

From far away, I heard a crash of chords from the piano.

A crash, loud and angry, as angry as the door slamming shut. A moment of heart-shaking silence followed, as though Sara had startled herself. Then came a series of single notes, slow and tentative at first, but gathering speed and assurance, like the flood tide I'd once witnessed up north in Canada. My knowledge of music was like my knowledge of cooking and art—enough to care about the details, not enough to call myself an expert. But this piece I remembered from one of my last outings with Angela. *Appassionata*, the piece was called. By Bach—no, Beethoven.

Chord by chord, the melody rose upward like a host of angels toward a grand and glorious redemption.

I was no Christian, nor was this a sacred song.

But this. Yes, this.

If I were a god, I might ask for such a joyous noise.

I listened a few moments longer to that oh so glorious music, then picked myself up slowly from the floor. A list, I told myself. All I needed was a list to start. I sat down at my new desk and my tablet, opened up a new text document, and began to type.

5

SEPTEMBER 17. Redemption. *Funny word, that. It
dropped into my head this morning as I was negotiating
the deluxe coffeemaker in apartment 2B. Dictionaries say*
redemption *means "deliverance." And, oh, those days I
spent hiding with my patients in a ditch, I would have said*
deliverance *had the loveliest syllables in all recorded time.
A couple of entries down, you come to a different definition.
"Atonement." Christ's blood for ours. Punishment
transferred, not grace bestowed. I think a lot about grace
and punishment these days. Maybe next week, when I'm
not so wrung out, I'll have something profound to write.
Not today.*

I wrote in my journal today. That I managed to write anything, and at six A.M., was almost worth recording by itself.
The entry was nothing more than a quick scribble, but I had
needed the act of writing itself, more than the particular
words. I had needed the feel of my favorite pen between my

fingers, needed to see the bright green ink trace patterns on the page, patterns that made words that made a string of sentences that echoed, however imperfectly, my thoughts. Epiphanies could come later, if they came at all.

But I knew the root and reason for choosing that particular subject. Today was my first day flying solo at the VA Medical Center, with no nurse supervisor dictating my every word or action. Today was just me and the patients in that interview room. It would be hard, maybe harder than my first day of residency at Georgetown, because I had to remind myself constantly that these were not *my* patients. I was only a technician.

One day, one victory at a time, I told myself. Each victory to tip the scales weighed down by Alton. Each day to bring me closer to a new device, to my life redeemed.

I drank off the last of my coffee and scanned my tiny domain to make sure it was ready for inspection. Counters cleared and wiped down. Check. The roll of exam paper in its slot and a fresh segment draped over the table. Check. Keyboard, screen, and electronic pen, ready for use. The inventory of equipment and supplies signed by the previous shift supervisor. Check and check. For the next seven and a half hours, minus lunch and federally mandated breaks, this would be my world.

It's part of the new VA, my nurse supervisor had told me that first day.

A VA driven by the need to economize, what with Congress so anxious for funds, and the White House unwilling to spend its waning political capital in this difficult election season. And so they had instituted this new system, where medical technicians interviewed the patients, took their blood pressure, and handled dozens of other tasks once assigned to the nurses and physician assistants. Our time was cheaper than theirs, and since we worked thirty or fewer hours a week, we cost the VA no benefits.

I closed my eyes, felt the roiling in my stomach subside. The heavy scent of antiseptic hung in the air, familiar and welcome, and from the corridor came the hum of equipment, the voices of nurses deep in a technical discussion. Even the blank white sterility of my surroundings felt like a coming home of sorts.

"Watson."

My supervisor, RN Roberta Thompson, stood in the doorway.

I set my mug aside at once and paid attention. You did that with Thompson. She was tall and lean and brown, with a nose like a hawk's beak, and a temper that came and went, like summer thunder. She spared one glance toward my coffee mug—a breach of regulation, but one so frequently broken that everyone ignored it—then made her own survey of the room.

Apparently, I passed, because she gave a brisk nod of approval. "Your first patient wants a follow-up consultation," she said. "I showed you the procedure yesterday, but we'll go over it again now. Are you logged in? Good. Click menu option VAQF-03. Patient questionnaire number 0400 is the one you want. Memorize this form, Watson. Love it as you love your mother. Oh, sorry. I forgot about your mother. Well, as you love your paycheck. Got it? Now tap that icon to copy the patient ID to your personal list."

I worked through the menu options with my electronic pen until I reached the screen showing the appointments scheduled for today. Confirmed appointments were blue. Patients who had checked in were marked green. From here, I could select the next one for their interview. The joke about my mother had left me sweating, but I contained myself.

"Got it," I said.

Thompson regarded me with a long stare. "Do you, now? Listen anyway. This is the standard questionnaire we use for follow-ups. I told you this before. I will likely tell you six more times this week. This form has all the necessary input fields—which you *will* enter completely or I *will* chew your sorry ass into a million pieces. If you think you need more information, *Dr.* Watson, you only need to click one of these happy icons to the right. Green for patient history. Yellow for details about their previous visit. Red connects you to the laboratory portal to request any tests or look up results. If you decide to request any tests—and you better have a damned good reason—you need my okay or a doctor's. Got it?"

I knew that tone from my residency days. "I do."

Thompson grinned. "I like your attitude, sunshine. Don't disappoint me. Good luck."

She left me to inspect the next technician and room.

The clock on the wall flipped silently to eight forty-five A.M.

According to regulations, my official workday started at nine A.M., but I knew from VA gossip that *official* had an elastic meaning. Once a patient had completed the initial check-in procedure, they were often led directly to an interview room. So I stowed my coffee cup in a bottom drawer, then double-checked the status of my terminal. My duties were simple enough—ask the questions from the screen, pick this answer, check that box, type a few notes, then record their vital stats, and send the poor scrub off to the next waiting room.

"Med tech?"

One of the office staff stood outside my door. Alice, that was her name. She indicated the patient standing behind her. Sergeant Michael Williams. Ex-sergeant Williams, here for a follow-up exam. I picked up the electronic pen and gave him my best professional smile. "Good morning. Let's get you started."

☙

Name and date of birth, please.
    Military ID.
    Date of discharge.
    Date and location of your last medical exam.
    Any changes in your medications?
    Any new symptoms?

The questionnaire guided me through the questions, with only a few variations, depending on the answers I tapped with my electronic pen. I needed to type any personal observations, however, and with the scant fifteen minutes allocated for each patient, I found myself keeping more and more to the lists and menus. Regulations also stated I was to double-check those answers against the patient's medical history. One of the senior med techs—the only one who didn't glare at *Dr.* Watson—told me I would spend at least half an hour at day's end catching up on the required follow-up work. "Unpaid oversight and training" was how the employee manual described it. I could log the time for pay, but I might risk an official reprimand. I'd most certainly risk unofficial displeasure.

A faint hum from the digital clock caught my attention.

The numbers had ticked over to 11:43. Two minutes to the next patient. Seventeen until my lunch break. I rested my head in my hands and wished for a cup of strong coffee. I'd been at work three hours. It felt more like three hundred.

I had just enough time to massage my temples before Alice appeared with the next patient, a small woman, brown skinned and compact, her hair shaved close to her skull. She might have been in her twenties, but it was hard to tell from the lines of pain etched on her face.

"Doctor?" she said.

My pulse jumped at the old title. And her accent, a liquid lilting rhythm, called up memories from Alton and the attack.

"I'm not the doctor," I told her. "I'm here to review your history first."

I pointed to the examination table. She limped over to it and awkwardly took a seat. A part of me registered the loose camouflage pants and olive-green T-shirt, clothing that closely resembled a soldier's uniform without crossing over that invisible line. And unlike so many other patients that day, she didn't argue when I ran through all the usual questions about her service history and recent medical symptoms.

"Name and date of birth?"

"Belinda Díaz. September first."

She gave her birth year. Only twenty-five, then.

"Military ID."

I typed the number she provided. The system chimed to signal a match, and the screen blossomed with new information. Belinda Díaz had graduated from high school in Charleston, West Virginia, part of the growing population of Latinx in that state. She joined the army the next day and, after the standard training, served thirteen months in the Crimea. When President Sanches recalled the military from abroad, Private Díaz transferred with the rest of her squad to Tennessee. On June 3 of this year, she lost her leg from the knee down during a reconnaissance mission in enemy territory. The surgeon in the closest medical unit had fitted her with a device. Her last visit to us had been just one week ago. Dr. Patel had been the physician.

Díaz kicked off her shoe and pulled up her trouser leg.

The device before me was an ugly collection of metal rods with boxlike compartments at the knee and ankle, which housed the primitive electronics, and a foot that looked like blunt pedal. The last time I had seen a device like this, it was over ten years ago, and even then it had been an outdated model. The thing enabled her to walk, but not much more. If she had been a dancer, a nurse, she would have lost her career. As it was, she could only stand two hours at a time.

But that was life for our soldiers these days. That was our whole economy tumbling down into the black hole called the New Civil War.

"I want to work," she said.

"I understand."

Díaz glanced at my left arm. "I guess you do."

There was not much I could say to that.

"You came to us last week," I said.

She nodded.

"Any problems with your medication?"

She hesitated. "No. Nothing wrong."

There was a long, long mile between wrong and good, our nurses had told me, during my intern days. I could also sense the tension radiating from Díaz, and I knew better than to press her for answers.

"I'm glad to hear that," I said, my tone and expression carefully neutral. "Now, I just need to check what I typed here, Private. My left hand isn't so good as it used to be, so it might take me a few minutes. Why don't you tell me a bit about yourself?"

There wasn't much to tell. After the army had discharged her, Díaz had returned to her family in West Virginia. To no one's surprise, there weren't many jobs for someone like her. Now she lived with a cousin in DC, where she had signed up for all the VA's recommended programs. She had also enrolled in classes at UDC, so she could get a certificate in data entry. But she had trouble sleeping and eating regularly.

I know how that goes. Lord, I know how that goes.

I kept those thoughts to myself as I typed in her comments

about sleep and appetite under the section labeled *Preliminary Observations*. Anderson and Wright were the physicians on duty this morning. Both men had a reputation for ignoring comments from the medical technicians, but regulations required me to fill out the section, so I did.

"Just a few more things before I send you on," I told Díaz.

Weight, 130. Pulse, 80—well inside the so-called normal range, but edging toward the high end. Still, visiting the doctor often did that. The blood pressure, though, measured 135/90. Not dangerous, but not good for someone her age and weight. It all depended on her current diet and medical history. I glanced at the yellow icon, then the clock on the wall. Two minutes left, unless I wanted to cut my lunch break short.

"Tell me why you came to us last week," I asked her.

Her voice came softer and slower now, wary almost. "Nothing to tell. I can't sleep. I can't . . . Dr. Patel gave me some meds. I don't remember what they're called, but he told me to come back if they didn't help. They didn't. Not much anyway."

I laid a hand on her shoulder. Felt a tremor that could have been simple nervousness, could have been something more.

A standard suite of blood tests might uncover the problem. Hopefully Patel had done that. I'd have to check her history and the laboratory portal later. For now, I recorded the numbers for weight, pulse, and blood pressure, adding the notation *Borderline on the last two. Consult records to compare previous readings.* Wright and Anderson might ignore my entries, but Thompson would pay attention. She could make the doctors listen, if she thought it necessary.

"Is there anything else you'd like to tell me?" I asked.

Again Díaz hesitated. "No. Nothing. I just want to see the doctor."

My instincts told me she was lying. But I was no internist,

nor a counselor. My job was to record the patient's symptoms and send her on to the next waiting room.

I logged out at four P.M., as the regulations required. And as regulations required, I spent the next forty minutes double-checking my records for the day, comparing each patient's symptoms and vitals against their history. Williams, Reyes, King, Mendoza, Young, Guzman . . . I could match each face against their fifteen-minute slot in the day. Out of curiosity, I navigated to the screen for details about Belinda Díaz's visit today. No blood tests, today or the week before, which surprised me, but perhaps there was a quota. Anderson had prescribed a drug with the company code LP#2024016.

A click on the link brought up a summary of LP#2024016. Approved by the FDA a couple months ago. Originally intended to treat high blood pressure, it had a better score treating stress-related disorders.

Stress-related disorders. Call it PTSD, why don't you? Call it the disease of war.

A drug like this was almost tailor-made for these times. Livvy Pharmaceuticals owned the patent, which usually meant a higher cost, but they supplied the drug at a discount as part of their contract with the VA. One of the senior med techs had made a passing joke the other day about big pharma and their endless government contracts, only to get reprimanded by one of the doctors. Another, more nebulous memory about Livvy—or was it about another company?—hovered just out of reach. A conversation I'd had . . . When? Last month? Last year? It would come to me later, I decided. I made a note in my personal log to check the drug's details, then went on to the next patient's records.

At four forty-five, Thompson arrived to review my performance. Her critique was brief and to the point. I hadn't made any outright mistakes, she told me, but I needed to improve my patient-to-hours ratio. By the time I changed from scrubs into my own clothing and started for home, I was trembling from exhaustion.

Home. More like a temporary shelter. A damned expensive one.

It's better than a dirt farm. It's better than that goddamned hostel. It has air conditioning. And sometimes Sara cooks.

What an inadequate word. To say that Sara cooked was to say that Dalí used a paintbrush. I had watched her at work, plucking fresh herbs from her miniature garden, dashing sesame oil into a shallow pan, her hands moving rapidly as she diced and chopped and stirred.

Do you cook? she had asked me that first day. Yes, I did, but nothing like that.

Tonight, however, she had sent word through her texting gadget—the gadget she refused to take back—that she had obligations elsewhere that evening. I could order ahead to Hudson Realty's concierge service, or I could fend for myself.

I allowed myself the very brief fantasy that I could afford the concierge service. That fantasy went along with my dream for a new device and higher pay. The regret lasted as long as it took me to travel half the distance along my usual route home. My path took me between the stark white buildings of the medical complex, around the silver-threaded expanse of the reservoir and its grassy banks, then past the brightly painted row houses on Harvard Street, with their slate roofs perched like conical hats above yellow and red faces. Those gave way to larger houses set back from the sidewalk, and in turn to the small shops and diners on Columbia Road.

I stopped by one of the grocery stores on Columbia for

chicken breasts and fresh greens. Rested my feet a bit when I came to a bench. By the time I climbed the steps to 2809 Q NW, the sun had dipped behind the rows of brick houses, and the first breath of coolness cut through the late summer air. Even so, my feet ached from the long walk, and invisible claws gripped my skull.

I need a Metro card. I don't care what it costs. I don't care how many times I have to transfer.

Next paycheck, I promised myself. *Next paycheck* had become a promise to me. Oh, the luxuries I would indulge in then. A Metro card with extra zones included. A journal with thick creamy paper, bound in leather. And a genuine fountain pen, the kind I used in my residency days. My imagination rolled on to the paycheck after that. Better shoes. A jar of that expensive hair cream I once saw in a shop window. An insulated carafe so I could drink hot coffee all morning long. And I would treat Jacob to his favorite diner, then a night at the theater.

I balanced my bag of groceries against my hip and pressed my right thumb over the door's security reader. There was a glimmer of green, a spark, and . . .

. . . And nothing.

My heart gave an uncomfortable jump. A fault in the system, I told myself. Hudson had warned us about glitches on the hottest days. Security was working on the problem. I wiped my hand dry against my trousers and tried again. This time, the light flickered a moment before turning red.

"Security breach," announced the device. "Contacting precinct. Please stand by."

Goddamn it.

The last thing I needed today—any day—was a conversation with the local police.

I leaned against the doorframe, trembling. The rage I had

locked down these past two weeks pressed hard against its invisible cage. *Do not shout. Do not make any kind of show. Do not, do* not *look over your shoulder to see if anyone is watching.*

From what Jenna Hudson had told us, I had five minutes before the local cops showed up.

I needed to fetch my metal keys from my pocket, but my right hand shook too hard, and my prosthetic had begun to tremble from the electric pulses of my panic. *Breathe,* I told myself. *Let's take this one step at a time.*

There was an option the med techs had described to me, almost reluctantly, in the last week of therapy, but not anything I had tried for myself. Saúl himself had warned me the mechanism for this particular model was not reliable. It might fail. It might never unlock.

At this point, I did not care. I set my arm in position around the bag of groceries. With a flick of my thumb, I opened the control panel and pressed the keys to initiate the lock sequence. The arm twitched once before the mechanism clicked over and the arm went rigid.

It took me a count of ten before I could trust the lock was secure. Another interval after that before the trembling throughout my body stilled. Only then did I unzip the pocket of my trousers and fetch out my key ring. *Do not hurry,* I told myself. I had at least three more minutes.

The key slid into the slot and turned. I dove through the door and shut it after me. By now I was counting the moments until I could hide in my bedroom. I chose the stairs over the elevator, purely to keep in motion. Once I reached the second floor, I didn't even bother with the biometric reader at the apartment. I unlocked the door with my backup keys and hurried inside.

The living room was empty, another blessing. If my luck held, Sara would not return until morning. But as I rounded the corner toward the kitchen, I heard voices coming from Sara's bedroom. Damn. Another one of *those* nights.

I had lived with Sara Holmes for twelve short days. I had *expected* a series of infuriating confrontations, mostly variations on that first and very uncomfortable encounter we had in front of Dalí's extravaganza. Difficult, yes, but in the ordinary sense of the word, even though Sara herself was anything but ordinary. It was the price for this luxurious apartment, I had told myself over and over. The penalty for my foolish love of beauty.

But I had never imagined the visitors.

Oh, those visitors.

Every couple or three nights, Sara entertained. Or at least that is how she explained the matter to me. Two days after I moved in, I came home to find a dozen strangers in the parlor. Rich people, judging by their clothes. I had not waited for introductions. I had fled into my rooms, where Sara had left an exquisite meal, which she had clearly cooked herself. An apology? A bribe?

The visitors had stayed until dawn. The following morning I demanded an explanation, or at least a promise that she would warn me the next time. I got neither. Instead, another party arrived the same night, smaller and quieter, but no less an intrusion. After that, the pattern continued. A night or two of quiet, followed by several noisy ones. Once she had met me at the door with a handful of hundred-dollar bills. "Go," she whispered. "The Fairmont has a room waiting for you. I'll send over a bag with your things." After those first few incidents, they left no traces behind, these visitors, which I found more unsettling than their presence.

A man's laughter echoed from Sara's bedroom.

Ignore her. Ignore them. Eat your dinner, then hide in your room.

I hauled the bag of groceries onto the counter and slumped

against the cabinets. My anger had leached away, along with it the temporary surge of strength, but the drills from my physical therapist had now kicked in. I unlocked my arm. It fell to my side, as limp as metal could be. The clock on the microwave read 6:20. Fourteen hours until the next workday, with its lists of questions and carefully measured-out parcels of attention for our patients. Thompson had called my work adequate—a compliment, actually—but what had I accomplished? Other than earning $150, minus taxes?

You have delusions of importance, my sister had once told me.

The same delusion that had led me to volunteer for the army.

Maybe Grace was right, after all.

Or maybe I was just tired and sore from a long, unaccustomed day. I rested my head on my hands and let the air conditioning work its healing upon me. Gradually my headache receded. Much more gradually, the sweat evaporated from my skin and I felt a brief resurgence of energy. I unpacked the groceries and fetched a cutting board from its latest hiding spot.

A sudden swell of voices caught my attention. Holmes's visitors had emerged from her bedroom and were heading for the parlor. It was a smaller crowd than usual—four strangers, plus Sara herself. One man was holding forth in a language I couldn't identify, but I could recognize someone expounding on a much beloved topic. A woman interrupted him. A question? An objection?

Their footsteps slowed as they passed by the kitchen. They must have noticed my presence. I bent over the counter and concentrated on chopping up the chicken breasts.

Sara made a comment in that same language. Her companions laughed and continued onward to the parlor. The outer door slammed once, and the apartment fell abruptly silent.

I blew out a breath of relief. Only then did I realize I had begun wrong. I needed to set the rice boiling before I sautéed the chicken and greens. I set the cutting board to one side and rousted out the deluxe rice cooker from one of the bottom cabinets.

I had not dared to confront Sara since that first incident, but that didn't mean I had stopped having questions. Worrisome questions. Who were all these visitors? Was Holmes a drug dealer, perhaps? What if the police raided our apartment and considered me an accomplice?

After that first incident, I checked my lease. The section covering terms and conditions went on for several pages of legalese, all of which translated to *You are stuck for twelve months, and ain't no way to get around it*. The fine print said I could terminate the contract with two months' notice, plus a forfeit of my security deposit, which equaled another month of rent. I'd spent a few evenings cursing my trusting nature. Perhaps I could convince Jenna Hudson that Holmes had misrepresented herself to me and to Hudson Realty. Was there an exception clause if your roommate turned out to be a criminal?

I dumped a cup of rice into the cooker, then rummaged through the cabinets for the liquid measuring cup. I had just located one when Holmes strolled into the kitchen, whistling softly. She wore a rumpled brown tunic and trousers, the cloth shot through with threads of gold. Her locs hung loose today. The scent of sandalwood perfume was stronger, the memories of Angela almost irresistible.

Almost.

"You work too hard," she said.

I filled the cup with water. "Is that another deduction?"

"No. Simply an observation."

She reached out and laid a hand on my arm before I could pour the water into the cooker. "What do you say to dinner out? I heard about an exquisite new Thai restaurant near the diplomatic quarter. It would be my treat, of course."

I froze. She had never touched me before. Her fingers were like flames, warm and ephemeral. It was not so much that I found her attractive—though I did—but that she seemed so utterly unconnected with the physical world. This reminder of her being flesh and blood unsettled me. I took a moment and cleared my throat. "Why?"

Holmes shrugged. "I've had some luck this week. I'd like to celebrate."

"With me?"

"You're restful. Or, if you don't believe that, you're useful."

Useful. I wanted to laugh. And yet, I'd questioned my usefulness not an hour ago.

"Who were those people?" I asked instead.

Sara laughed. "You don't want to know."

I slammed the cup onto the counter, sloshing water everywhere. "Yes, I *do*, goddamn it. Who are they, Sara? And don't tell me they're just friends. Friends like that are usually called business associates. Maybe I should expect the police to come sniffing around next week. Or maybe the FBI."

She regarded me with an expression I could not decipher. Amused? No, not that. As if she were gauging my competence. Only now did I see the faint lines etched beside her eyes and mouth, lines of laughter, yes, but others that spoke of great anxiety. She was older than I had guessed. But how old?

"Is that what you believe?" she asked.

I found a rag and mopped up the water. "I don't know what to believe."

She nodded. "Fair enough. Come with me to dinner—"

"No. That's not good enough."

"Ah, but what if I promise to answer three questions?"

Oh. The breath fled my body at the offer. How had she guessed?

I recalled myself. "You won't tell me the truth."

"Perhaps not. But you won't find out unless you say yes."

I said yes. Five minutes later I regretted it.

Sara came into my bedroom while I stared at the very few, very inadequate dresses and suits in my closet. Without a word, she unfurled a mass of shimmering dark blue fabric and let it settle softly over my bedspread.

"I thought I might lend you a dress," she said.

My hand reached toward it without volition, and I needed all my willpower to pluck it back. Such a lovely thing, custom sewn from a dark blue silk that reminded me of a storm-ridden sky, with sleeves constructed from a loose fall of matching blue lace, gathered at the wrists. Sara and I were of a height, but where she was blade thin, I had the heft and muscle of my father.

"That is not one of your dresses," I said flatly.

"I never claimed it was," she replied.

"Where did you get it?"

"Is that one of your questions?"

"No."

"Then I see no reason to answer you." In a softer, rougher voice, she added, "I have bracelets and rings to match. Would you like to see them?"

I closed my eyes. *You can always say no.*

But there was the matter of those three questions.

"I need to shower," I told her. "Please leave the room."

Holmes laughed. "As you wish. Our car arrives at seven fifteen P.M. You have half an hour."

The door clicked shut. I eased out a breath. Glanced down

at the shimmering dress and ran my fingers over the impossibly soft fabric. *It's not a gift,* I told myself. Or if Sara believed that, she would find out how temporary gifts could be.

I retreated to the bathroom to shower. Sara had vanished into her own bedroom, but not for long, as I discovered once I returned to mine. In spite of my refusal, Holmes had left a set of silver bracelets on my bed, along with stockings to match the dress, and a pair of low-heeled shoes.

I slid the dress over my head. Just as I suspected, the fit was perfect—too perfect—and I had another moment when I reconsidered accepting these gifts, even temporarily. But beauty was my weakness, and Sara had gauged my tastes with unsettling precision.

It's a challenge, I told myself. *I've faced harder ones.*

Besides, she had promised to answer three questions.

I drew a deep breath to steady my nerves and slid the bracelets onto my right wrist. The bracelets chimed softly. The metal felt cool against my skin. Ready, then.

Holmes waited for me in our parlor. She too had dressed for the occasion, in a suit cut from a gleaming black silk that flowed over her lean frame. Her ordinary earbuds had vanished, replaced by a new set of polished silver. An enormous pearl hung from one earlobe. She had tied back her locs with a silver ribbon, but loosely, as if they could not be adequately contained.

She reached out a lace-covered hand. "Shall we begin our adventure?"

The car waited by the curb, a discreet black limousine, with an equally discreet driver, who ushered us into the luxurious back compartment. I thought I glimpsed one of our neighbors watching from behind the curtains of their upper-story window, and felt a flutter of laughter at their likely astonishment.

We rode in grand state to the restaurant. There was time

for a glass of champagne, and a conversation mainly supported by Sara Holmes, who seemed strangely exhilarated. Once we arrived at the restaurant, she waved the driver away and handed me out of the car herself.

"Look happy," she said softly, in her low voice. "For my sake."

The steward greeted Holmes by name and escorted us to a seat underneath a window overlooking Dupont Circle. Sara ordered a bottle of wine to be served immediately while we considered the menu. That accomplished, the waiter and his attendants withdrew. Sara lifted the glass in my direction. "I promised you answers," she said. "You will have them. Or do you need more time?"

"Do *you* need more time?" I asked.

She glanced up from her hooded eyes. Once again, I caught the hint of tension before she granted me a flashing smile. "I never need more time, my love. But since you offer, I shall ask a few questions myself. Point for point, of course."

Cold washed over me at the thought of what kind of questions Sara would ask. "I am *not* your love. And that was not our agreement."

"Not originally, but you implied a change with your words. No? But I insist. I have so many questions for you, doctor. It would not be fair to tease and taunt me with possibilities. However, if you like, you may start."

Her voice was light and mocking, very much a replay of our first encounter. My first impulse was to walk out the door and back to Q Street. I suppressed the urge. Q Street was a very long mile and a half away. Sara had dismissed the driver when we arrived, and I had no money for a taxi or the Metro. So and so. Very neatly planned. Very well. If I was trapped here, I might as well use the opportunity to extract some information about the enigmatic Sara Holmes.

A dozen questions presented themselves at once. I suspected she would refuse to answer them. I would have to conduct this conversation as I would a diagnosis. Choose questions that might define the overall shape of the disease, or in this case, the mystery.

"First one," I said. "How much do you— No, tell me this. What is the true rent for our apartment? Not what we pay, but what Hudson Realty would charge anyone else?"

Holmes's eyes narrowed with amusement. "Excellent choice, doctor. Very well. The apartment normally rents for sixty-two hundred dollars a month. I negotiated a lower price. I then requested several additional options, none of which concern you. All in all, the total cost is fairly close to the original."

I let the breath trickle from my lips. So, I had been correct with my suspicions.

Holmes was grinning, as if in anticipation. I braced myself for her question.

Instead, she fluttered her hand at me. "Next one?"

I had not expected that, and I needed a few moments to decide. She had answered honestly at first—a tactic calculated to disarm me. Yes? No? I could not tell.

"You are thinking," Sara said. "How unlike you. Except I know from your diaries that you do think. About redemption, and Dalí, and—"

I slammed a fist against the table. "You spied on me."

"Hardly. You left your journal in the kitchen this morning."

"If you had any honor—"

"I never claimed I did. Ask your next question."

"Fine. Question number two. What work do you do?"

Her laugh was a soft chuckle. "As little as possible." She glanced around, and I was suddenly aware of the many eyes pointed in our direction.

"That was no answer," I whispered.

"It is all I can say. My turn. When did you first know you didn't love Angela Gray? And why did you tell everyone you did?"

The breath fled my body. Angela. How did she—? Except I knew how. Not from my journals—I had not written about Angela in weeks, and all my older journals were safely locked away—but Holmes had connections to any number of databases and online records, none of them very secure, apparently.

I took refuge in argument. "Those are two questions, not one."

Sara nodded. "True. Pick one or two and answer them. We'll total up our accounts later."

"What if I refuse?"

"Then we leave at once, starved of information and dinner both. And I believe you are very hungry these days, Dr. Watson."

She met my gaze directly, without any hint of amusement. This was no bluff.

Eleven more months until the end of my lease, I thought. Eleven more months of the madness that was Sara Holmes. Briefly, very briefly, I considered abandoning Washington, DC, and my quest for a new device. Forget the goddamned lease. I could vanish into New York City. I could take up a new career, under a new identity. Bookseller would be nice.

Before I could succumb to my impulse, the waiter appeared with an array of appetizers I didn't remember ordering. He refilled our water and wineglasses, then politely faded away. I selected several of the chili shrimp and nibbled on them between sips of wine, conscious of Sara's gaze all the while. She did not press me, however, and with food a small portion of my fury leaked away. "Very well. I loved Angela until she stopped loving me. There was no reason to tell anyone anything."

Holmes regarded me with a long, considering look, and I had the feeling I had admitted more than I intended to. I stared back at her, which only brought her closer to the edge of laughter.

Have you loved anyone in your life? Or are we all game pieces to move around as you like?

But I did not have the courage to ask her those questions. Not yet. We worked our way through the appetizers, then a delicious first course that I could barely recall afterward. But once the waiter cleared away the dishes, I could not resist.

"I have a question that is not one of my questions."

"That is not part of our agreement."

"It isn't," I agreed. "But what if I decide to walk out now? What if I decide your games are not mine? Because whatever you think of my intellect, I know you want me here, in this dress, and if I do not cooperate, your plans will suffer."

Her amusement became a barely contained laughter. "I see. Ask then. I shall not count it against you."

"Very well. Why did you call me restful?"

For a moment she did not answer. She raised her wine-glass, almost in the attitude of a toast, and studied the pale golden liquid. "Because you are. Restful, that is. No, that is not a genuine answer. Because you keep regular hours. Because you take pains with your work. Because you have not yet attempted to murder me."

At that I could not help myself. I laughed. "Three answers for nothing. Thank you."

Holmes's eyes glinted with shared humor. "You have one more."

The glee faded. *So do you,* I thought. Two more, if I wanted to be honest.

I finished off my glass of wine and felt the warmth, the pleasant and seductive warmth, spread through my body.

I sensed Holmes's attention, like that of a wildcat that had sighted its prey and was waiting for the moment to strike.

Perhaps that was not fair.

Perhaps it was not true.

And yet I had learned to trust my instincts.

"No," I said softly. "Thank you, but no. I'll save my last for another day."

I expected her to insist, but Sara almost immediately turned to a different subject and asked me how I liked the restaurant. From there our conversation wandered into more commonplace topics. The late summer weather. The overloaded Metro system, the quirks and difficulties with the new driverless buses, and how the outlying routes only added to the burden of the inner-city lines. Sara spoke as someone quite familiar with the city, which I had not expected, and with the grace and skill of a person used to making social conversation.

It was as though she had deliberately muted herself. Become almost . . . ordinary.

A part of me doubted her motives, even now. Did she want me lulled into complacency? Or had she already accomplished her mysterious purpose simply by coaxing me to this restaurant?

In the end, I was too weary to keep up my suspicions. And when we returned to our apartment at midnight, I was happy to retreat into my bedroom and close the door.

The silence continued as I undressed. Then, then came the first notes of *Appassionata,* a wondrous crashing set of chords. One single thunder of music that stopped abruptly. I waited, my own heart echoing that thunder. Silence came after that, or so I thought. Then I heard the soft, soft opening of Pachelbel's Canon. A melody calculated to unwind the tangled cares of the day and let me drift slowly into sleep.

6

Early the next morning, I returned every borrowed item to
Sara Holmes. I did that face-to-face, confronting her in the
parlor before she could escape into whatever mysterious errands she had planned. First the dress, carefully folded. The
shoes, with any small scuff marks polished away. The stockings, hand-washed and hung to dry overnight. I laid each
item on the parlor table, as though I were checking off my
inventory sheet at work. Last came the jewelry, piece by piece.

The jewelry cost me a small pang. As I said, beauty is my
weakness.

Sara accepted them without comment, unless you counted
that tiny twist of her mouth, as though she could detect how
my fingers hovered over the rings and bracelets, wanting to
touch them one last time.

I hurried off to work before I could regret the act.

🔍

I should have suspected that smile.

Every single gift came back to me, returned secretly and

with obvious mischief. That same evening, when I kicked off my shoes into my closet, I discovered the dress among my suits. The rings and bracelets turned up the next morning in my underwear drawer. Apparently a closed door meant nothing to Sara. I shouldn't have been surprised. If she could gleefully trespass my thoughts by reading my journal, why would she balk at invading my bedroom?

I sank onto the bed and fingered one of the bracelets. The scarcely visible pattern etched onto its surface, like the pattern of raindrops on the surface of a lake. I remembered that time Angela bought me an expensive gift, for no reason other than it pleased her and she hoped to please me. Such an innocent act. I terrified her, I think, with my anger.

Gifts are temporary, I had said. I was shouting.

Am I temporary too? Angela had shouted back. She was crying.

In the end, I proved us both right.

September . . . What? Same year, same month as the last entry. All the days are smeared together in an ugly murky cloud. I can only keep track by the paychecks. Two so far. I feel disconnected from DC, from life outside my hours at the VA Medical Center. Whenever I listen to the news reports on the break room TV—news about Sanches, the war, the elections—it's as though they are talking about the other side of the world.

The VA. God. Six <u>official</u> hours, plus time off the clock to double-check every form and lab result. Six hours with my supervisor reaming me out for every minor infraction of the rules, even if those rules leave a patient undiagnosed. God forbid the doctors actually help someone. Except . . . I believe they do want to help. So do Thompson and all the med techs. We are just fucked by the regulations.

(NB: <u>Fuck</u>. A word as old as Chaucer, once innocent and now forbidden. Swearing, Thompson tells me, gets you a reprimand, but only if the doctors hear you. There's a power play of privilege at work. It must have been the same when I was a resident, but either I don't remember or I never noticed. And I'm ashamed of that. I do know that men hate it when women swear. They

get scared, and scared makes them angry. #notallmen
#yesallwomen to use the old hashtags. But whatever.)

And what about those regulations? Christ, I have no
idea what to say, or if what I say matters. It's all so personal.
Then again, that's what a journal is all about, isn't it?

So. List fashion, here is what's going on with me:

- I sit all day long, but my feet never stop hurting.
- I never did buy that Metro card. Maybe next month.
- Six emails from the VA about "readjustment" counseling.
- Three official reprimands from Thompson. One each
  from Drs. Patel and Wright.
- Two emails from Saul to my new email address,
  asking me how things do go. I didn't respond. Maybe
  I will next month, when I've grabbed a victory from
  the government bureaucracy.
- No word about a new device. No word from the VA job
  portal about "openings suited to your skill set." (And
  yes, I check daily.) I didn't expect either one. But I let
  myself hope.
- Two more evenings at trendy restaurants. Every time
  I returned Sara's gifts, they found their way back into
  my bedroom. I finally gave up. Victory for Sara. I
  wore them for those next two evenings, but when

she tried to give me a second dress, I refused and she didn't insist. Does that count as a victory? Not sure there is such a thing as victory with Sara Holmes.

One more thing, not a list:

I saw a black man today in Georgetown—a rich black man, with his black wife and two black daughters, walking along Q Street. A young Barack Obama, translated to the civilian class. I was so surprised, I didn't say anything. We looked at each other, me all tired and sweaty, them in their beautiful clothes. I saw no hate in their faces, not for me or my color, but I saw a whole lot of pity. Intersectionality wins again.

I am so angry.

But why? Why am I angry with this black man with his money and his wife and their two perfect children? Okay, I do know why. For all I wish them joy, and I really do, I can't stop thinking about the mud and shit and absolute terror from those four days in April, when I was certain (1) I would die, and (2) no one would care.

Fuck this. Fuck, fuck, fuck, fuck. Fuck, fuck, fuck—
holding tight to my new sheets, soaked in sweat
holding so hard it hurts

I am so angry. I thought I was past that. I guess not.

7

"You believe you deserve more," my therapist said. "Let's talk about that."

Her name was Faith Bellaume, as she told me when I arrived at seven thirty for my appointment. Like me, she was black. Like me, she was born in the South. Her parents had abandoned New Orleans for Houston after Hurricane Katrina, then migrated state by state to Virginia. Bellaume herself was born in Mississippi, and she had studied psychology at Mary Washington before taking a job with the VA Medical Center. She had given me this résumé during the walk to the counseling room, adding that she was not a doctor herself, though she had a degree in psychotherapy. I could guess why she had shared these particular bits of information with me. An offer of trust, from her to me. Reassurance that she understood what brought me here. A way to break down the natural reticence that any patient felt.

She was right about the reticence. No matter how long and loud I had argued with VA services for an appointment, my throat squeezed shut at the thought of answering her truthfully. We had spent a cautious forty-five minutes, she and I, dancing toward this moment. I had not expected her to ask for honesty quite so soon. I sipped from my glass of water as I considered how to say what I needed.

"*More* isn't the right word," I said at last. "Better. I deserve better."

She nodded. "Tell me what *better* means to you."

I allowed myself another sip of water. Felt the cool liquid slip down my throat, which was raw and thick from a night spent weeping. I considered asking for a refill, but I knew I was avoiding the moment.

You might find it hard to talk with me at first, Faith Bellaume had said. *And I won't make you.*

No, she would not. But for all her gentleness, she was as stubborn as I was. I indulged myself with one last sip of water, then set the cup to one side. "Okay, then. I want—I deserve a better device. I've earned one. Ten times over. And not . . . not just . . . not just for what happened in April."

I pressed my lips together and glared at the carpet. My fingers had twined themselves together, metal and flesh, and I felt a sharp ache traveling along an arm and hand I no longer possessed. The room was blessedly quiet for several more moments, without even the hum of electronics I had come to expect throughout the VA Medical Center. I could almost imagine myself back in apartment 2B, with Sara absent and even the infrequent traffic on Q Street muffled by the thick glass windows.

"And what did happen in April?" Bellaume said softly.

My fingers unlocked. I slammed my fist against the table. "I served my *country*, dammit. *That* is what happened."

All at once a black cloud fell over me. I launched myself to my feet. Shouting. Swearing. My voice, already hoarse, cracked as I cursed the VA and the rebel soldiers. Cursed the troops who had failed us for days and days. Cursed the politicians who blamed us for their failures, and the squirts and feeds that used the story to boost their ratings. Faith Bellaume did not stir from her chair until I took to clawing at my device. She grabbed my right arm. I wrenched myself free and punched her in the chest.

We faced each other, both of us breathing hard. Tears were running over my cheeks.

"I am so angry," I whispered. "It frightens me."

My knees folded and I collapsed to the floor. Faith knelt beside me. Not touching me, but there, palpably there with me. "You are angry," she said. "I am not surprised. You lost an arm. You lost . . . a sense of yourself."

Yes and yes.

I was trembling now. My stump ached ferociously, and I felt the sting of electricity through the cloth sock. Vaguely I wondered if I had damaged my device. If I had, would the VA grant me a new one? Or had I destroyed even the small, small victories of these past few weeks?

"I can't say anything more," I croaked. "Not about the war. Not about anything."

She shook her head. "Not until you're ready. Make an appointment for tomorrow," she told me in that soft, stubborn voice of hers. "We can talk about proper medication then. But not," she added, "about the war. No, tomorrow I want you to tell me about Georgia."

Georgia. Oh, well, that made a difference. Talking about Georgia meant talking about my childhood. About the farm and my grandmother, and the whole history behind my parents leaving the South for DC. These were difficult topics as well, but not nearly as difficult as the war.

I did not resist as my therapist helped me to my feet, then led me into a smaller room somewhere in the maze between her office and the outer world of the VA Medical Center. The room was an empty cube, sunk in quiet and painted in a soothing pale green, with a padded bench along one wall. Bellaume brought her hand up to my shoulder, not touching me. I suppose we said good-bye to each other, and I suppose I promised to make an appointment for the next day, but I found it difficult to track one sentence to the next. My pulse echoed loudly in my skull, and it felt as though my thoughts had turned fragile, crumbling into fragments and spinning away into darkness.

Abruptly I sat down and concentrated on not throwing up. I heard the door open and a soft conversation between Bellaume and another woman. The other woman disappeared momentarily, only to return with a cup of water and damp towel. Then I was alone.

My stomach heaved. I sipped the water slowly. Pressed the towel against my eyes. The rage had vanished, leaving behind an ache and an emptiness. *Breathe, breathe, breathe,* I told myself. My stump continued to throb and tiny electrical impulses flickered through flesh and metal, like the aftermath of a storm. Moments ticked by. Gradually I found myself, and with that, a measure of badly needed control.

"Captain Watson."

The assistant had returned. She waited until I acknowledged her, then collected the empty cup and the towel. Her movements were unhurried, as if she were handling a frightened cat. Well, perhaps she was.

"Do you need more water?" she asked.

I shook my head. She vanished again, only to return with the receipt for my visit and an appointment card already filled out. "Tomorrow?" she said. "Same time?"

"Tomorrow, yes."

Jacob Bell waited for me in the corridor. Or rather, he leaned against the wall while he chatted with one of the janitors. His hair stood up in all directions, as though he'd been grabbing at it in frustration, and he wore a set of ugly green scrubs and white running shoes.

The janitor poked his arm and pointed at me. Jacob grinned. "Hi, Captain. Thought you might treat me to breakfast."

"Don't you have a job?" I said.

My throat felt like raw hamburger, and my voice came out barely above a whisper. The janitor shook her head and continued to push her mop down the hall. Jacob shrugged. "I'm working the midnight shift these days."

I wanted to throw a brick at the man. Or hug him tight and cry. I settled for checking my watch. Damn, 8:37.

"I need to run," I told him. "Thompson wants us on station by quarter of."

"What about dinner? I have the night off."

Oh, dinner. Yes. Holmes had taken to vanishing without warning. And I had promised myself to treat Jacob. "Meet me outside after my shift," I said. "Four thirty—no, make that five. You choose the place."

The new wing, which housed physical therapy and the counseling services, dated from ten years ago, but the elevators were just as slow and crowded as the rest of the hospital. I skimmed past the bank of doors and ran down the six flights of stairs. The electronic clock outside our wing blinked eight forty-five as I pressed my electronic ID against the reader at the employee entrance. Five minutes to change into my scrubs and bang the locker closed. Giulia Antonelli, one of the senior med techs, whistled softly as I hurried past her station to my own interview room.

Where Thompson waited for me.

"Five minutes late," she said softly. "No, don't make any excuses. I can guess why—I heard something through the grapevine—so I won't give you a warning. Not this time."

I felt the rage piling up in my chest. Not the black cloud, but bad enough. I swallowed and nodded. "Thank you."

Her mouth twisted into a smile. "You're welcome. I prepped the room. All you need to do is check the inventory list and sign it. And, Watson . . ." Her voice dropped to a whisper. "Do what you must. But tell me first, please. I hate surprises." With a glance over her shoulder, she said, "Log in. Quick. You have a patient."

I fumbled through the sign-in, my electronic pen tapping all the wrong choices at first, until I stopped and closed my eyes and breathed, breathed, just as they told me back in the Alton hospital. Okay, then. Log-in name. ID. Password. Thumbprint.

The almost inaudible clock hummed. Eight fifty-seven. I glanced up to see my first patient standing in the doorway.

It was Belinda Díaz. I nearly did not recognize her.

Her eyes were bloodshot, her face had taken on a pasty gray cast, and the bones of her face and neck stood out, as though someone had scooped away the flesh. She stood unsteadily, one hand gripping the doorframe, and stared at me.

It was that look of desperation that plucked me from my own self-pity.

"I remember you," I said. "Come in, Private."

Díaz nodded once and fixed her gaze on the examination table, as if it were an enemy stronghold. She pushed off from the door and limped toward her goal, her prosthetic leg clicking and thumping over the tile floor. A few steps away from the table, she stumbled and had to lunge toward it. She missed and grabbed the edge of the counter. Slowly she pulled herself upright, breathing hard, and turned back to the examination table.

I did not attempt to help. I knew better. Instead I watched as she hauled herself onto the table and let her shoes drop to the floor. Her T-shirt was soaked through with sweat from her efforts, but she offered a smile for me. "I know you. You're the doctor who's not a doctor."

I flinched and hurried to cover my reaction by scanning her patient history. Díaz had visited the medical center the week before. Hicks was the med tech who screened her. Turner was the physician on duty. Turner had ordered a basic panel of blood and urine tests, and prescribed a refill of Díaz's medication for stress-related symptoms, ten milligrams daily with the comment to try a second half tablet when needed. She had also added a new script for a combination hydrochlorothiazide to lower her blood pressure. There was the usual recommendation for counseling and a note that the patient was advised to take aspirin at night for pain relief. Nothing unusual. Nothing that explained Díaz's strange transformation.

When I looked up from the screen, I found Díaz watching me anxiously. "I'm sorry I offended you," she said. "Only, the nurse outside told me you were a doctor once."

"I was," I said. "Back in Alton. Maybe again, someday. But let's talk about you."

I ran through the required list of questions. Belinda Díaz answered as quickly as I asked. Perhaps she too heard the clock humming toward the quarter hour and the end of our allotted time. With three minutes to go, my pen hovered over the observations field. What could I ask that I had not asked before? Anderson was on duty today. He would see the difference himself. Or would he?

"Talk to me," I said. "Tell me what's bothering you. You haven't slept much, have you?"

That was not part of the standard list, and she knew it, because she hesitated.

"I'm tired," she said at last. "Tired and . . . and angry."

I nodded. "Like a black dog hunting you."

Her eyes widened and she nodded back. "Yes. Except I can't sleep, and I didn't used to be so angry. Not until . . . It's like everything went wrong one damned day."

The day an enemy IED blew up her leg and her life. I held my breath, willing her to continue talking. Eventually she did.

"We did good," she said softly. "We did *real* good, me and my squad. They told us after . . . after what happened that we were heroes. I believed them. I had to. But I guess we weren't heroes, after all. Not really."

She paused, and her gaze turned blank, as though she were watching those invisible memories. I nearly told her she probably was a hero. I didn't. She wouldn't believe me anyway. Just as I didn't bother to ask her what had taken place that day with her squad. She wouldn't talk about it, same as I didn't want to talk about Alton.

"Goddamn war," I murmured.

Díaz shook her head, but I could tell she wasn't listening. "They warned us," she said. "Those counselors back in the unit. You act all fine a couple months, a year even, they said. Then it's like someone ripped you to pieces. You can't remember the good, you can't forget the bad. Dr. Anderson gave me those pills, but they don't do shit. They used to, back in Tennessee, but now? One isn't enough. I tried two and that went better. I could breathe. I could . . . I could almost sleep a whole night. But I got scared because Dr. Turner said that wasn't safe. The doctor back in Tennessee said the same thing. She said—"

Her voice broke off and she was holding her head in both hands, weeping.

"It hurts," she said. "If it only stopped hurting, I could sleep."

They told me, back in medical school, and later, in my residency, that sympathy was a dangerous thing, that my patients would suck all the empathy from me, then die anyway, no matter how much I cared.

Belinda Díaz deserved better. Even as a lowly med tech, I had mechanisms, much like the swords of knights of old, at my disposal. I only needed the courage to use them.

"Díaz," I said. "You are sick. I know that. Will you let me find out why?"

Her gaze flicked up to meet mine. "Can you?"

Truth—that was as important as hope.

"I think so. But I can't guarantee anything. It's like war, Private. We make the best plans we can and see what happens."

That calmed her, I could see. She submitted to the blood pressure cuff, and then a blood draw and a urine sample. The blood draw left her dizzy, which bothered me, so I told her to sit quietly while I filled out the necessary screens.

A few clicks brought me to the laboratory portal. Capitol Diagnostics had two entries for Belinda Díaz, both from her visit the week before. The blood and urine tests had not flagged any obvious problems. I checked off that option anyway and worked down through the more specialized tests.

Lipid profile. Creatinine levels. More tests for hormone levels in adrenal and thyroid. And because I couldn't rule it out, the standard run of toxicology test panels to catch any drug addictions. Every single order required authorization from an RN or doctor before the medical center would transfer these samples to the diagnostics lab. I couldn't be certain I'd get that authorization, but I had to try. Goddamn it, if I had the authority, I would have added in an ultrasound and ECG.

The clock was ticking toward 9:28 by this point, almost fifteen minutes past the maximum allowed for each visit, but I didn't care. I clicked *OK* for the last form, labeled the vials, and headed out to find Thompson. It turned out I didn't need to go very far.

"Watson."

Thompson pinned me with that hawk gaze just as I exited the interview room.

"You have samples," she said. "When did I authorize that?"

"You didn't. Or at least not yet. I thought—"

"You thought. Did I authorize that, too?"

I closed my eyes and counted to twenty. Thirty.

"Well?"

The rage hovered at the back of my skull. I told it to wait. Díaz needed me.

My eyes flicked open. Thompson flinched back. A part of me noted that for later satisfaction. Very calmly I held up the tubes of blood and the plastic container of urine, all carefully labeled with patient ID and a bar code for the requested tests. "I am a doctor," I said. "Whatever you think. This patient . . . She's lost twenty pounds in the past two weeks. Her blood pressure is up twelve points. The medicine is not doing her one fucking bit of good. I want her blood and urine tested and the results sent back to Anderson, Turner, and any other doctor who happens to wander by, tagged vital and cc'd to you. If that means another black mark, I do not care."

Thompson regarded me for a long count, her expression strangely puzzled. Then she laughed softly. "No black marks. And no arguments from me. Get back to your patient, Dr. Watson. I'll make sure those test orders go through."

_____

Promise me you'll go back tomorrow, Jacob said.

We were in a cheap hole-in-the-wall place. Dirty linoleum. Bad lighting. The cook with his locs tied back, smoking cigarettes and sweating hard as he worked over the grill. Best damned food in DC, Jacob had told me when we met outside the medical center. I don't even know if it had a name.

Jacob had started off talking about nothing in particular. What he thought about his supervisor. What he thought about presidential candidate Donnovan and the man's speechifying during the latest debates. But then, in the middle of that, his face went old and grim. Promise me, he said. Say you'll go back tomorrow, and the day after that. Say you won't quit, Captain.

He would not shut up until I said those exact words. Why do you care? I almost shouted. Right off I wanted to smack myself. I knew why he cared.

Turns out I only knew part of the story. Jacob told me the rest.

It was Hannah, he said. I had my own troubles. You know about them. I come home to Portland and nobody fit me and I don't fit nobody else. So I come down here and get this job. Doing better, I told myself. Don't need no counseling. I even met this woman. Hannah was her name. She was service like me. Had a tour in Syria before things went bad in Oklahoma. She came home to the Texas border until her squad got ambushed. They took Hannah. Did to her what they did to me and then some.

She told me she didn't need help, that she was getting better, Jacob said. She told herself that same story right up to the day she swallowed a bottle of sleeping pills. That goddamned war left her ragged inside. You know how that is.

I did. That I did.

But then he told me something I almost couldn't believe.

I nearly did the same thing, he said. Told myself Hannah died because I didn't do enough. It was Sara Holmes who got me through the worst. She stuck with me. Listened to me when I needed that. Talked when I didn't. Kept quiet when it mattered. Funny that. I never thought I could talk to a rich woman. At least, she comes from a rich family, which isn't the same thing. Times they remember her. Times she remembers them. Is she giving you trouble?

No more than you do, I told him.

We laughed, both of us.

Jacob had the night off. I badly needed a friend's company. We stayed in that place until midnight, eating ribs and catfish and sweet potato—the kind of food I remembered from Georgia—and drinking shots of what tasted like moonshine. Home brew, the waitress called it. Finally we both got some sense and went home.

Apartment 2B was empty when I got there. No Sara. No piano. At some point I'd texted her to say I would be late. She never replied.

But I saw the gift the moment I switched on the light in my bedroom.

A book, set in the exact center of my bed. I picked it up carefully. The cover was thin, supple leather, dyed to the darkest blue, with the spine and corners reinforced by polished silver. Inside, the pages were a thick cream-colored parchment, blank and lovely with promise.

A journal. She bought me a journal.

Inside the front cover, Sara had pasted a bright green sticky note that said: _In recognition of a difficult day. —S._

Oh. This was a gift I could not bear to return.

I'm writing all this as though it's easy. It's not; this

being six A.M. and me with way too much hangover and nowhere near enough sleep. Not to mention keeping my promise to Jacob. Should I tell Faith Bellaume about Sara and the journal? I think no. Not yet. Today we talk about Georgia.

But I'm not done with my real entry.

So there I was. Drunk. Exhausted. A headache pinching my skull. And this inexplicable gift from Sara. I didn't even bother to ask how she knew about my day. She just did.

That's when I saw the other gift. A fountain pen of stainless steel, with a plain square nib. I touched the nib and it was as though the pen bled for me— blue-black blood that stained my fingertip. Everything ready, I thought, except the words themselves.

And then it came to me. A proper first entry.

And so I wrote what I repeat now:

I WILL HAVE MY VICTORY. I WILL HAVE MY LIFE BACK. I SWEAR IT.

8

The next day I kept my promise to Jacob.

It was, after all, a necessary step for the promise I made to myself.

If Faith Bellaume wondered at my bloodshot eyes, she said nothing. We talked for the requisite fifty minutes. About Georgia. About the arguments I had overheard between my father and my grandmother. About the differences between a dirt farm in Georgia and the one-room apartment where we first lived in Suitland. I didn't have any grand epiphany, but neither did I expect one. At least I didn't punch her this time.

The third visit was more difficult. The fourth nearly impossible.

But I kept at it.

The younger technicians, the ones who had not served in Oklahoma or any of the Russian Conflicts, whispered when I arrived—disheveled, often tear-stained—from my therapy sessions. The older men and women, most of them veterans, offered me a practical kind of sympathy. Sometimes they handed me a cup of strong coffee to gulp down before my first patient. Or they restocked my supply cabinets. The days when I failed to arrive at eight forty-five—those days when I could not, absolutely could not, spring fully formed like Athena from the skull of therapy—the techs or Roberta Thompson did a sweep and made everything ready.

Between us all, we managed, and for that I was grateful.

❡

Eventually, Faith Bellaume told me, *you must learn to make the hard decisions. You never have, not really. You've pretended. In school. With your family. With Angela. A very good pretense, I admit, but you kept running away. You will never reclaim your life unless you confront what truly frightens you. That is the truth.*

Laboring at this almost unthinking job was not enough.

Nor this daily scouring of my soul.

When I argued, she was pleased I could fight back with words and not a formless rage. Still she insisted. I would have to choose a goal, lay out the steps, then follow them. Only then could I reclaim my life, in all senses of the word.

❡

It was the middle of October—not quite two months since I rode that crowded Amtrak from Pittsburgh to Union Station. President Sanches's speeches, when I had the spoons to notice, had taken on a didactic quality, as though she would lecture the nation and the rebel states into obedience. Jeb Foley called her a failure, and the conservative news feeds used the word against her like a blunt relentless weapon.

Except she had not failed. Not as I saw it.

From that very first day, when she announced her plans for federal oversight of the police, when she launched her campaign for gun control, Alida Sanches had achieved all kinds of victories my parents once called impossible. She had argued and negotiated, along with her third-party allies, until we had universal health care and equal rights for gay and transgender people. And when the rebels had taken to bombing hospitals and airports and federal buildings, she had not backed down.

But still soldiers died. Still the New Confederacy fought against what they called the tyranny of the left. And still there were rumors that Texas and Arizona poured money and arms into the civil war. Aided, some said, by certain foreign governments, though the names of those governments changed from week to week. Russia, our enemy. China, our ally except when our goals differed. Unless Sanches could end this war, and end it without dismantling every gain she'd made, I knew how history would write these past eight years.

Two weeks after my first visit with Faith Bellaume, I presented my photo ID to the receptionist at the VA headquarters and told her I had a ten A.M. appointment with my caseworker, Terrence Alexander Smith.

Making the appointment had taken five days of wrangling by phone and email. The VA could not accommodate me earlier than ten A.M., they said, nor later than two P.M., unless I wished to defer my appointment until December. I did not wish to. Momentum, I told myself. Keep moving. Do whatever it takes. In the end, I worked out a plan with Roberta Thompson to make up the lost hours during the evening shift.

My escort appeared within moments and brought me up the same flight of stairs and through the same maze of corridors to Smith's cubicle. Little had changed since my last visit, including Smith himself. I sat down and waited while he shuffled through a stack of papers, then consulted his computer display. He glanced toward me, with my new haircut and my freshly pressed suit, the one I had bought during that mad week after meeting Sara Holmes.

Clothes are like armor, Faith Bellaume had murmured when I told her about my plans. *They can protect you. They can also act like a challenge to the enemy.*

I smiled at him. He stared at a point over my shoulder.

"You have a job?" he asked.

"Medical technician at the VA Medical Center."

He sniffed. "Permanent or temporary?"

"That information should be in my records."

His glance met mine briefly, then flicked away. "Yes. I see. It is."

Smith scrolled through the rest of my file. At one point, he paused the display and his eyes narrowed while he studied the screen, now carefully angled away from me. I wondered if he had noticed my new address, which certainly did not match a technician's salary.

"When you applied for this interview, you said you wanted a reevaluation of your case," he said at last.

"Not exactly. I'm not contesting my pension or my benefits. No, I want . . ." And here I had to remind myself of the script I had rehearsed these past three days. "I want a reliable device. A replacement for the one installed under emergency conditions on the front."

Smith blinked. I felt a trembling inside my gut and its electronic echo through my left arm.

Say nothing. Wait for him to speak first.

He leaned back in his chair, tapping one hand against the other, as though he were reviewing his supply of government-issue replies. Finally he offered me a sanctimonious smile. "I understand your concerns, Captain Watson. However, as you know, the military action in the central states has not been kind to our economy. The VA does not have the funds to outfit all our veterans with the newest prosthetic limbs—"

"I don't require a new one. But as my medical record

shows, this particular device took excessive damage when its previous owner died in combat. The operating surgeon installed it as a temporary measure, but he recommended a replacement, as did the physical therapists in Decatur. And there is a market of used and refurbished limbs."

He was about to object—I could see that—so I hurried into my next argument. "There is also the matter of my return to service."

That caught his attention. "You wish to reenlist."

Stop now, you idiot. Do not promise them anything.

But one lesson I had learned in my morning sessions was to heed my instincts. I would not sacrifice my soul for our civil war, not even for a new left arm, and not even if I believed that victory served a higher purpose than a Progressive Party win this November. But I did believe in honor. And in using my hard-won skills to heal the wounded, to make them whole.

"I want to serve my country," I said. "But I'm a surgeon. I need two good hands to do my work."

Smith stared at me with his watery eyes, as though amazed by my speech. No, not amazed. Disturbed. Abruptly, the old bored expression fell over his face again and he returned to studying the computer screen. For several long moments, the cubicle was silent except for the hum of the ventilation fans and the *tap, tap, tap* of his fingers over the keys.

"You applied for counseling, I see."

Oh. Oh, *damn* him for using the VA's own services against me. I drew a deep breath and pinned my thoughts upon my goals. Even so, it took me a moment before I could trust myself to speak in an ordinary tone. "The VA recommends counseling for all returning veterans."

He gave a little wave of his hand. "It's standard for combat veterans, not medical personnel."

I was in combat. You know that. You choose to forget.

"I'm not sure I understand what you're saying," I said cautiously.

"Just a concern," he said. "Nothing more. How many weeks did the clinic recommend for your case?"

Another question he had no right to ask me. But if I lost my temper or refused to answer his questions, he could label me uncooperative, unstable, and therefore a risk, just as a hospital might deny an organ transplant to an alcoholic.

I pretended to smooth out the sleeve covering my device. My fingers were trembling. Rage. Frustration. None of them useful emotions. I shut them away in a mental box for later, and met Smith's gaze with as pleasant and bland an expression as I could muster. "The clinic did not specify, but you could ask them for access to my private records."

Which they would not grant, but neither could he claim I had refused him.

Smith examined his fingernails with a frown. "I can't promise anything."

"I know," I replied. "Until next month, then."

He glanced up, startled.

I smiled, sure of myself for once. "Regulations grant me regular reviews. No?"

The frown turned into a scowl. "Correct. Until next month, Captain Watson."

P

We smiled, shook hands, and silently wished each other to eternal hell. At least I did. Smith did not strike me as the imaginative sort. Most likely he simply wished for an early lunch break. He handed me over to my escort with little more than a shudder and disappeared into his cubicle. By now I knew my way, but I dutifully followed the young woman through the maze of cubicles, back to the public regions of VA headquarters.

Outside, the air felt damp and cool, and ugly gray clouds hovered low above the city. The skin over my forehead felt too tight and my prosthetic arm buzzed with suppressed emotion. I checked my watch. Ten thirty-five. Thompson did not expect me until eleven forty-five. I briefly considered taking a cab back to 2809 Q Street, but that would be a mistake. I had work to do, patients to interview, a paycheck to earn.

I set off on foot for the VA Medical Center, with second thoughts trailing close behind.

Fail, fail, fail. I had failed completely. Smith would never recommend me for a new device. Bellaume was right. I had challenged a man who did not like being challenged. All through the ten blocks from the VA headquarters to the medical center, I replayed every exchange, every moment where I could have chosen more diplomatic words, a more conciliatory manner.

Impossible.

The word came to me in Sara Holmes's voice. I felt a brief bubble of laughter in my chest. Of course she would view any compromise as a mistake. Had she ever once conceded anything in her life? I doubted it.

Five blocks along, my rage died down to embers and sparks, helped along by a rain shower. Perhaps I had not lost completely and forever. I had laid out my wishes without excuses. I had offered the gift of my continued service in exchange for an arm and hand that would allow me to perform that continued service. I only needed to call up the stubbornness I'd once possessed, which I knew to be my inheritance from my father and mother, and the grandmother who still lived in Georgia.

The rain died off. The clouds scattered long enough for

the sun to break through. It glinted off the cars in the street and the dirty puddles on the sidewalk. A few electronic billboards advertised movies and cars alongside the men and women campaigning for whatever political office. I marched on, my duffel bag thumping against my back.

I arrived at the medical center drenched in sweat and chilled by the early autumn air. Eleven o'clock. My shift started in forty-five minutes. I used that interval to down a cup of strong coffee and a double dose of Advil, then take a hot shower, before changing into my scrubs. I arrived at my station in time to run through my checklist and hand over the signed inventory to Roberta Thompson.

"Good news?" she asked.

I shook my head.

"Ah." She left without saying anything more.

Just as well. Pity might undo me.

For once the unending routine of the day helped. Sixteen veterans presented themselves in turn, each one with different symptoms, each with a disease you could trace back to the war. The young man who had turned drug addict in the face of blood and terror on the front lines. The pilot shot down in enemy territory, rescued after torture. The others with no visible injuries, who had served their tour of duty and returned home, only to find the war had not left them behind. They complained of toothaches, or migraines, or ulcers. An endless litany of small, ordinary illnesses, all much easier to categorize and treat than the invisible wounds the war had inflicted.

At 3:58 P.M., the last patient exited my interview room. I leaned against the counter next to my console and massaged my forehead. Half an hour to review and update records. The evening shift started at five thirty. That left me an hour for dinner in the hospital cafeteria.

I swallowed two Advil, then scrolled through the day's re-

cords. Sixteen patients interviewed. Three repeats. One transfer from a different district. Of the twelve new patients, seven
were medical discharges. The war was not going well, but
when could you ever say that any war was? I double-checked
the two records where I had entered observations. Patel had
clicked the box marked "read" for both but made no comments of his own. Had he actually bothered to look at them?
Or did the system automatically check that box for him?

My headache eased. I drank another cup of water and
brought up the list of patients scheduled for that evening.

First on the list was Belinda Díaz. My heart skipped to
a faster beat. *Again? And so soon?* Then I saw the entry was
grayed out, which meant she had canceled. But the entry also
said she had confirmed the appointment the day before. I
tapped the icon to find out why she had canceled.

Deceased. DOD October 15.

The breath caught in my throat.

She died this morning.

I fumbled twice with my electronic pen before I could tap
the right icon to bring up the screen with more details. The
screen flickered once, then hesitated, as though it didn't want
to divulge that information. I tapped again, harder.

Medical reports can be so cold, I thought as I read the short
summary. I had written a few of those myself, and that had
taught me to read between the lines of the dry accounts to
uncover the grief that so often lay behind them.

According to the EMT on duty, Belinda Díaz had collapsed
at seven A.M. Her cousin had immediately called 911, and the
ambulance crew had transported the patient to the hospital
without delay. Further questioning of the cousin revealed
that Díaz had not slept well the previous week, and had complained she felt tired and overheated.

The records after that were sparse and blunt. Patient admitted to the VA hospital at 7:40, breathing but otherwise unresponsive. Oxygen and intra-arterial tPA administered. Patient declared dead at eight thirty. Diagnosis: blood clot leading to heart failure.

Impossible, was my first thought. She was too stubborn, too strong, to die that easily.

Except I had witnessed any number of deaths where the young and strong had died.

Medical contraindications. The VA doctors had prescribed all kinds of drugs for Díaz to combat her PTSD and her blood pressure. It was just possible . . .

I scanned through the records of Belinda Díaz's last four months. It was all painfully bare, painfully average. Her records, copied into the VA system on her discharge, detailed her combat injuries. Her four visits to the VA Medical Center, including Anderson's diagnosis of PTSD and his prescription of LP#2024016, my own observations about Díaz's blood pressure, and the ever-increasing dosages of sedatives and hypertension medication that Turner had prescribed.

But nothing about the blood and urine tests I had requested. I scrolled back to see if I had missed the relevant entry, but no. No results, not even a mention of my original request. Thompson had promised to authorize those tests. Had she lied to me? I almost laughed at the thought. Thompson never lied. She told you to your face if she thought your ideas were stupid. It was one of her charms.

I logged in to the laboratory portal, in case the data had failed to make the hop from one system into the other. Not likely. Capitol Diagnostics had won their contract with the VA by guaranteeing reliable service, with penalties for every failure, no matter how small. Rumor said the CEO subtracted those penalties from the salaries of those at fault.

My search turned up nothing. The log showed eight tests

submitted that day—none of them mine. Thompson had authorized one. RN Francis Meade had authorized two. The rest came from Dr. Patel. In case someone, somewhere, had mis-entered the dates, I checked the log for two days before and after October 2. Again, nothing.

She's dead. What do those tests even matter?

It mattered because I hated any kind of mystery. Especially a mystery about someone I considered my patient. I stared at the screen, fiddling with my pen. Four forty-five already. Unless I logged off now, I'd end up skipping dinner, the same way I had skipped lunch. Besides, they had probably archived the results when they marked her as deceased. It was even possible they had deleted the records after her death.

Except the VA never deleted any records. We might all die in Oklahoma, but we'd live on forever in pixels, bits, and bytes.

And Díaz trusted you.

It was a matter of thoroughness, I told myself as I called up the advanced search page. Find out the results and I would find out how we had failed her. And we had to find out, so we would not fail the next patient who came to us with the same symptoms.

I entered Díaz's military ID and clicked the *Find similar* option. I added both my employee ID and Thompson's. I set an impossibly huge date range, in case someone had botched that as well, and I included the option for offline records. When the system demanded the laboratory name and the specific tests, I typed the code for all records. Then I clicked the button to execute the search before I logged off.

Dinner, check. More coffee, check. A pointless argument with another technician about the need for online voting options. Another argument about the war and whether we ought to consider China a threat to our national security.

Donnovan said no. Foley said yes. Personally, I suspected Russia was feeding money and arms to our New Confederacy. The rumors fit what I heard over the newsfeeds. The U.S. unbalanced within its borders. Russia aiming to win what were known as the Russian Conflicts—the outright wars in the Ukraine, Crimea, and Syria, as well as their clandestine activities in Serbia and Greece—by demolishing its enemy internally. They'd had success with those tactics before, after all. But what did I know for certain? Not much. At least the debate gave me a badly needed distraction.

At five fifteen P.M., I checked my supplies and signed the inventory sheet. I logged in early for the evening shift. My private dashboard showed a blinking icon at the bottom of the screen. Search still in progress.

Six thirty P.M. The first hour brought us a flood of patients, the ones who came to us between the end of their workday and the start of their evening shift. I tried. Oh, dear lord, I tried to help them. None of them would die before dawn's break—or at least, I hoped not—but they were, all of them, floundering in a sea of panic. What could I do?

Seven thirty P.M. My regulation fifteen-minute break. And I do mean regulation. Darnell, the senior RN on duty, nagged me when I didn't leave the interview room fast enough. But even those few patients during the evening hours didn't want much. They had nightmares. They couldn't sleep. They only wanted the right pill to help them along. If I could pass along a good word to the doctor . . .

Seven forty-five P.M., back to my station. My next patient had an ulcer. I sent him to the doctor in five minutes, then returned to my search results. Nothing. Not even an error code. I tapped through the menu option to review Díaz's latest visits, only to discover that her records had been marked Deceased, unavailable.

Nine P.M. End of shift.

I stared at my screen a very long ten minutes before I realized Thompson would not be along to rag me about the accuracy of my reports. RN Darnell did want to see all my comments and recommendations, but I already knew her standards were much, much lower than my expectations. We discussed a few difficult cases. The rest she ignored.

By nine thirty I had changed into my own comfortable T-shirt and jeans. My scrubs went into the hospital laundry. My black linen suit, hopelessly wrinkled from lying at the bottom of my locker, disappeared into my duffel bag, along with a few paperback books I had stashed there the previous day. The details of my fruitless search pursued me through the doors and onto the sidewalk outside the hospital.

October 15. Wednesday for me. For Díaz, her last day on Earth.

My steps slowed until I came to a halt at the curb.

The cold dank October air clogged my lungs. I had to will myself to drink in the night air, laden with the sharp scent of electronic billboards, the faint, softer scents of mud and autumn leaves from the nearby reservoir.

It's not my business.

Except it was.

Díaz bothered me. Her death, her useless and inexplicable death, bothered me. *The day everything went wrong,* she had called it. Days like that happened all the time in war, sure, but for Díaz, her death had been a long slow free fall since June. Too many goddamned things had gone wrong for me to ignore.

I turned around and headed back to the employee common area, where the hospital had installed a few computers for us to use during breaks. One was free. I dropped into the chair and logged in, then clicked through to the internet portal and my private email account. My left hand was jittering as I typed: Dear Saúl, I'm sorry I didn't get back to you sooner. I have no excuse except work and more work. Better than no work, you could say. Anyway, I'm sorry I've been invisible these past two months. I promise to do better. Love, Janet.

My finger hesitated over the *Send* button. Saúl had emailed me twice since I left Decatur. This was my first attempt to answer those emails. He deserved better than this.

P.S., I added. I lost a patient today, and it hurts. Hurts so damned much. Her name was Belinda Díaz. I don't even know why she died or what I could have done to fix things. (And you know how I love to fix things.) Maybe I couldn't do anything for her. The doctors in her unit and the ones here gave her drugs. The VA told her to sign up for all the usual rehabilitation programs, but it's never enough, is it? The war broke her life into pieces, called her a hero, then dropped her into a dark hole when she proved to be only human. And that's the real reason I'm writing to you. I need to talk about her. I need to figure out what went wrong. So maybe I'll know how to save the next one. Call me Saturday or Sunday, if you have time.

I added my cell number and sent off the email. I didn't know how much would make it past the censors, but as long as Saúl got the part about talking this weekend, that was good enough for me.

One bus transfer and half an hour later, I disembarked at the corner of Connecticut and Q Street. I set off along Q Street with my duffel bag over one shoulder. The night air was cool and damp. The embassies lining the street were like brilliant jewels set in dark velvet. I crossed the bridge over Rock Creek into an emptier, darker section and picked up my pace.

My route took me past the parkland surrounding the creek, then through a neighborhood of brick houses converted into offices occupied by lawyers and doctors and various political organizations. The sidewalks here were empty and the streetlamps stood far enough apart that I hurried through the dark gaps between them. Twenty-Eighth Street was just ahead, with its series of close-set apartment buildings. I had just slowed down when a shadow hurtled toward me from the alley on my left.

Instincts kicked in, hard and swift. I swung my duffel bag around and caught my assailant in the chest. He grunted and lurched to one side but came after me again. I sidestepped his first punch, missed the second one aimed at my gut. I went down into a heap, breathless and retching. My attacker seized my left arm and twisted.

Electricity burned through my flesh. I shrieked, a wild animal cry that ripped itself from my throat. My assailant landed a blow to my head, then flung my device to one side. I tried to catch my breath, but I was too busy retching up my supper. My ghost arm felt as though it were on fire. My metal one lay some distance away. Above me a knife flashed in the moonlight . . .

The blow never came.

Even as the knife arced toward me, I heard the sound of rapid footsteps. My assailant cursed and swung around. Someone's fist thudded against someone else. Someone else thudded back. I had the impression of dozens of footsteps dancing around me, quick and light, and a laugh that sounded so like Sara Holmes's that I wanted to laugh myself, even gripped by agony as I was.

At some point, I realized the noise around me had fallen away. In the distance, a dog barked, but here on this street, all was muffled and quiet, except for my own harsh breathing.

Sara knelt beside me and looped my right arm over her neck. One hand gripped my wrist, one arm circled my waist. Very carefully, she raised me to my feet.

I drew a breath and sobbed in pain.

"Hush, hush," she said. "Do not cry, my love. You will frighten our oh so respectable neighbors."

"I wish I could," I said fiercely. "And I am *not* your love."

Holmes laughed, but I could tell, even through my agony, that she was anxious. I gave up the struggle and let her hurry me along to 2809 Q Street, where she urged me up the steps and through the front doors to the elevator. It wasn't until she had laid me down on my bed that she truly relaxed.

"I disappointed you," I wheezed.

"Hardly." She too was breathless from her exertions. "Though I confess I never expected to rescue you from the street on a Wednesday evening. It seems too outré for such a middle-class creature as yourself. How did you attract the attention of this incompetent criminal?"

"I don't know. Walking home?"

That provoked another laugh. "Reason enough, I suppose. Wait here."

Not that I had a choice. When I tried to lever myself upright, I doubled over, spewing bile and what little else remained of my supper. Sara returned within moments with a damp cloth for my forehead and a bundle of paper towels for the floor. She returned a second time with a cup of fragrant tea, which she helped me to drink while she supported me with one arm. The tea settled my stomach and its warmth eased a few of my aches.

"How did you know?" I whispered.

"Know what?" she replied.

But she understood what I meant. I could tell by the momentary stillness, the almost imperceptible tension in her arms as she held me. Just as I knew she would not admit to anything.

"You saved my life," I said instead. "Thank you."

She made a dismissive gesture. "You're welcome. You should know better, though. You grew up here."

"I do." At least, I thought I said that. My brain was too muddled and my tongue too uncooperative to make much sense. This was not natural, I thought. I was tired, yes, but not this tired, not this confused. I wanted to demand some explanation from Holmes, but I found my head growing heavy. "You drugged me," I mumbled.

"Of course I did."

I wanted to say more—much, much more. But my eyes disagreed with me. My entire body did. *Damn, damn, damn.*

Before I could do more than mutter a curse, I dropped into sleep.

9

From far away the helicopters hummed over the broken land. The enemy had taken our camp early that morning and since then, they had secured the grounds for several miles around us. Now they were hunting down the survivors and throughout the afternoon came the crackle of rifle fire, the hum of electronic weaponry, the strange mix of ancient and modern that had come to represent the New Confederacy.

I glanced around to check my patients. Abruptly, memory and my dreams shifted. No longer did I see a muddy ditch filled with bodies and dying soldiers wrapped in blankets. My patients had thrown off their bandages. Many of them walked to and fro with an abstracted air, as though they were listening to a stream of talk beyond my hearing. It was only when one turned to face me that I realized she was a patient who had died on the operating table, the day before That Day. Another stood behind her—a corporal who had survived his surgery only to die later that night. There were others: the dead from that first day, and those who survived until our rescue only to die in the hospital . . .

A great loud cracking noise yanked me awake. I rolled out of my cot and—

—my legs folded underneath me. I flung out both hands to break my fall, only to plunge through my invisible left arm. My right arm crumpled under my weight. My stump hit the floor. I cried out—just once—and bit through my lip to stop another cry, still thinking the enemy would find me if I made a sound.

I curled over and around myself, breathing hard. Red splashed against my tight-shut eyelids. The *thump, thump* of explosions echoed inside my skull. The ghostlike tendrils of pain extended from my shoulder down through the fingers I no longer possessed.

Eventually I stopped thrashing around. Eventually the waves of pain receded. I lay there, sweating, my face sticky with drying tears.

It's over, I told myself. *It's nothing but a dream.*

But I could still hear the echo of that explosion, and a whiff of burnt flesh lingered in my brain.

Funny thing, memories. Faith Bellaume said we couldn't rely on them. Time, and their very strength, distorted our recollections, blurred and altered them in ways that made them useless as a record. What we do, she told me, is trust them as signposts for our emotions.

Records are facts, she said. But so are emotions. People tend to forget that.

Slowly, oh so very slowly, the last traces of my dreams evaporated. I was in DC, in a luxurious apartment in Georgetown. Last night, I had come home late, weary and careless. Sara Holmes had rescued me from a stranger's attack.

I unfolded my body and levered myself to sitting. Even that little bit left me gasping with sudden stabs of pain. I collapsed against my bed and forced myself to breathe slowly, steadily, until the agony receded and I could take stock of my injuries.

First and easiest. My right hand ached. My wrist, when I rotated it carefully, gave a twinge. That was from this morning. The scrape along my forearm, however, came from my sliding over the pavement when I tried to scramble away from my attacker. It was only now that I realized I no longer wore a T-shirt, but a long-sleeved pajama top, and that my arm was bandaged.

My gut felt tender when I gently probed. That punch I remembered. I drew a deep breath. Another twinge registered, this one around my rib cage. I drew a deeper breath and was relieved when the twinge was no worse. No cracked or broken ribs, then. Only bruises.

My left knee ached when I flexed my leg—I had an image of myself twisting away from my attacker—but again, nothing that would leave me incapacitated. My jaw was a different matter. It was not broken, at least. But I could trace the swelling along the right side of my face, courtesy of another blow I didn't remember. And my stump . . .

My stump ached ferociously. Sara had bandaged it neatly, an event I did not recall, but even without visual cues, I could detail every bruise and abrasion, from when my attacker had ripped the thing off.

I twisted my shoulder around to see what other damage he'd done. Pain, like a thin sharp blade, lanced through my skull. *God, god, god.* How could I get through work today?

Work. A sudden panic overtook me. The light from the window—it was far too bright. And the faint noise of traffic seemed too regular for the early morning. I rubbed a hand over my eyes. Carefully maneuvered myself onto my knees and swiveled around until I could see my alarm clock.

Ten fifteen. Shit, shit, shit.

Thompson had drilled us endlessly on the regulations. Call

the front desk by eight A.M. if you were sick. If you couldn't call, send an email. No excuses.

I lurched to my feet and stumbled over to my duffel bag. Even now, if I called Roberta Thompson and told her about the assault, she might put in a word with the hospital management. It wasn't as if I had spent the night carousing.

My duffel bag lay unzipped and open. I felt a pinch in my gut at the sight. It was possible I had forgotten to fasten the bag before I left the VA. Or that Holmes had opened the bag to check for medical supplies. The pinch turned into a knot, however, as I searched one-handed through the bag's contents. All my clothes were there, a paperback from the used-book store, other odds and ends. But no cell. And the text device she had slipped into my pocket at our first meeting, and which she had steadfastly refused to take back, had also disappeared.

I stood up and kicked the bag.

I nearly kicked the bag a second time when I realized I must have heard Sara leaving the apartment just moments ago. That loud crack was the door slamming shut.

Fine. I don't need her help. I can tell Thompson face-to-face what happened.

I stomped off to the bathroom for a shower. Our rental contract guaranteed an unending supply of hot water, and I tested that guarantee to its limit this morning, twisting the nozzle to needle sharp to sluice away the fear sweat, then ratcheting the dial to what Jenna Hudson called the rainfall setting and letting the heat soak into my bones. I ignored the stings from my cuts and scrubbed myself clean with a nub of soap that smelled of ginger. It was in moments like these that I could forgive myself for succumbing to the seduction of such an apartment.

But once I toweled off and returned to my bedroom, I discovered a few more surprises.

My attacker had ripped off my arm and tossed it aside. I distinctly remembered that. I also remembered Holmes picking up the device and tucking it under one arm, while she half dragged, half carried me through the streets. The device, however, was nowhere in my room, nor the bathroom.

A quick glance around showed me that my device was not the only item gone from the room. My tablet was missing as well. In its place on my desk was a sheet of paper anchored by a glass of water and two large yellow pills.

> *I phoned your excuses to FB and RT. FB has rescheduled you for next Tuesday. RT expects you back tomorrow at the usual time. I have some errands to run, but I should return by six P.M. Until then—soup in pot on warmer, coffee in thermos, bread in oven. The yellow pills are harmless, I promise. I tried one myself. —S.*

I crumpled the note, swearing softly. She had no right to order my life around. It had probably never occurred to her I needed these precious six hours of pay. She probably thought she was doing me a favor. No, scratch that. She was doing herself some strange and mysterious favor.

A second and more thorough search confirmed what I thought—she had not simply hidden the cell and other items. I continued into the parlor, where I discovered the outer door locked and bolted. The security panel flickered yellow and orange when I pressed my thumbprint to the reader. When I tried a second time, the recorded voice said, "Technological malfunction. Please contact security support by phone."

My skin rippled with a sudden chill. This, this was not another of Sara's whims. She had gone to great and detailed lengths to shut me away from the world.

I have to get out of here.

I rested my arm against the door and considered what to do.

Epiphany came almost at once. The *other* telephone, of course. The apartment had its own landline—another perquisite that older residents favored. I could call the Hudson offices and tell them about the malfunction.

I hurried back to the parlor, to the cabinet that housed the landline device, and snatched up the receiver. *Yes.*

No, dammit.

The receiver was dead. I slammed the useless thing onto its cradle and checked the wiring for what I already knew. Sara had left the phone but removed its cord.

I retraced my steps to my bedroom and tried the windows. It took me a few struggles, but I wrestled one open as high as my head. The screen itself was easy to yank from its frame, but I had forgotten about the metal grating and the electronic barrier beyond that.

I leaned as close to the grating as I dared and studied the gardens below. They were a stew of crimson and gold and crackling brown. On any other day, I might have drunk in the heady scents of moldering leaves and damp earth, but today was not any other day. If I tried to break through the metal grate, I would only injure my one good arm. Or get arrested.

For form's sake, I searched the rest of the apartment. Sara's bedroom was locked. All the closets, cabinets, drawers, and shelves contained only the usual collection of coats and boots and umbrellas. My efforts brought me at last to the kitchen, where the promised soup and coffee and bread waited for me. Sara had laid out plate, mug, bowl, and silverware on the counter, making it easy for a one-handed person to serve herself. She had even sliced the bread before setting it in the oven to keep warm.

I poured a mug of coffee and drank it. Hot. Strong. Delicately flavored with a spice I could not identify.

From the coffee it was only a minor compromise to try the bread. The bread woke my appetite. I finished off all the slices, then the soup. By the time I had drunk the last of the coffee, I was thinking more clearly. So. Right. Sara Holmes meant to keep me here until she finished whatever mysterious errands she had. I set the dirty dishes in the sink, then returned to my bedroom, prepared to wait.

Only to find a new surprise.

I remembered clearly how I'd been in a rush the previous Saturday. There had been groceries to buy, a visit to the bank to dispute various fees, a prescription for sleep medication that Faith Bellaume had eventually, under duress, provided to me for the worst nights, and other items I no longer recalled. However, I could clearly picture the brief visit to the used-paperback store, where I'd picked out three new books for the week. When I returned to the apartment, Sara had just finished serving out a dish of spiced noodles. I had dropped the books in a heap on my bookcase and run back to the kitchen.

Now that same heap was a neat double stack. And there were ten books, not three. I picked up the topmost one. It was *Cold Magic* by Kate Elliott, one of my three. The second, however, was a mystery by P. D. James. Inside was a folded sheet of paper with a note: *Look behind me.*

Behind the double stack of books was an old-fashioned, battery-operated AM/FM radio, the kind my grandfather had talked about building from a kit when he was ten or thereabouts. It operated by a wind-up crank, and you set the station with a series of switches and dials. These days, there were only a few broadcast stations left in the U.S. Most of the commercial ones had died off in the late 2010s, courtesy of Trump's most paranoid days, when he turned the FCC into a hammer against his enemies. The few that had survived were independent operations run by cranks or activists. My mother always said it was often hard to tell the difference between them. My father always replied it was worth the effort.

I had the sudden image of my parents, then, bending over the radio inherited from Grandpa Benjamin. One bright and lovely picture that made my breath catch. The sharp electric scent of the old device. The warmer scents of that house they had struggled so hard to buy, and even then, it was little more than a square surrounded by other squares, and the higher walls of the nearby shopping mall, with only that field of weeds and wildflowers to interrupt the concrete.

I carried the radio and an armful of books back into the parlor. The books I set off to the side while I fiddled with the radio controls.

WFED, the Federal News station, was entirely dead.

WAMU, from American University, was nothing more than a steady hiss.

Irritated, I spun the dials. A squawk of golden-hit rap music poured out. I stabbed the controls until the noise died to a whisper, then cycled through the stations. In the end, the only one that didn't offer noise or right-wing commentary was an indie station that alternated between jazz and the occasional segment on world news.

While the radio continued to deliver its stream of music and news reports, I stared at my haphazard collection of books. One by Martha Wells. Another by Delia Sherman. The volumes by Le Carré, Butler, Sayers, Nisi Shawl, and Nalo Hopkinson. I leafed through them, finding scribbled notes in the margins dissecting the plot's accuracy, as well as the author's views toward race and sex and gender. The commentary was so typically Sara. Under different circumstances, I might have found it entertaining.

The indie station had begun another news segment, so I listened to reports about the war in Oklahoma, which in truth was a war that had grown, like a tumor, throughout Missouri, Mississippi, Arkansas, and Kansas, with tentacles reaching into Colorado and Tennessee. They replayed a speech by Sanches, then another by Jeb Foley, who argued for reconciliation. Sanches's voice sounded weary to my ears, as though she had already laid aside the burden of her office. Foley's speech disturbed me, with its call for a more Christian nation, one where "true Americans" could be proud. My parents had lectured me and my sister, Grace, about those dark days in the late 2010s when white supremacists had taken over our country and the world. Maybe those days had come back. Maybe we had never left them behind.

Jeb Foley was a legacy of those goddamned dark days. Like our forty-fifth president, like that weasel Paul Ryan and the rest of the GOP, he was the kind of man who would abandon a veteran like Belinda Díaz even while he called more soldiers to war. I had volunteered my service freely and with passion. I believed myself a patriot, or at least a foot soldier in the unending battle for civil rights. But I hated how my service—*our* service—had been misrepresented in this election season.

The news gave way to a segment of piano concertos from a modern composer. I relaxed back into my chair with the Butler, which discussed a world where Earth had destroyed itself, leaving behind a remnant of humankind, now captive to a strange alien species. The protagonist was written in such a matter-of-fact voice, and yet I could hear the anger beneath her so reasonable accounting of the events that destroyed her life and her world. I read on, half-listening to the radio as it cycled through another news segment about the elections . . .

I must have dozed off, because the next thing I heard was the click of a door. A cool hand pressed over mine. My eyes blinked open to see Sara Holmes's face a few inches away. There was a whiff of rosemary and cardamom in the air, a fainter one of Sara's favorite perfume. Her eyes were dark, her expression difficult to read in the fading light of this damp October day.

"Do you want salad with your steak?" she asked.

"What?" I tried to lift my hand to my eyes. It was the wrong hand. By the time I realized it, Sara was stalking toward the kitchen. She flung a leather satchel to one side as she went.

"Whiskey is in the bag," Holmes called back to me. "Pour us both drinks."

She vanished around the corner before I could protest.

Right. Of course, Sara. I don't mind being locked up without any explanation.

But arguing with Sara Holmes was like arguing with a tornado.

I decided I could at least get a drink, and possibly a few answers, before the storm whirled past. I dragged the satchel closer and dug through its contents.

Several real estate brochures lay on top. A couple advertising leaflets with coupons. Then a dozen election pamphlets of all flavors. *Covering our bases, are we?* I thought. I had never questioned Sara's politics before, but then, I had not offered to discuss my own.

Underneath the pamphlets, I found a bottle of Macallan Sherry Oak, wrapped in sheets of bubble plastic. Next came two crystal tumblers with heavy bases. There was also a packet of clove cigarettes and ten lotto tickets.

I unwrapped the whiskey and the glasses. It took some doing without my device, but I managed to unstopper the bottle and pour drinks for us both. The alcohol was buttery smooth but left a faint smoky trail down my throat and into my stomach. I sank back into one of the parlor chairs and stared out over the star-spattered sky. It was a dark and moonless evening. City lights cast a halo over the horizon. High above, a faint contrail marred the pure black of the night. I could almost imagine myself as Lilith aboard the alien spacecraft, looking across the vast distance to an Earth that was no longer hers.

Fifteen minutes later, Sara returned carrying two platters with steak and salad. The one she set before me was bleeding rare, just as I liked it, and cut into bite-sized portions. She took the seat opposite me and picked up the second glass of whiskey.

"Eat," she said. "Then we talk."

"What if I'm not hungry?" I said.

"Liar. You ate the soup and bread, but you've had nothing since. Eat and we talk. Refuse and I shall sally forth in search of more congenial company."

Fine. I tested a bite of my portion. It tasted of cumin and orange juice and a strong helping of fresh pepper. I decided I could be noble another day and dove into the steak and the salad. My jaw still ached, but not enough to slow me down. Halfway through our meal, Sara vanished into the kitchen and reappeared with a hot baguette, which I used to sop up the dressing and juice from my steak.

"I have a question," I said. "It's multipart and it is *not* one of your magical three."

"Tschah, so many questions I never agreed to."

"What you agreed to doesn't matter." The idea had come to me earlier, as I considered how thoroughly and absolutely she had isolated me. *A professional job* was the phrase that occurred to me. "Tell me this, Sara Holmes. Are you FBI, CIA, or any entity related to them?" Then a horrible thought occurred to me. "Or someone else?"

A very long pause followed before Sara answered.

"Call me a freelance operative," she said. "Local, not foreign."

"What do you mean by local?"

Her smile, the smile I knew so very well, that hid behind her carefully cultivated blandness, ticked up a notch. "I mean our own U.S. federal government."

"Then what are you doing here?" I asked.

"Resting."

In other words, she wouldn't tell me. "Fine. How did you know I was in trouble last night?"

She shrugged. "Call it instinct. Are we done with your questions, Dr. Watson?"

"No! Why did someone attack me?"

A longer silence. "I don't know yet. My investigations today were inconclusive, though certain individual details intrigued me. I plan to find out more tomorrow. But first I want you to answer a few questions."

I glanced at her, startled.

"Oh, yes," she said. "I don't do anything out of the kindness of my heart. You know that. So. Tell me all about your day at the VA this Wednesday. Everything you can remember. What you did. What you thought. The people you talked to. Don't leave out anything, even if you believe it's unimportant."

"And why should I cooperate?"

"Because you are as curious as I am. Because I cannot discover the grains of truth unless I sift through all the sand upon the shore."

Like a doctor diagnosing their patient. I felt a strange urge to comply—brought about, I suspected, by the whiskey and dinner—but I could see her point. Very well. I started with my appointment with Terrence Smith and how that shifted my schedule at the VA Medical Center. And because she had insisted on all the details, I told her about Smith's attempts to extract information he was not privileged to hear. I told her about my frustration with his attitude, and my fear that I had sabotaged my case, even though I had not meant to.

And, a miracle, Sara listened without interrupting. Her eyes went hooded. Her entire self went still. Only once, when I mentioned my offer to reenlist, did her gaze flicker up toward mine, but she did not speak.

From Smith, I continued my very boring account of my day. The patients I interviewed. RN Thompson's compliment about my work. Sara continued to listen with all her attention, and, no doubt, all her electronic devices.

Until I reached the point where I learned about Belinda Díaz's death.

"You say she confirmed her appointment the day before?" she asked. "Is that typical?"

I shrugged. "Some do. Some don't."

"How much simpler if humans conformed to expectations," she murmured. "But then my work would be far less interesting. Tell me, what did you write in that message to Dr. Martínez?"

I hesitated. Sara smiled, that same infuriating smile I remembered from our first meeting.

"Do not be shy," she said. "I promise not to judge you, at least not in your presence. Was he your lover? Did you mention any salacious tidbits of your times together?"

I slammed my right fist onto the arm of the chair. "He is my friend, dammit. Not my lover. All I said was that I missed him and I wanted to talk with him by cell on Saturday if he had time. And no, I did not mention you."

Sara was unfazed by my outburst.

"That was exactly what you wrote?" she said.

"Yes. Well, no. I said I had lost a patient."

I said it hurts. I said I wanted to fix things, if not for Belinda Díaz, then for the next one who came to me with their life shattered by war.

But I could not say those things to the cool and aloof Sara Holmes. I paraphrased as best as I could, certain even so she could read the true text behind my words. She did not smile, however, nor did she seem at all amused.

She nodded. "What time did you email him?"

"Right after my shift. Nine thirty or thereabouts."

"Hmmm. The timing . . . But never mind about that. Was the connection secured? Tell me right away if you don't understand the terminology."

I wanted to throw my steak knife at her but resisted the temptation. "I understand the terminology just fine, *Agent* Holmes. I used my personal account and his service email. The computers in the common room are connected to the medical center's systems, so we have to use our employee password to use them. Any email traffic gets routed through the military servers and the government censors."

"What about the laboratory portal? Do you need a second log-in? What kind of encryption does the connection use?"

Meaning, could a foreign agent intercept my search request.

"It's a secure line between the VA Medical Center and Capitol Diagnostics," I said. "I doubt anyone could hack into the connection. I doubt anyone cares."

"You would be surprised what people care about," Holmes replied. "But I appreciate your honesty and your excellent memory. Tell me more about the security measures for the computers in the common area."

I told her. She had several more questions, all about seemingly unconnected issues. The whole exchange took little more than half an hour, by which time I had finished off the last of my steak and salad. Telling the story had reawakened a host of questions as well, but between my isolated day and the whiskey, I found it harder to insist on questions and answers.

Apparently Holmes found it equally difficult, because she poured herself a second glass of whiskey and stared at it with an unfocused gaze for several long moments. "Yes. I think I see the problem," she said. Then her gaze snapped back toward mine and she gave me an enigmatic smile. "Thank you. Yes. Thank you very much."

She refilled my glass, then lifted hers in a toast. "Drink up. And let us celebrate enlightenment."

She drank down the whiskey in one swallow. Without thinking, I followed her example.

Only to realize that she had drugged me once again.

10

Dreams came to me in the night. Dreams of a sort. Wisps and scraps of images, bloodred, fluttering into view, only to be snatched away by an invisible wind. Voices, too, but their speech was garbled, strange, and distant, as though a veil had dropped between me and the dream world. I cursed that veil and tried to rip through it, one-handed. I had the strangest notion that if I could break through the veil, if I could only hear what those voices talked about, I would learn an important clue.

Then a brilliant wedge of light broke through the gray, like the sun breaking through the clouded sky. The bloody images of war vanished, along with the voices.

This time I truly slept.

11

I woke to the hush and whisper of the ocean, to the gray haze of dawn and a bird whistling in the distance. For a moment, I thought I was a child again, ten years old, lying on that hard narrow cot next to my sister, the summer my parents had bargained for a cottage on Maryland's Eastern Shore. It hadn't mattered we had to clean the other cabins to earn our stay. All I remembered was the heavy tang of salt, the amazing, entrancing sight of waves rolling toward me from the infinite. Five sweet days in August away from the city that I still hated.

Like a digital clock, memory flipped over from past to present. I caught my breath, remembering the day before, the night before that. Then, as the air escaped my lungs, I tensed again, recalling my strangely muted dreams, then the dark void of deeper sleep that was empty of nightmare—empty of any dreams at all, as though someone, or something, had switched off my brain without my consent.

I lurched upright from the depths of the couch and surveyed the parlor with bleary eyes. The hour was early, the apartment still washed in shadow, though the sky had taken

on a silvery cast. A full moon hung low over the horizon. By
that faint light, I could make out Sara Holmes lying curled
around herself in one of the overstuffed chairs. A metallic
gleam caught my attention. It was a gun, tucked between her
bare feet. Her hand rested on its grip.

My guardian demon.

The hiss and surge of waves grew steadily louder. I finally
located the source of the noise—a portable alarm clock on the
table, surrounded by the remains of our dinner. Very carefully, I reached over and switched off the alarm. The display
read 6:12. I had slept almost twelve hours.

I rubbed a hand over my face, recalling more details of the
previous day. Holmes had rescheduled yesterday's appointment with Faith Bellaume until next week. Good. I was fresh
out of the ability to examine my soul. Thompson expected me
back today. That I could manage. I had to. I braced my right
hand on the arm of the couch, ready to launch myself, however unsteadily, into my day.

And froze.

Holmes's eyes were open, bright and glittering in the rising dawn. The gun had vanished, and she was studying me
with that self-satisfied expression I had come to know, as if I
were one of many game pieces that she had maneuvered for
the win.

My good intentions of getting to work, of *managing*, vanished. This was a conversation that could not wait. "You," I
said softly. "You drugged me." More clues shifted into place.
"You drugged both of us."

She smiled that ghost of a smile. "It was safe enough."

"That's *not* what I meant. I—" I stopped and felt all my
muscles tighten into knots. "Why did you drug me? You'd already locked me up. You jiggered security and made damned
sure I couldn't call anyone."

You even stole a part of my body. A part constructed of metal and wire and plastic, but that doesn't matter. You treated me as a thing.

Holmes must have guessed that last thought, because she dipped her gaze in uncharacteristic agreement. "I apologize. But I'm not sorry," she added. "You badly needed the sleep."

The breath trickled from my lips. True enough. It still did not erase the sense of violation.

"What about you?" I said. "Did you need the sleep too?"

She shrugged. "I wasn't certain you'd take the drink otherwise."

In spite of everything, I had to suppress a snort of laughter. It was so typically Sara, buying a whiskey that cost $80 or more, and serving it to me in a crystal goblet, just to deliver a knockout drug. I remembered the seal crackling as I broke it. She must have replaced the seal herself after doctoring the contents with . . . something. I swallowed but tasted nothing beyond a smoky memory of the whiskey itself. Whatever kind of sedative she had used, it had acted slowly and left no residue behind, only a deep dark void of memory.

"What did you give me—us?" I said.

"It won't affect your work," Holmes said at once. "Trust me. I've used it before."

Another clue, another hint of her character. But I had already wasted enough time on the mystery of Sara Holmes. Thompson and the VA hospital expected me at eight forty-five. "We finish this conversation later," I told her. "Tonight. Tomorrow. And no games with counting questions."

I didn't wait for her to answer but stalked off to my bedroom.

My tablet was still missing from my desk. My device, however, lay in the center of my bed, next to my cell. Curious, I switched on my phone. The screen flickered a few times before it displayed the message "Limited Service."

Oh yes, we would definitely have a conversation tonight, Sara and I.

I showered, then hurried through the drill of tending to my stump. In another of the many contradictions that made up her character, Sara had laid out all the necessary items for restoring my arm—powder, antiseptic, a fresh cotton sock—on the counter. Once I had secured the device, I let myself breathe a moment, and I could let myself feel . . . almost whole.

The mirror was still cloudy from the steam. I wiped a circle clear and stared at the blurred reflection of my face. The swelling along my jaw had subsided, leaving behind a mottled trail of bruises, like purple shadows lurking beneath my dark skin. I worked my jaw carefully from side to side. It twinged, but not as badly as I'd feared.

I took stock of the rest of my injuries. My stump still felt raw from the abuse it had received, and the knee would give me trouble for a day or two, but the rest was bearable. Scrapes and bruises. Minor stuff.

What my coworkers would say was another matter. They would gossip, in whispers that died whenever they saw me. I knew what that gossip would say, too. When I told them I'd been mugged, they would remember all the times a patient rushed to explain how they weren't in a fight, no, not them. It was some stranger who had attacked them for no reason at all. Or the others, who didn't want to talk about the lover who beat them.

Sara and I weren't lovers. We weren't even friends.

But she saved your life.

I shivered. Of all the images that had remained of the attack, the clearest ones were of Holmes, like a deadly viper, striking hard and fast at the enemy.

As I headed toward the kitchen, I heard a soft melody

from behind Sara's closed door. A quiet, thoughtful piece, with long pauses between measures. In the kitchen, fresh coffee and an omelet waited for me, both steaming hot. Next to the plate was a heap of five-dollar bills and a note that read, *Take a taxi. Thank me later.*

The bills were crumpled and worn. Several had coffee stains, and when I sniffed them curiously, I smelled a whiff of clove cigarettes. They were perfectly anonymous, these bills. Almost too much so, as though she had manufactured them for the occasion.

For every clue you give me, you add a dozen mysteries.

I used the apartment landline, now restored, to call a taxi. By eight o'clock, I had finished my omelet and the last of the coffee. I set the dishes in the sink, packed my duffel bag with clean scrubs and a paperback. It only took me two go-arounds to convince the driver that I was the person who had called.

Outside the hospital, Jacob Bell waited next to the employee entrance. He had taken the familiar parade rest stance we all knew, even the medicos. As I turned away from the cab, he rolled onto the balls of his feet. He looked alert and angry. "Captain. I heard you had some trouble a few nights back."

The accusation was clear: *You were hurt. You didn't call.*

I didn't bother telling him I was fine. Or that Sara Holmes had made it impossible for me to call him or anyone else.

I sighed. "Look, I was stupid. I walked home late at night, and I wasn't watching. I was lucky we made enough noise the neighbors opened their windows. Damned lucky, and I know it. He ran."

It was the truth, I told myself. Or pieces of it. As much as I hated to lie to Jacob, certain aspects of that night concerned secrets I knew I wasn't allowed to share.

Jacob cocked his head and studied me with narrowed eyes, as though he suspected the direction of my thoughts, if not the exact details. "Damned lucky is right, Captain," he said softly. His gaze flicked down to my left arm, hidden, except for the hand, inside my jacket sleeve. He looked about to tax me with more questions, but then he shrugged. "Let me know if you want to have dinner tonight."

I nodded. He took a step back, and I walked around him and swiped my security card. The door hissed open.

Just beyond the entryway, Faith Bellaume had set up her own roadblock. Before she could say anything, I held up a hand. "No. I'm sorry, but I cannot be late to work. We can talk Tuesday."

Her stare was uncomfortably like Jacob's. "I can hardly wait. Until Tuesday, then."

"Until Tuesday," I repeated steadily.

After she left, I allowed myself a moment to *breathe, breathe, Watson,* before I hurried on to the locker rooms to change into my scrubs. The clocks were just clicking over to 8:43 as I slid my employee badge over the reader and pushed through the double doors into the wing.

Three med techs and two nurses clustered around the duty desk. Medina was handing out paper cups from the Ethiopian coffee shop on Irving Street. Hicks was telling another story about her boyfriend and his dog. For one infinitesimal moment, I had a picture of a quite ordinary day, with its strictly laid-out hours, routine questions, and complaints shared with my coworkers, who had gradually begun to follow Antonelli in treating me like just another tech and not a surgeon temporarily displaced from her world.

Hicks happened to glance up. Immediately she gave a soft exclamation. Everyone else noticed me and went silent.

"I was mugged," I announced, a bit too loudly. "I still have a headache."

The silence continued a heartbeat longer. Then . . .

Medina grinned. "So you're saying if you screw up, you don't want us yelling at you."

"Especially you," I replied.

"And what about me?" Roberta Thompson said.

Like a thin brown ghost, she had materialized from around the corner, clipboard in hand. She was smiling that edge of a smile that passed for amusement with her.

It was because of her smile, and my giddiness at the fact that, yes, I was alive, and yes, I would spend a perfectly dull and ordinary day, that I replied, "Oh, you. I wouldn't dare tell you what to do."

And that was all. The other med techs vanished to their own interview rooms. Thompson gave me my assigned station, then left me on my own. I was grateful for that. I wanted, badly, those fifteen minutes alone in between the surreal quality of the past two days and my most ordinary job.

Checklist reviewed. Supplies counted and ticked off one by one. The quiet routine, the sharp familiar scents of rubbing alcohol and disinfectant, steadied my nerves. My job was boring, but right now, boring looked marvelous.

"Watson."

Thompson loomed in the doorway.

"Did you file a police report?" she asked.

I shook my head. A few excuses flashed through my brain. The light was bad. I couldn't see his face. He got scared off before he could steal anything. None of them sounded believable.

Thompson made a grumbling noise. "Just as you like." She turned to continue on her inspection tour but paused on the threshold. "By the way, you're eligible for sick leave for yesterday."

That startled me. "How? I thought—"

"Regulations, Watson. Overtime. Combat injuries." Her

mouth twisted into a smile. "Don't get so excited. It's not for the whole day, just a couple hours."

She was gone before I could do more than stare.

She was lying. She had to be. Unless she had uncovered some obscure exception, a subparagraph of a subparagraph, located in the several pages of addendums that lawmakers and special interest groups had grafted onto the original legislation. But that meant . . .

"Watson." Alice knocked on the doorframe. "Wake up, Watson. Private Jenkins to see you."

I jumped. Alice grinned at me as she ushered my first patient into the interview room. Private Jenkins, twenty-two years old. Blinded in one eye by shrapnel when rebels attacked his outpost in Ohio. We were seeing more of these injuries from outdated weaponry. Some of the nurses and med techs believed this meant we had broken their supply lines, at least for armaments. Others, including most of the doctors, said it didn't matter.

I recorded the details from Jenkins's previous visit and his most recent symptoms. Headache. Phantom images when he shut his good eye. The nightmares we all had. Within ten minutes, I had shunted him through the doors to the next waiting room.

♀

My giddiness at having such an ordinary day lasted until noon. My gratitude remained, but more a shadow than the substance. *Better than the other choices,* said a thought in my sister's voice.

Grace, dear Grace. For such a little sister, she sure liked to lecture me. Times were I liked her better in the abstract. Still. We hadn't talked for over a year, and that was all about our parents' house and her plans to move west.

Memo to self: Buy a new cell on the way home. Don't tell Sara.

By four thirty, I had reviewed all my cases and updated their records where necessary. Everyone else from my shift had gone, except for Antonelli, who waved at me absentmindedly as she stared at her screen. Ah, no. RN Thompson was reviewing the newest med tech's work, while the newbie herself hovered in the background, looking anxious. Poor newbie. I hoped she would last.

I was in the locker room, changing into my street clothes, when I heard the buzz from my duffel bag.

Sara's text device. She must have sneaked that into my bag last night. I fumbled through every pocket and zipped compartment, until I finally located the damned thing. It had stopped buzzing, but a green light flashed the new message signal. I tapped the screen and whispered, "Sara?"

The screen turned bright. A message scrolled past. Hurry up, it said.

I hissed in irritation. "What the hell do you mean, *hurry up*?"

As if the thing heard me, another message scrolled past: You said you wanted to talk. Let's do it.

Within ten minutes I was racing out the side door of the hospital, the text device clutched in my left hand. The sidewalk was empty, the skies rapidly fading into an inky dusk. One by one, the streetlamps blinked on, like stepping stones of light around the medical loop. My breath caught in sudden apprehension, even as I told myself that Sara liked to play games.

I stuffed the text device in my jacket pocket. Fine. I would take the bus home. Nice and regular.

A few hundred yards away from the entrance, the device buzzed again. Make a left at the next intersection. Do not pause, do not look behind you.

By now my pulse was thrumming in my ears. I forced

myself to continue at a normal pace down the loop to First Street, where I turned left as instructed. Soon I heard the ring of footsteps behind me. I stumbled, caught myself, and kept walking. The footsteps continued to trail me from a distance, slowing down to match my pace, so that we made but one set of echoes along the pavement.

When I reached the turnoff for the Children's National Health System, I deliberately dragged my feet, not quite coming to a halt. I heard a huff of laughter, then my shadow companion overtook me.

"Are you hungry?" Sara asked in that low rough voice that said she was amused.

"No," I said.

"You are. You just forgot. Turn right ahead, then stop by the reservoir."

"By the reservoir? Won't that look odd?"

"Not your problem. Just do as I say." But when I shook my head and stubbornly planted my feet, she glanced around. Nervously? Yes. I had not mistaken that flicker of apprehension. Perhaps the amusement was more to reassure me, or even herself. "Very well," she said. "We walk together, you and I."

She hooked her arm around mine and we continued together. We turned right onto Michigan Avenue. Half a block ahead, an ordinary yellow cab waited underneath a streetlamp. Sara spoke to the cab's driver while I stared over the reservoir in the direction of Howard University, where I had spent four years.

An image of my younger self came back sharp and strong.

Who was she? I wondered. *That tall and stocky girl who dragged her suitcase up the stairs that hot and rainy August afternoon? Would we recognize each other?*

Nostalgia had a funny sharp edge when you came down

to it. I liked that young girl with her attitude and her belief she could conquer the world. I wasn't so sure she would like me back.

Finally Holmes finished her conversation with the driver. Within moments, we sat in the cab's enormous backseat as it sped west toward our apartment. The driver flicked on the radio and reggae music vibrated through the vehicle.

"Takeout or diner?" Sara asked. She had to speak directly into my ear before I could understand the question.

"Does it matter?" I said.

"Of course it matters. I discovered a few interesting things about a friend of yours. I need to investigate them, but they'll take me out of state. Would you like to come with me?"

My breath stopped in my throat. "Is it part of—I mean, why?"

"Reasons."

A passing streetlamp reflected off Holmes's eyes as she glanced toward the driver. So. More secrets.

"I need to hear those reasons," I said. "Over dinner."

"That means takeout."

She pulled a cell from her pocket and spoke into the receiver. Then she punched in a second number, where she rattled off . . . an order for food? Directions? I couldn't identify the language. She clicked off before we crossed Sixteenth Street. For the remainder of our ride, she stared out the window, arms crossed and her body tucked into the corner. Remote. I almost told her I had changed my mind. I didn't want to know her reasons. I didn't want to know anything about her life or her work.

But I didn't say anything. It was a different kind of challenge, one I couldn't refuse.

Faith Bellaume would have something to say about challenges and risks, and the thin divide between them.

A battered black Hyundai waited at the curb by 2809 Q Street. Sara paid off our driver with what looked like a fifty-dollar bill. I had my hand on the door latch when her hand closed over my wrist and she leaned close. "I'm going to push you out," she whispered. "When I do, say *San Juan*. Make it a question. Make it angry. Then shut up."

Before I could argue, she hooked a hand around my neck and pulled me into a kiss.

Her lips were warm and impossibly soft. For a moment I lost myself in the scent of her perfume and the sensation of her body pressed against mine. But only for a moment. I could tell it was an act—by the precise angle of her head, the finely calculated pressure of her hand against my neck, the way her body never succumbed to intimacy. This was not passion. This was yet another performance from the incomparable Sara.

Holmes ran a series of kisses along my jaw. "San Juan," she whispered, her breath feathering my skin. "Say it."

She unlatched the door and pushed me out of the cab. I stumbled and landed on my hands and knees. "San Juan? What the hell—?"

Sara was grinning, a maniacal grin. I glared back. "You are insane," I said loudly. "And I mean that in a purely clinical way."

"You're overreacting."

"Not yet. I should, though. It might be interesting."

"Doubtful." She swung out of the cab and offered me a kiss on the cheek before sauntering over to the Hyundai. The driver of the Hyundai rolled down his window. The streetlamp told me almost nothing. Holmes handed the person a wad of bills, and they passed over a large paper bag with the name of a local grocery store on the side.

The driver obviously said something, because Sara laughed.

Then the car was driving away and she was walking toward me, swinging the bag by its handles. "Who was that?" I asked. "A long-lost lover?"

"Don't be jealous. I don't want a lover, lost or found. I'd rather have you."

Briefly, I considered taking off my device, so I could beat Holmes around the head and shoulders. But first I wanted some answers.

So I tamped down my rage and followed a whistling Sara up the steps and into the building. When we were inside the apartment, doors shut and locked, Holmes pointed at the couch. "Sit. We'll eat first. Then we can talk."

"I'd rather eat and listen while you talk."

"No, I'm hungry."

She unpacked several containers from the bags, then fetched plates and silverware from the kitchen. There were several ceramic pots with vacuum-sealed lids. Sara dumped one container on each plate, and the scents of garlic and red chilies and lemongrass filled the air. Two smaller pots followed, these filled with sweet mango and sticky rice. Huh. Not the usual paper containers you got with the usual takeout. Yet another item to file under *Mysteries, Sara Holmes's, One of Many*. And tonight she served us tap water instead of wine. So, a serious conversation.

We ate steadily through our first serving of every dish. Then Sara ladled a second helping of noodles onto her plate and refilled our water glasses. "You have questions, of course. Ask away. I shall count none of them against what we negotiated before."

I had expected more games, more evasion. It took me a moment before I could organize the hundred thousand questions I had about Sara Holmes. "Why did you lock me up yesterday?"

"To keep you safe."

"You think I'm in danger. That's why you met me outside the hospital."

"Yes. No. Possibly."

"But *why*?"

Sara took up a pair of chopsticks and expertly lifted a mound of noodles to her mouth. Her eyes closed as she ate, and in the lamplight, the folds beside her eyes were more pronounced. "I cannot say—in part because you do not have the necessary security clearance, in part because . . . I don't know why. Not yet."

I made an exasperated noise. "What *do* you know, then?"

She smiled, reminding me of a cat. "Too much for a single night of conversation. Here is what I can tell you. Your friend Private Díaz was an other-than-honorable discharge."

I sucked down a breath. "OTH? But—"

"But she had full veteran benefits. Yes, I know. And yes, I know, it's almost impossible to keep your benefits when you're OTH. The circumstances were unusual, according to the official reports. Which," she added with a fleeting smile, "are a matter of public record. If you know where to look."

She went on. "About those circumstances. On June third of this year, two squads attached to the Second Infantry Division, currently stationed in Tennessee, were ordered out on a standard reconnaissance mission. The Red Squirrels and the Badgers were their names. The assignment was nothing out of the ordinary. What was extraordinary is that the squads crossed into enemy territory and retook an important outpost from the rebels."

She paused and poked at the remnants of her meal with her chopsticks. "Or rather, one squad retook the outpost. The rebels outnumbered the squads by five to one. They fought back hard, too. As she later reported, the staff sergeant of the

Badgers judged the situation outside of their original orders and called her soldiers to retreat. There were repercussions for her decision later, but that isn't important. What matters is that Díaz and her mates fought against impossible odds and won—at a great cost. Half the squad died that day, the rest were badly injured and discharged within a month."

They told us after . . . after what happened that we were heroes. I believed them.

"She *was* a hero," I breathed. I wished I had told her myself, no matter if she believed me or not.

Holmes nodded. "They all were. Every single member of that squad received a medal and a commendation. However, between the medals and their discharge, there were several incidents. Unruly conduct. Drinking. Drugs. Díaz herself punched another soldier without provocation."

Oh, yes. The other part of her story, the part where all her life went wrong.

I didn't used to be so angry. It's like everything went wrong one damned day.

All of these were very intriguing details, as Holmes said, but what did the Red Squirrels and Tennessee have to do with me and what happened Wednesday night? Unless . . .

I remembered Sara's questions about security for the VA computers. Her insistence on knowing exactly when I emailed Saúl and what log-in I used for the laboratory portal. If the New Confederacy could hack into the VA system, that could do more harm than another Alton.

"You believe we have a different kind of security breach," I said.

"That is one possibility," she said. "But I have a few more details you should hear. Two members of Díaz's squad died last week in a shootout in Miami, Florida. A third went into intensive care this morning, in a hospital in Michigan. I intend to find out more, starting with Florida. I'm going there tonight." She leaned forward and rested her elbows on the table between us. Her face was still as stone, but I saw her pulse beating at her neck.

"It might be coincidence," she said. "There are other factors involved that I can't talk about. It's a question of parallel lines of investigation. That is all I can say."

"Oh, there is much more you could say," I breathed. "You want me to come with you to Florida. Why?"

"Perhaps your presence would reassure the people I need to question. Perhaps I want a companion in my madness. Perhaps," she went on, "they might attack again."

He had become *they*. I shivered at the implication.

If we could prove a connection between the New Confederacy and Belinda Díaz's death, it wouldn't bring her or her squad mates back to life, but it might tell the world what heroes they were. It might undo the day when everything went wrong.

And if she is redeemed, then perhaps I will be too.

Holmes stood up. "My plane leaves in two hours. If you wish to come, you have twenty minutes to pack. Personal items, nothing more. Whatever you need for your arm. I'll take care of the rest."

⚲

We reached Dulles by nine P.M. Our cab dropped us off at the International Arrivals Building. We ducked through the doors and swung right into the main terminal, then up to the ticketing level. We bypassed all the counters, however, for a small office marked CUSTOMER SERVICE next to the British Airways section.

"Professor Smith?" A woman in a dark blue suit approached us with one hand outstretched.

Holmes accepted the handshake. "Anderson. I'm so glad you could accommodate us."

"Bribes and threats are always effective," the woman murmured.

"I wouldn't use them if they weren't necessary. Do you have the IDs I asked for?"

Anderson's gaze flicked over to me, then back to Holmes. "Of course. But are you certain—"

"I've done due diligence," Sara said, a bit crisply. "And I'll take precautions. You know me."

Anderson shrugged. "That is what worries me. However . . ."

She handed over a leather-wrapped parcel, then a second slim portfolio with an emblem that indicated microchipped documents. Holmes leafed through the contents of both and nodded. "Good. I'll let you know what happens."

"Don't," Anderson said. "I'm happier that way."

Holmes laughed. "You always were. Thanks again. And tell the chief I'll deliver my report in person Sunday afternoon."

Anderson took us through a door marked SECURITY PERSONNEL ONLY, along a winding corridor, to a steel hatchway leaking cold and damp. "The pilot has his orders," she said. "You won't have any trouble with him."

She swung the hatchway open, letting in a spatter of rain. Holmes and I climbed down the metal stairs and crossed the tarmac to a small twin-prop airplane with a commercial logo painted on the side. We each took a seat inside the otherwise empty cabin and strapped ourselves in.

We refueled once, at a nondescript airport in North Carolina, where Sara held a brief conversation with the pilot. I overheard the words *Fayetteville* and *visibility*, then Sara's telling him to chart whatever course he needed to.

It was midnight before we landed a second time. I had dozed off shortly after North Carolina. When the plane touched down, I started up, still entangled in dreams. I wiped the sweat from my face and drew a breath of the thick humid air. "Where—oh. Florida."

"Miami," Holmes said.

But not the main airport. The pilot handed us a flashlight, and we used it to cross the tarmac to an almost deserted parking lot, where a taxi waited.

The taxi brought us to a motel on the outskirts of the city. There, with Sara negotiating the terms, the night clerk handed over a set of keys in exchange for $300 in cash. There was no guest registry, no demand for a credit card or driver's license. I followed Holmes down a musty-scented corridor to a room on the outside corner.

The room contained two single beds with barely enough room for the bedside table between them. What I had first taken for a closet was the bathroom, with sink, toilet, and shower crowded into a five-by-five square. A pair of narrow windows overlooked the parking lot. Holmes noticed my staring at them.

"We paid extra for that view," she said as she dropped her bag into a corner.

I shrugged, unable to find an answer to that enigmatic comment. The first surge of energy, from when Sara told me her plans to investigate Belinda Díaz's death, had faded, and doubts were crowding in. Sara admitted the connection between my patient and my assault was tenuous. One of several parallel lines of reasoning, she had called it.

I'm tired. And frightened. And tired of being frightened.

A state that had begun in the war, with intermittent bouts of healing. Another topic for Faith Bellaume.

I changed from my T-shirt and jeans into the cotton pajamas I had packed. I could sense Sara's gaze upon me, steady and unblinking, as I jammed my clothes back into my duffel bag. My stump felt bruised and tender. I had packed my kit for tending to my stump, but I couldn't bear the thought of Sara's watching me. I unlocked my device and laid it on top of my bag.

Meanwhile Holmes had stacked several extra pillows against her own headboard. She leaned back with a plastic flask in one hand. I didn't see a gun, but I suspected she had one.

"What's tomorrow's agenda?" I asked.

"Nine A.M., an interview with the senior doctor on duty the night our boys died. Depending on what he tells us, we ask a few more questions here, or we proceed directly to our next suspect."

"But we're home Sunday afternoon, right?"

"Oh, much earlier than that. Barring any accidents." She raised the flask to her lips and took a long swallow. Twelve forty-five A.M., said the alarm clock.

"We should sleep," I told her.

"You should. I need to think." Sara drank another swig. "Don't worry. I'll wake you in time."

"*That* is not what worries me."

Sara laughed, a soft rasping laugh, and tipped the flask back one more time. I closed my eyes and hunkered under the musty, threadbare sheets, wanting the weight and presence of the cloth in spite of the warm damp night. I heard a creaking noise from the direction of Holmes's bed. The lamp clicked over to a lower setting, and Sara eased back onto her mattress. I could hear her soft breathing, like that of a patient who waits out a lonely pain-filled night.

12

"Wake up, my love. Rise and show the world your glorious face."

Holmes grabbed my shoulder and yanked me onto my back. In the seconds before I recognized her, the old panic overtook me, and I swung a wild punch. Holmes stopped the blow and shoved the windup clock in my face. Only then did I realize the alarm was buzzing. Loudly. "You have thirty minutes to dress and make yourself human," she informed me. "Our appointment is at nine, remember."

Her eyes were red rimmed, and she had a strange manic air. I sucked down my breath, convinced she would kill me if I said a wrong word.

"Afraid?" she said softly.

"Give me one reason not to be."

"Ah," she said. "That I can't do."

She released her hold on me and hurled the alarm clock at the floor. It bounced down the lane between our beds and crashed against the door. The buzzing hiccupped once, then started again, louder than before. Someone in the next room thumped the wall. "Shut that fucking thing up!"

Holmes's gaze flicked toward the voice. She scooped up her gun from her bed and exited the room, slamming the door behind her.

There was one more burst of pounding on the wall, then abrupt silence.

I froze, and waited for the gunshot.

None came.

Very slowly I eased myself from bed. I located the alarm clock and pressed its buttons until it stopped buzzing. The room stank of whiskey and sweat, and the damp air seemed to stick to my skin. It was almost impossible to remember the cool of midnight and the sense of our being wrapped in a bubble of companionship.

Thirty minutes, Sara had said.

My duffel bag was still at the foot of my bed with my device draped over it. I dumped the bag and the device onto my bed, fished out my soap and the oil for my hair, and headed into the bathroom.

The shower was a tiny stall edged in black mold that produced a lukewarm spray. The setup reminded me of the showers at camp. I had just enough time to lather myself thoroughly before the hot water died completely. I rinsed off in cold water and reached for the nearest towel.

Through the *drip, drop* of water I heard a click and the brief influx of noise from the outside world. Sara, back from her adventures. Had she left a trail of dead bodies behind her? Did I really want to know?

I toweled myself dry and wrapped one around myself before I opened the door.

Our bedroom was empty, but Sara had left behind evidence of her visit. A metal carafe, placed in the center of our tiny bedside table. Next to it, a stack of paper cups, a container of yogurt, and what appeared to be a genuine French baguette. On the bed was a complete set of clothes.

One cup of coffee, bitter and strong, got me through tending to my stump. Sara had not arranged my supplies, so there was more awkwardness as I fumbled through powdering my stump, then reattaching my arm over its new sock.

Now I turned my attention to Sara's other gifts. Oh, and oh, and oh. More evidence that this woman did not view the world as I did. There was a linen suit of dark gray trousers and jacket, shot through with threads of burgundy. A cream-colored silk tunic. Elegant flat shoes that seemed to wrap themselves around my feet. The suit and tunic were perfectly fitted for my height and for my device, as if she had secretly taken my measurements while I slept.

She is a demon. A spy of my soul.

I was shivering, in spite of the summer heat. I had asked for this, back in August, when I accepted that first challenge and visited 2809 Q Street. And yet, I had not truly understood the challenge. I could not have predicted its outcome.

Holmes returned as I finished the baguette and my third cup of coffee. She was dressed in a dark blue skirt and jacket, with her locs coiled into a low crown. The mad look had vanished, replaced by a strangely contained expression. I tried to remember if she had been dressed that way before, but terror had erased all memory except the gun and her manic grin. I did notice, however, that she wore her earbuds and the lace gloves that signaled her connection to her mysterious data sources.

"Taxi is waiting," she said. "Don't bother packing. We'll come back afterward. Oh, and here are a few items you need."

She extracted a medical bag from her satchel and a leather ID case. I glanced at her, then opened the bag. It contained all the standard items of a medical field kit—antiseptic, bandages, tourniquet, scalpel, probe, suture kit—plus a number of unlabeled vials with pills and liquids.

"Are we drugging anyone today?" I asked.

"Only if we need to. Read your ID packet. Memorize the details."

The ID packet said I was Dr. Adrienne Wilson, an internist associated with George Washington University Hospital, currently serving as an adviser to the Federal Bureau of Investigation.

"This reads like a document invented by a crime-thriller author who hasn't bothered to do any research."

Holmes smirked. "As if you knew what a genuine ID looked like. Come on. The driver tells me traffic is terrible this time of day."

♀

Our taxi battled through the traffic of I-95 until the highway dwindled into U.S. 1, aka the Dixie Highway. They still called it that, even in the twenty-first century, and the utility poles still carried the old logo with red and white bars and the letters *DH*. Several of them also had the old Confederate flag painted underneath. Not anything official, of course. But nothing about the KKK and its supporters was.

Stop it. This is not the backcountry of Georgia. And we are not two anonymous black women. We are representatives from the federal government.

I still didn't feel any better.

We exited the Dixie Highway for the streets connecting U.S. 1 with the beachfront roads. Here there were fewer cars, and our cab soon turned off Miami Avenue into a complex of driveways. We drove past several buildings with signs indicating various specialties to the main hospital itself, where the driver shut off his meter.

Mercy Hospital. A tall gorgeous building, its walls gleaming white under the brilliant Florida sun. Palm trees decorated the landscape, and next to the entrance was the statue of a saint. A hospital founded out of compassion, according to the literature I had come across.

A hospital for rich people, I thought. How had my two veterans found their way here?

Beside me, Holmes was staring up at the pale blue lettering of the hospital's name with a strange, almost fey expression. "And may God have mercy upon our souls," she said softly. "And forgive us our sins."

She paid off the driver and told him he didn't need to wait. We climbed the few steps to the entrance and through the doors. I allowed myself one glance around the glittering entryway, then followed Holmes.

"We're here to speak with Dr. Garcia," she said to the woman behind the reception desk. "We have an appointment."

The woman frowned. She was pale, for someone who lived in Florida—pale blue eyes, pale white skin dotted with freckles, and hair fading from gray to white. Ghost people, my sister called them, when we first moved north. That had earned Grace a spanking and a lecture from our mother.

Our own ghost woman took in my presence, just behind Holmes. The suits apparently made no impression on her, because her frown deepened and she pretended to consult the papers on her desk. "You say you have an appointment, miss?"

Holmes slapped her ID case onto the counter. "Agent Harris. It's an official matter."

Her voice was too loud, too flat. The woman jumped in her seat. I sensed movement rippling throughout the reception area. The white people staring at us. The few blacks going still and tense as they stared anywhere but in our direction.

Holmes touched her gloved hand to the earbud in her right ear. She tilted her head and her gaze went diffuse for a moment. Then she smiled. "Abigail Lampert. Married. Expected retirement date is next year. No record with the police except for a few traffic violations. Ms. Lampert, I would like you to use that pretty console on your desk to notify Dr. Garcia that his nine A.M. appointment has arrived."

Lampert fumbled with her e-pen and tapped the display screen. It had gone utterly silent around us, except for a faint whispering at the far end. I felt a flutter of nervous laughter behind my ribs. Sara's extravagant display with the earbuds, the not-so-subtle threat about our ghost woman's record. It was a farce of all the spy movies Angela and I had ever watched together.

Meanwhile, Abigail Lampert was speaking in low tones into her headset mic. She nodded once and tapped the display. "Dr. Garcia is on his way. Please . . . Please make yourself comfortable. He will only be a few moments."

Holmes, still smiling, replaced the ID case in her jacket. We took our seats in an ocean of unnerving quiet. No whispers now. Only the hum of electronic equipment and a muted beeping from beyond a set of double doors. Small, anonymous hospital sounds.

I had forgotten, truth be told, how it was in the Real True Genuine South of these United States. Maryland did and did not qualify. Illinois most definitely did not. I had lived too long in states where you could—for the space of one blink, one breath—pretend there was no difference between white and any other color. My mother said that this belief was more dangerous than the in-your-face racism of the South. And yet she had died in the South, at the hands of those people who were nothing but in-your-face.

I wished I could talk to her about that. How we were both

right, both wrong. How I missed her. Even her lectures about proper behavior, her disapproval of Angela. How I remembered that stricken look—gone in a flash—when I told her I had volunteered to join the army.

When I got back to DC, I would buy a new cell. I would call Grace. And we would talk about our mother and father, about our grandmother who still lived in Georgia, angry and proud. We would argue. We might even shout at each other. But we would talk.

Next to me Holmes waited, apparently wrapped in that same impervious blanket of cool and calm she carried with her. I wanted to speculate on where she had acquired it. Was it an artifact of her own upbringing? A clue to a background unconnected with the U.S. and its history? Or simply her own arrogance? The white security guards eyed us from time to time. Lampert glanced in our direction whenever I chanced to shift in my seat. The white patients were blind to us both. The black and brown ones sent us covert glances as if they feared we might cause more trouble, trouble that would wash over them as well.

"Agent Harris." An older man, dressed in a wrinkled gray suit, stood at the door beside the reception desk.

Holmes stood up in one easy fluid motion. "Dr. Garcia?"

He nodded. "Come with me. If you please."

Garcia led us through what felt like a mile of corridors until we reached a newer complex of offices and glass doors. After a few more turns, we came into a bright office with windows overlooking gardens of azaleas, irises, and gardenia trees. Garcia's medical degrees and certificates of honor decorated the spaces between bookshelves crowded with reference books.

He gestured toward two comfortable chairs before taking the seat behind his desk. "I received word yesterday to expect your visit," he said. "Though I'm afraid I don't have much information myself. The two men in question . . ." He consulted the papers on his desk. "Victor Molina. James Walker. They weren't regular patients of ours. The ambulance—"

"I know the particulars," Holmes said. "Or at least the particulars of their arrival. Molina and Walker were brought here last Saturday, Mercy Hospital being the nearest facility. They died, or were already dead, having been caught in the middle of a shootout in Bayfront Park."

"Then you know more than I do," Garcia said.

"Possibly." Holmes waved a hand to one side. "I'm here to fill in a few missing pieces. Molina and Walker . . . No, let me back up. You might've heard the reports about the drug trade between Miami and Central America. What you might not know is there's a new drug cartel with operations in Quintana Roo, various Caribbean islands, and Miami. Our analysts came across a list of names. Molina and Walker were on that list. The purpose of my visit today is to determine if our department needs to investigate these men further."

It was a masterful performance of lies constructed from selected truths. Was there a new drug cartel? It was plausible. The mainstream media newsfeeds carried any number of articles about the connection between Miami and the Mexican drug trade. It was even possible Molina and Walker each had a history of drug use. Too many veterans did.

I suppressed a shudder at the thought of that possibility. Garcia seemed pleased. An easy explanation? A solace for him and his staff, knowing they could not have prevented these deaths?

"There's not much more I can tell you," he said. "Both men were DOA. The cause of death was obvious—each body had a dozen bullet wounds. Internal injuries in both were severe.

One man had nearly bled out by the time the EMTs arrived at the scene."

"Did you have any blood work done on them?" Holmes asked.

Garcia shrugged. "No. We saw no reason for that."

No doubt it was the end of the case in his eyes, but I hadn't missed his unthinking dismissal of these deaths. "I have a few questions," I said, "concerning the cause of death. Did you perform an autopsy?"

He swung his gaze toward me. He took in my expensive suit, then my battered device, which rested uneasily in my lap. "We received no request from the family for one."

Did you bother to contact them?

I suppressed that surge of anger. I recognized Garcia's attitude from my years at Georgetown. *Why borrow trouble?* a senior surgeon told me once. Find the simplest cause and treat that. You'll be happier. So will your patient.

Clearly Garcia believed the same. I smiled at him. "Thank you. And could you tell me the official cause of death? Was it blood loss or internal injuries?"

"It's irrelevant," he said sharply. "They died because they were shot." Then he drew a long breath and collected himself. "If you want my opinion, however, I'd say internal injuries edged out the blood loss. Those bullets left a mess behind that I'm not certain we could have repaired even if they hadn't bled out. Is that what you needed to hear, Agent Harris?" he said to Holmes.

Holmes nodded. "It will do, yes. Thank you."

We went through the usual round of handshakes and polite commentary. Garcia offered us coffee, which Holmes declined, then the courtesy of summoning a taxi, which she accepted. The entire episode had lasted an hour.

"That was useless," I said.

"Not entirely," Sara said. "Though I expect our next interview will be more productive. The police headquarters," she said to my questioning glance. "And please, continue to ask any questions that occur to you."

Her optimism about the usefulness of our next interview was misplaced. When we announced our presence at the front desk, the sergeant on duty immediately sent a minion to fetch Detective Fletcher. Another minion brought us coffee and doughnuts, and told us the detective would be along soon. Eventually Detective Fletcher, dressed in a wrinkled black suit, took us away to his office on the third floor.

"I only heard from your people last night," he said. "Not much notice, but you could say I'm used to that when the FBI gets involved. Here's what we know."

He recited the details of the police record in a dull, flattened voice. No, there had been no previous drug-related incidents in Bayfront Park. The principals involved each had a record with buying marijuana, and Walker had a quite legal prescription for painkillers, which sometimes indicated a deeper involvement with drugs. When Sara pressed him, he admitted there had been no other complaints or arrests.

"But let's get back to the night when there was a complaint," Sara said. "Can you tell us anything beyond the official report?"

"Not much more," he said. "We got an anonymous tip about a disturbance. Gunfire in the park, five or six guys at least, shooting at each other. Our caller thought it might be a drug deal gone wrong. By the time our people arrived, the shootout was over and we had two dead bodies and nothing else. Whoever else was there had disappeared. We made a sweep of the area, of course. All that got us was a collection of nine-millimeter bullets. And before you ask, yes, yes, we checked the local clinics and sent out a broadcast. Nothing showed up. No ER visits from people with gun wounds. No word about trouble between gangs."

"Is that unusual?" Holmes asked. She had already given him the spiel about drug cartels and the list of names with Walker and Molina.

"Eh," Fletcher said. "*Unusual* is too strong a word. Let's call it odd. If it was an argument between two drug dealers, we generally hear about it. But that's with the local boys. You say they were connected with a drug cartel, no? That might explain things."

Holmes shrugged. "They might be, they might not. Our analysts are sometimes more suspicious than they need to be. However, if we confirm the connection, my department will let you know."

Fletcher shifted his gaze to the paperwork on his desk, his expression noncommittal. Obviously he expected as little from us as we did from him. I left the usual courtesies to Holmes as we negotiated further exchanges of information and records, then took the offered escort back through the precinct hallways to the front entryway.

"Do you need a taxi?" our escort said.

"Thank you, but no," Holmes replied. "I've called for one already."

The relief in the woman's face was all too obvious. Miami, or at least the doctors and police of southern Miami, wanted us and our inconvenient questions gone. Can't say I blamed them.

A car waited outside, no doubt summoned by Holmes through the network she wore. I hardly cared. I murmured a good-bye to our escort, then followed Holmes to the sleek black car that waited at the curb. It was far more elegant, and therefore far more expensive, than the taxis we'd used from the motel. Another deliberate choice on Sara's part? Did she intend to confuse our audience as much as she confused me?

By one P.M., we were back at the motel. Holmes paid off the driver and unlocked the door to our rooms. "Checkout was at noon," she said. "I bought us an extra two hours."

I dropped my useless medical bag, with its equally useless IDs, on the unmade bed. "No doubt I ought to be grateful," I replied. "Can you tell me what you found out from those pointless interviews? Or was there something I missed?"

"It's not important," Holmes said.

"It fucking *is* important," I said.

She *tsk*ed at me. "Such language, Dr. Watson."

I slammed my fist into the pillows of my bed. "Fuck language. You know Belinda Díaz died for no good reason. You said there was a connection—"

"I said no such thing. I merely agreed there might be one. Which we have not proved. Yet. Now, if you are done with your speeches, we need to pack. Our next plane takes off within the hour."

Our car had vanished, replaced by a nondescript taxi. The driver was Latino, his meter appeared to be stuck at the $20 mark, and the few legible city license stickers dated from ten years ago. There was a pattern to these choices, but I was too weary and frustrated to work it out. I let myself doze in my corner of the backseat while our driver veered from lane to lane as he sped along the Dixie Highway. We made one stop, where Holmes ducked into a small shop plastered with signs in Spanglish. She returned five minutes later with a large bag and two large bottles of water.

"Eat," she told me. "We have another stop to make before we head home."

We shared the bag's contents—several Cuban sandwiches, a paper bucket of spicy fries. By two P.M., we had finished our lunch, and the cab had dropped us off at the south terminal of the Miami airport.

"Where is our next stop?" I said once the driver had pulled away from the curb.

"Someplace cold," Holmes replied. "Don't worry. I brought coats."

"Coats," I muttered under my breath. Coats were the least of my worries, I thought as I followed her through the nearest door.

Our brief encounter with Miami International was a replay of Dulles. A man in a dark gray suit met us by the ticket counters and led us into a windowless office, bare of anything except a battered desk. Holmes handed over an ID—a different one from the one she had displayed to the hospital and police officials. This one was smaller, the size of my palm, and had a row of embedded chips along one side. Our new escort slid the card into a small device strapped to his wrist. A sudden image of assassins in the ancient world, with daggers in wrist sheaths, flashed through my mind.

"Holmes," the man said. "I've heard of you."

"But I haven't heard of you," she replied.

He laughed softly. "Fair enough."

He offered Holmes his own ID. She clasped it between her lace-covered hands and paused, apparently listening to the results from her earbuds.

"Have we collected any new friends?" Sara asked.

"None so far," he said.

She nodded. "Is the plane ready?"

"Ready and waiting this past half hour. Come with me."

We made a long trek through the back corridor, followed by a hurried exit through a back door onto the tarmac, where our plane sat—the same plane from yesterday, but with a different pilot and a second man who took charge of our bags.

Once more we strapped ourselves into our seats. The plane took off on a jolting run down the airstrip. There was a hesitation, a sudden leap into the air. Then we were shooting through a brilliant blue sky I had not even been aware of. Our pilot circled around over the ocean, then angled the plane to the northwest.

On and on we flew through the afternoon. Two stops to refuel: once in Raleigh; once, much later, in Pittsburgh. I heard the *tick, tick, tick* of sleet against the windows. When she saw me shivering, Holmes unbuckled her seat belt and staggered to the back of the plane. She returned in a couple of minutes with two coats. Mine was a wine-colored down coat with a hood. Holmes had one of dark blue wool. I tucked my hands into the pockets and discovered black wool gloves.

Had she forgotten no detail?

And what would happen if she did?

By five thirty we landed at a small municipal airstrip outside Lansing, Michigan. By six P.M. we had arrived at our destination, a hospital whose name I missed as we hurried from our cab into the warm, bright reception area.

It took me several moments before I shook off the cold and took in my surroundings, only to realize we were the only black people there. Oh, yes. We had traveled into a different world. I tensed, ready for another confrontation.

One or two visitors glanced in our direction. I caught a hint of surprise, or perhaps uneasiness, when they noticed my device. No one challenged us, however. No one questioned our presence. When Holmes gave our names, the pale blond woman behind the desk tapped a few keys on her console, then smiled. "Dr. Allen will be right out. She was afraid the weather might have delayed you. Would you care for anything? Coffee? Tea?"

"Water, thank you," Holmes said.

Answers to our questions, I thought. I kept that comment to myself, however, and accepted a cup of weak coffee. We had only a few moments to wait. Dr. Allen, an older woman, soon appeared to lead us to her office.

It was a dreary interview, even worse than the one with Garcia. Allen told us that the veteran in question, Private Deborah Geller, had died late Friday night. Primary cause was heart failure, she said. Secondary cause, blood clots leading to dementia. Other than a prescription to regulate her blood pressure—and the script had lapsed three weeks ago—the patient did not have any unusual pharmaceutical history, official or unofficial. Holmes appeared unsurprised. She handed over two official orders. One, she explained, for a copy of the existing autopsy. The second, to retain the body until a second autopsy could be performed.

"As for now, we only need to clear up a few loose ends," Holmes said cheerfully. "Did you run the usual tests?"

Allen shook her head. "The cause of death was obvious, at least without any evidence to the contrary—"

"—so you forwarded the body to the funeral home. Good enough. We only need to know the name—"

"You don't understand," Allen said. "Private Geller has been cremated. A personal request, found among her papers."

Oh. Yes. That was a final decision.

We, all three of us, spent a silent moment in remembrance of Geller's death and destruction. I had no doubt that Allen and her staff felt true remorse. It did not make anything better. Deborah Geller was dead, her body transformed to ashes because her flesh and her bones had proved inconvenient.

We rode in silence to the airport and boarded our plane. The sleet had died off, but clouds muffled the stars and moon. I stared out the window at the lights from the terminal. I felt curiously empty, empty and colder than mere physical cause could explain. A thought niggled at me, that the circumstances of Geller's death felt off, but I could not pinpoint why.

Inconvenient. The word popped back into my mind, but I was too weary, too distressed to make sense of that.

Sara laid a hand on my shoulder. "Steady now," she said softly. "We're almost home."

"Tell me that when we land safely," I said.

"If I can," Sara replied. "If I can."

We were both speaking in allegories, and we knew it.

Our pilot returned us to Dulles by midnight. By one A.M. we were climbing the outside stairs to 2809 Q Street. We negotiated the outer locks, the elevator, and finally the locks to our own apartment. It was comforting, having to work through so many layers of security. More comforting knowing that Holmes could take care of any infelicities with the local police.

When we finally broke through the last barrier to our apartment, Holmes marched onward to her bedroom. I made it as far as the parlor, where I tossed my duffel bag to one side and dropped into the nearest chair.

The rooms smelled of wood polish and the scent Hudson Realty's cleaning service liked to use. And someone had built a fire from well-seasoned beechwood. The flames burned bright and hot. A few logs had crumbled into ashes and embers, but one on top had not yet caught fire. Interesting. However, I was too exhausted to dissect the clues.

Holmes was picking out a desultory tune on her piano, crisp single notes, from a work I couldn't recognize. It started off slow at first, then gradually picked up speed until the notes were like a waterfall of music. Sharp, yes. Not like knives, but like pinpoints of rain. I let my eyes fall shut and thought about what I had seen and heard and survived the past few days.

Four veterans dead this past week. Four veterans from the

same squad. A coincidence? Impossible, according to the gods of statistics. And yet I had no proof, not even a clue about why they had died, only the tug of truth in my gut.

Truth, as Saúl Martínez would tell me, didn't matter once you were dead.

My friend, you are so wrong, I thought. *But I'll let you argue the point when we talk.*

Half an hour or so, and the music came to a gradual and natural conclusion. I wondered, briefly, who was this Sara Holmes. Did she have a history, recorded in painstaking detail, in the annals of the FBI or CIA, or wherever she called home? Or was she pure invention, called up by the nation's need? A Peter Pan of national security?

As if summoned by my thoughts, Holmes came into the parlor and took the chair opposite me. "So," she said. "What did you think of your first spy mission?"

"Useless," I said. "Useless, pointless, and a grand waste of time and the federal budget."

"On the contrary," Holmes replied. "We found out a great deal. For one thing, no one attempted to kill us."

That provoked a laugh from me. "Which means?"

"Which means this is not a professional case. Or rather, it's not from the true professionals."

My breath caught at the implication, even though I had suspected the same.

"You believed the New Confederacy was involved," I said, just to make sure I understood her.

She hesitated a very long moment. "Let us say I needed to eliminate certain elements in our mystery."

Right. All those parallel possibilities.

"So these trips were nothing more than . . ."

". . . to give whoever attacked you last week a reason to attack again. They did not. Which means you were an accidental target. It also means they had no access to my activities and conversations on Thursday and Friday."

Now more clues slid into place.

"You used me as a decoy," I said softly. "Not because of Belinda Díaz, but for that other case you cannot and will not tell me about. Because I have no security clearance in these matters, even if they concern my life."

For once, Holmes seemed ashamed. "I did. I'm sorry. Well, no, not really. You would be in danger no matter what I did."

Liar. If I had stayed in that awful hostel room, if I had never met you, I would be in no danger at all.

There was no need to say that out loud, however. Holmes knew that as well as I.

"Let's pretend," I said, "that last Wednesday night was a coincidence. What about that other case? You have adversaries there, no? What if they find out your identity? Can you guarantee my safety then?"

A pause followed that question, one that continued so long I realized that silence itself was her answer.

October 19.

Sunday, according to the world's electronic calendars.
My body insists at least a month of terror, rage, and
frustration has taken place since last Wednesday.
Perhaps I was right. Perhaps Sara does have the special
talent of turning time inside out. Time and lives. I
suspect I am not her only victim.

No, I'm no victim. Belinda Díaz is a victim. So are
Molina and Walker and Geller. Accidental companions
of war, failed by their commanders, their doctors, their
nation.

By god, I want a name and a face to blame. Forget
Alton. What about the Red Squirrels, those who died
that day to make their impossible victory possible? Or
the ones who lived on, branded with dishonor?

After I left Sara alone with her silence, I lay awake in
bed wondering how much she knew that she refused to
admit to me, to herself. I am certain she knows a great
deal more about Belinda Díaz's heroic squad and the
reconnaissance mission that ended their lives. I told
myself that I would confront her again the next day.

Only the next day arrived with Sara already gone
from the apartment, and a text message saying she had
errands to run.

Errands. A report to her superiors? Or simply avoiding my questions?

You overthink everything, Angela once told me.

That was near the end, after I told her I intended to volunteer for the army. When we spent our days not in making love, but in argument and regrets.

My parents made other, more pointed comments.

My sister rolled her eyes. It turned out we were already moving in opposite directions, quite literally, and she relocated to the West Coast two years later.

Huh. Overthinking again.

So let's keep it simple. I am exhausted in heart and mind, if not my body. I grieve for the dead. I want answers. Justice. An end to the gray smothering my life. I want this cup taken away from me. I want . . . any number of contradictory things.

For now, I'll settle for breakfast.

13

Sara returned my tablet Sunday night, between that dark midnight hour when I lay awake and staring into nothing, and when my alarm clock sounded. As with everything else, she had arranged the scene with a careless artistry. Power cord connected. Electronic stylus off to one side. And the tablet was tilted down over its keyboard, almost but not entirely closed, as if I had left in a hurry. A faint blue glow leaked around the edges, ensuring I would notice the moment I rubbed the sleep from my eyes.

I stared at the thing, immediately suspicious. Everything looked so ordinary—too ordinary—as if Sara had re-created the scene from a photograph of my habits.

The blue glow rippled in time with the screensaver. I could picture the swallows in flight, wheeling around the confines of that ten-by-fourteen sky. The flickering caught the edge of a paper note, tucked underneath the keyboard.

Oh, no. Not obvious at all, Agent Holmes.

My first impulse was to ignore the note. Or burn the damned thing, and never mind any explanation or apology.

Luckily, I had no matches or lighter. A fire would set off the smoke detector, no doubt. I could just picture the emergency squad arriving with bells and whistles and a fire hose to extinguish the flames.

Meanwhile, the alarm clock was beeping its querulous reminder that morning had arrived. I slapped the button to shut off the noise, then wearily padded across the room. Sara never did anything without a reason. I might distrust those reasons, but if she offered me any clues, I'd be a fool to ignore them.

I extracted the note and awkwardly unfolded it with my single hand.

All that is yours is yours once more and without reservation.
   To answer your question: I did not, but others did and will continue to.

                                                                —S.

Classic Sara it was, the words splashed across the page in brilliant blue ink. I recognized those flourishes from all her previous messages. Like those previous messages, the note was written on milk-white parchment with the same mysterious arrangement of dots in the upper right corner.

I had discarded those other messages without thinking. This time, I wedged the sheet underneath my tablet to hold it open and ran my thumb over the dots. They were barely perceptible, just slight imperfections in the otherwise smooth surface of the page, but they appeared only in that top corner, nowhere else. I ran my thumb over the dots a second time, pressing harder.

There was a pause of nothing, a moment where I felt only the sweat from my nightmares, the panic and subsequent irritation of knowing that Sara Holmes had once more manipulated me. Then I felt a trembling against my thumb, a faint pricking that ran the length of my arm.

I plucked back my hand—too late. One moment, the paper lay before me, whole. The next, a cloud of white specks exploded around my fingers.

The grenade exploded only a few feet away. I was lifted off my feet and landed on my back, dazed and unable to breathe. Dust filled the air, obliterating the dawn. All I could see were shadows darting around me. Rebel soldiers. Our own troops and the other surgeons and nurses. And above me a cloud of burning motes that were surely the dead.

Images from the past dropped away. I was huddled in the far corner of my bedroom, trembling. I ran my hand over my face, felt the damp of tears and sweat. My ghost arm's presence was stronger, with a sharp ache just below the elbow where the bullet had shattered my bone. And in the center of the room, bits of Sara's message whirled around, white and glittering in the cold light from my tablet's screen.

Damn, damn, damn you, Sara Holmes.

I leaned back against the wall and stared at the patterned ceiling, waiting until my heartbeat slowed and the panic leaked away. Sara played a game. She always did. They all did, those agents of my beloved government. Why was I surprised?

I reconsidered the past few days, the truth of what had happened, separate from the script inside my head. So. The FBI had returned my tablet. Or rather Sara had, along with a warning. At least the message read that way.

I did not, but others did and will continue to do so.

Oh, yes. The code was obvious now. Her people had searched my tablet and its memory sticks. They had ransacked my cell for every call I had made. And they would continue to monitor everything I texted or emailed, especially now that Sara had shared certain secrets with me. Warrant-less searches were illegal, but no doubt the government could produce the necessary paperwork. Sara might even say it was for my own safety.

Abruptly I realized I had been rubbing my hand against my leg. Trying to scrub away the ashes. *Oh. Ashes. God.* Deborah Geller was nothing but dead and ashes now. The panic rose up again, bitter and strong. I slammed my fist against the floor.

No, no, no. Breathe deeply. Focus on one small thing. The voice of my PT nurse overlaid that of Faith Bellaume, and together they led me through the exercises to recapture my rage, to hold it lightly between my fingers, both ghost and flesh, then let it flutter away like the ashes still hovering in the air.

What do you want? Bellaume had asked me, time and again.

I want justice. I want the truth. Signed, Sentimental Girl.

What if the truth was nothing but a series of coincidences? Faith's own words, but they were very like the arguments Sara had given me early on Sunday morning.

Fine. Then we know, and we can move on.

Sara believed we knew the truth.

Or her superiors believed that, and Sara was being practical. They had dismissed Belinda Díaz's death as if it didn't matter. They had ransacked my life and my emotions, then tossed them aside. Even Sara had offered no more apology than *I did not, but others did.*

If I had a week to myself, I might . . .

Too bad, girl. You don't have a week. You have a job and bills.

One small bite at a time, I told myself. Wrestle with the angel later.

A cursory check of my tablet showed nothing added or altered, as far as I could tell. But then, the FBI would not leave an obvious set of tracks. I logged into my email account without any problem. There was no reply from Saúl, but I did have a dozen pieces of spam and one inventive phishing attempt.

My cell, which I found in my duffel bag in its usual pocket, showed no recent calls attempted, none received, and none missed. The "Limited Service" message had vanished. The cell itself was fully charged, which I would not have expected, not after three, almost four days in the custody of the FBI. A mistake? Or possibly Sara giving me an extra warning that someone else had handled my cell?

I need to be careful. But I can do that.

Later, after the workday was over, I could dig through the VA medical records for more clues about Belinda Díaz. Until then, I had to face the ordinary world of my workday, with its regulations and standard questionnaires. I could only hope I did someone some good today.

♀

The routine of Monday morning carried me along the next two hours. By 7:35 I had boarded the D2 bus for Dupont Circle. By 8:10, I had transferred from the Red Line onto the D8 bus, which crawled like a slug down Rhode Island Avenue. It was another gray October morning, the air outside dirty and damp, the air inside the bus dry enough to suck the moisture from my bones. I rested my head against the window and timed my breaths—*One, two, three, start again, Captain Watson, I know you can*—until the windowpane fogged up and I was confronted by a Washington, DC, smothered in silvery nothingness.

I swiped my hand over the glass and stared at the blurred vista passing by. Seven long hours stood between me and the day's end. Maybe I could bribe Alice to order an entire tray of coffee from the Ethiopian shop. She did that sometimes, depending on whether she liked you. I thought she might like me. It was hard to tell most days.

Exit the bus. Walk to the next stop.

The day was colder than I expected, even for October. Cold and raw. The dampness soaked through my fleece jacket, sending a ripple of goose bumps over my skin. Funny how none of my memories from childhood included damp or cold, only a few picturesque seasons of winter white. Most likely I'd never thought about sleet or gloves or heating bills in those days. Now, my belly tight against the raw wet weather, I wished I had kept the coat and gloves Sara had provided for our useless Michigan trip.

I stuffed both hands into my jacket pockets and stomped down Mount Pleasant Street toward Irving. My metal hand ached as much my flesh one. I ignored both and trudged past the thicket of election posters covering the lampposts and buildings. Almost November. Almost election day. Had I registered to vote? I needed a new Metro pass, too.

The sun ticked upward, offering no warmth. I boarded the H2 bus and bullied my way into another window seat. I would have to ask Thompson how to find out what happened with those samples she sent to Capitol Diagnostics. It wouldn't magically return Díaz to life, but it might *explain* things. I badly needed, wanted, an explanation, and if Sara refused to help, I would have to investigate on my own.

My bus arrived at the VA Medical Center only five minutes late. I jogged up the sidewalk, ahead of a dozen other stragglers, with my duffel bag drumming against my back. I pulled my employee ID from underneath my jacket by its lanyard and swiped it over the reader.

The reader beeped and flashed red.

Shit. The reader was notoriously difficult. Especially on days when you could least afford its antics. Swearing under my breath, I rubbed the card against my jacket and made a second, slower attempt.

The reader clicked, then emitted a series of red and white flashes. The orderlies behind me laughed. I twisted around to swear at them. They all flinched back, then their eyes went wide when the door snapped open. Mine did too.

Three security guards poured out of the entrance to surround me.

"Janet Watson? Please come with us."

"What? What did I—"

The white employees snickered. The black ones went quiet. Even those I counted as friends did nothing as the guards confiscated my ID and hustled me away from the employee entrance, around the corner of the building, and through another, smaller doorway. I only struggled once. The biggest guard twined his arm through mine and gave a twist. I gasped.

Do not argue. Never argue. A video does no good if you're already dead.

The guards thrust me into a cramped windowless room, in the outer ring of the medical center. The walls were painted dull brown. The floor was layered with scuffed gray linoleum. There were two plastic chairs, one plastic table. I noted a video screen mounted in one corner and a second doorway opposite the one my guards had used.

The lock engaged behind me. I leaned against the wall and stared at that second door. My head felt disconnected from the rest of me, as though someone had performed a savage operation upon my body. Ghost arm. Ghost head. I could still breathe, even if my ribs ached with every inhalation, and my muscles had locked in fear.

The second door banged open and two men marched into the room. One was a bureaucrat—yellow haired, his complexion like school paste, his soft belly spilling over his belt. The second was a stocky black man who wore a shoulder holster and a badge that read SECURITY. I glanced from one to the other. Both were dangerous, each in his own way.

Mr. Bureaucrat settled himself into the one chair. He gestured to Mr. Security, who took up a stance in the corner.

"Captain Watson," the bureaucrat said. "Please sit down."

"Who are you?" I said.

"My name is not important—"

"It is, dammit—"

The security man crossed the room in three rapid strides and shoved me against the wall. One meaty hand gripped my shoulder, the other pressed a Taser gun into my ribs. "Be polite," he said softly. "Can you do that?"

The gun was a sharp point digging into my gut. I gulped down a breath, tasted the salt flavor of sweat in the air. For a moment, I was back in Alton—an imaginary Alton where the enemy had captured me.

I jerked my head up and down.

The security man studied my face a moment. He must have been satisfied, because he stepped back to his guard position but did not holster his weapon. I remained pressed against the far wall. My left arm was trembling. Pinpricks of electrical impulses ran through my stump and all the way down my ghost arm.

Mr. Bureaucrat seemed oblivious to the exchange. "You have been terminated with cause," he said. "If you wish to receive a copy of the report supporting this action, you have the right to file such a request, but I must warn you that your status as a temporary employee precludes the guarantee of any reply. Do you understand?"

"I . . . What?" I could still feel the pressure of the Taser's snub nose under my ribs.

The man regarded me with a fishy stare that reminded me of Terrence Smith. "You are a temporary employee," he said slowly. "Government regulations state you may request a copy of your employee file, but you are not guaranteed any other explanation for your termination. Do you understand?"

I rubbed the shoulder the security man had grabbed. Or at least I tried to. My metal fingers refused to curl properly. "I do."

He handed over a binder of paperwork. "Sign here, please."

The top sheet was a standard form, stating I had been terminated from my position in a government facility, but as a veteran in good standing, I would continue to receive my regular benefits. I flipped through the rest—it was all government statistics for the VA in general and the VA Medical Center in particular, claiming that any recent reductions in staff were spread across age and sex and race. In the fine print at the bottom of the page was a disclaimer: The undersigned agreed to waive all action against the Veterans Administration of the United States. In return, the undersigned would receive unemployment benefits, and full payment at the ordinary hourly rate through the end of the current week.

A paycheck for this week. And unemployment checks after that.

I sucked my teeth, considered the various paths of action and consequence. I could argue. I could even refuse to sign and file a suit.

Mr. Security continued to watch me with the patient gaze of a trained military man. Arguing was a terrible idea, I decided. And Mr. Bureaucrat was right about those government regulations. I had even signed a form my first day, stating I had read and understood them. Could I argue coercion? Probably. But there was the not-so-small matter of my shrinking bank account.

Money, that damnable lure. My father had lectured me and Grace about honor and ethics. But we had also heard a different lecture from our mother about honor and debt and making our lives our own. I let my breath trickle from my lips as I considered my choices. A simple choice, really. Launch myself into an impossible battle. Or take the money and survive to fight another day.

I was no hero. Not anymore. I signed the forms. Mr. Bureaucrat pressed a button, which summoned a young minion, pale with responsibility. She returned within a few moments with my copies, which I tucked into my duffel bag.

"What about my personal items?" I asked.

"They will be held at the main desk until Friday morning. You also have until then to return any hospital uniforms in your possession. Failure to do so means you will be billed for their replacement value."

He handed over a check, printed in case I would prove agreeable. I glanced at the number—it was like all my other checks from the VA—and added that to my supply of paperwork.

Mr. Bureaucrat stood. "Thank you for making this easy. I wish you luck, Captain Watson."

He did not offer to shake hands. I was just as glad he did not. When Mr. Security maneuvered the door open, I made a brief show of checking over my duffel bag and other belongings before I exited the room. *Do not hurry me,* I thought. *I'll take my humiliation slowly, if you please.*

The man did not hurry me—perhaps I had proved I would go peaceably—but he did glide out the door just a step behind me. I wasn't surprised. I had watched others escorted from the premises, the ones whom RN Thompson had judged inept, the ones who showed too much attitude with the doctors. The troublemakers and the idiots.

I thought I was better than that.

But those past incidents had taught me not to argue when Mr. Security followed me down the driveway to the bus stop.

He didn't abandon me there, oh no. He waited by my side until the next bus arrived and its doors hushed open. Only when the bus pulled away from the curb did he turn back to the medical center.

I took the first open seat. The drunk next to me leered at me. I gathered my duffel bag onto my lap and made myself as small as possible. Tried not to think. That was easy at first. My brain still felt disconnected from here and now. It was only by habit that I made it through the first couple transfers. The same pattern I'd followed that morning, in reverse. But the pattern was already cracked and crumbling. By the time I disembarked at Dupont Circle, I couldn't remember which bus came next, or if I needed to walk to the next stop. I circled around aimlessly until I fetched up against a low concrete wall. Somewhere close by was the restaurant where Sara Holmes and I had played our game of questions.

Was Sara at home, asleep? Or had she left on further errands related to her current, mysterious mission?

Or had she vanished entirely? She would, someday. Her chief would assign her elsewhere. Hudson Realty would lease apartment 2B to different, more affluent tenants. Perhaps it was just as well my life had crumbled into dust.

I tilted my head back and stared at the sky. A steady drizzle wafted down from the clouds. Here and there a shaft of sunlight broke through, a brighter silver against the unremitting gray. Like the imagery Reverend Francis used, when he talked about God's redemption breaking through the gray clouds of sin to touch the sinner.

Weren't no redemption for me today, Reverend.

The rain misted down in heavier droplets. It washed away the tears on my face. No doubt a remnant of my altruistic, idiotic self. My unemployed self. Maybe it was time I took myself up north, to the border, where cheap rooms were more abundant than here. Maybe I could take that training and get a job as a real doctor, if not a surgeon. Maybe Thompson could give me a reference.

I don't know how long I stood there, hands clenched in my pockets, my eyes closed against the gray October sky. Long enough for the rain to soak through my jacket and for my skin to prickle from the cold. Long enough for me to speculate all kinds of dark thoughts. Faith would be disappointed if I failed her now. Ah, but Faith herself had insisted that I owed no one but myself in these matters. Perhaps I should call her today and—

"Captain! Captain Watson!"

Jacob Bell's voice yanked me back to here and now. I ratcheted myself around to face Jacob, half a block away, waving to me as he stumped along the sidewalk.

"Captain," he called out a third time.

I shivered but remained where I was as he crossed the boulevard.

Jacob stopped a few feet away from me. He still wore his dark blue orderly uniform and white running shoes, now filthy with street muck. He looked cold and wet, and from the set of his jaw, I knew his old injuries were bothering him. Jacob had his own half-healed wounds from the war, inside and out. I was ashamed that I kept forgetting them.

Jacob tilted his head. "Going home?"

I shrugged. "Soon. Maybe."

He shrugged back at me. "It's a wet day, Captain. Happen we'll both be more comfortable if we walk back to that apartment of yours. Maybe we can have a cup of the coffee you're always telling the other techs about."

He didn't touch me—he knew better than that—he only gestured along the street.

I took a step. Then another. It got easier after that. We left the madness of Dupont Circle behind, though not the morning traffic, and continued along Q Street, over the bridge that divided northeast from northwest.

"It wasn't Thompson," he said. "She didn't know herself until eight A.M."

I nodded. That would be the way.

"The official word was those black marks of yours. Most don't care as long as you don't get too many and as long as you do your job. But if they're looking for an excuse . . ."

"I know," I said. My voice sounded strange and rough to my ears. I tried again. "I know how it goes, Jacob. I was late. I didn't check this box or that on the forms. Or I checked too many boxes." I tried to laugh, didn't quite succeed. "They don't like that neither."

Jacob sighed. "No, they don't."

We crossed the bridge over Rock Creek and headed up Q past Wisconsin. The rain had died off, leaving a blanket of mist that obscured the boundaries between the pavement and the street. The air tasted clean and wet, the flavor of autumn. One of my neighbors had already ventured outside with her spaniel. She crossed the street as Jacob and I approached.

Damn you, I thought. *Damn you and yours.*

But the anger, though present, was muted today, as though I had used up my quota.

Next to me, Jacob muttered. "That happen a lot in this neighborhood?" he asked quietly.

"Every single goddamned day," I replied. "You need to ask?"

He laughed and shook his head. "Only surprised you put up with that shit. You never used to."

"I have. I do. From time to time. So have you."

I expected Jacob to argue. Or make a joke. But his steps had slowed unexpectedly. I paused to let him catch up, but he was staring hard in the direction of 2809 Q Street. A lean, dark figure lounged on the front steps, head tilted up. Sara Holmes. Of course.

Sara lifted a cigarette to her lips, took a long drag. Expelled the smoke in a thin stream that coiled upward to join with the mist. She gave no sign she noticed us, but I knew better.

Jacob made a noise of disgust. "Well, no good hiding from trouble."

We crossed the street. Sara glanced in our direction. "You found her," she said to Jacob when we reached the steps.

Jacob stared at Holmes with slitted eyes. "If you say so."

"I do say so, Jacob. Thank you for the favor."

All the softness of the rain-washed air vanished. Holmes was smiling that goddamned self-satisfied smile of hers, the one she used whenever her complicated plans unfolded just exactly so. Jacob . . . Jacob's face had folded into a frown and he was shaking his head. Watching them both, I knew what he refused to say.

"You knew about today," I said to Holmes. "You knew and—and you sent Jacob to fetch me back here. Like a dog, fetching a stick. And you—" I rounded on Bell. "You did that. You gallop when she says run. You say, 'Yes, ma'am, glad to fetch that stick.' Just like back in August, when she needed a partner to share the rent. You fed me that story like you believed it."

Damn them both. I spun around and started across the street. Jacob grabbed my arm. I cursed and aimed a punch at his face with my device.

Holmes was at my side in a heartbeat. "You need to come inside. Now."

She had captured my fist, the one made of metal. I tried to break free, but she gave a twist that sent an electric shock up my arm. I yelped.

"Hey," Jacob said. "Hey, now. You stop that."

"Go away, Jacob," Holmes said. "You did what I asked. You brought her home. This next part is none of your business."

He blinked. Then his lips curled back.

"Like a dog," he breathed. He was glaring at us both. "Well then, I will."

He stomped away. Holmes gave my arm another twist that brought us around to face the steps. When I struggled, she leaned close and whispered in my ear, "The neighbors are watching. Let's take our existentialist drama inside where we can talk in privacy. Or would you prefer we talk to the police?"

Her expression was inflexible. Her eyes were dark, all traces of molten copper subsumed in those wide black irises.

"Fine," I said. "We go inside."

Her lips quirked into a smile. "I thought so."

Even so, she did not release me until we had navigated the entryway and elevator and she had locked our apartment door behind us. Sara took my duffel bag from me and pointed toward the parlor. I locked my feet in ready stance and shook my head. "You knew they had fired me."

"Not until this morning."

Her voice was soft and colorless. A warning, said my instincts, but I pressed ahead, too angry to care. "Really? Your net connection must be slow today, Agent Holmes."

"It's not. I was occupied with a different new stream. Janet . . ."

She drew a shaky breath. Turned away, but even so I saw the pity on her face.

"I can find another job," I said. "And another place to live." My voice rose up, pushing away that pity. "I'm not your goddamned charity case. And no, it won't be easy, but—"

"Janet. Listen to me. Saúl Martínez is dead."

14

She tried to explain. A mistake.

With a cry, I flung myself at her. Sara fended me off with the duffel bag, tossed it aside, and with a few quick steps gained the parlor. Before she could turn around, before she could offer that pity again, or worse, some platitude about the necessity for Saúl's death and how I should be reasonable, I had ripped off my jacket and pried open the control panel for my device. I tapped out the familiar release sequence, then grabbed my device by its elbow and swung it around.

Sara leaped back, her mouth open in a wide O.

I almost laughed at the sight—Sara Holmes, taken by surprise—but the laugh came out as a growl.

Sara rolled onto her toes, arms loose at her sides. Her face had smoothed into a mask, and I saw the same blank and deadly stare my attacker must have faced. My pulse thrummed in my ears. Terror. Rage. Grief. A strange ecstasy that I could at last strike out at Sara. She would beat me down, but I didn't care.

Unexpectedly, the mask dissolved into the Sara I recognized. She lowered her hands and took a step toward me. "You're crying," she said.

"Fuck crying." I lunged forward and drove the fist of my device into her gut.

She made an abortive move to evade the blow. Too late. The fist rammed home. Sara doubled over with a grunt.

I flung my device to one side and sank to my knees. *Fuck, fuck, fuck.* The world had crumbled beneath my feet a second time. Whatever tiny victory I had over Sara changed nothing.

"You let me do that," I whispered.

"It . . . was the . . . only . . . way."

Her words came out breathless and halting—my blow had not been a light one. I wanted to laugh at her predicament, but I was weeping too hard.

Saúl. Oh, god. Saúl.

So many times Sara had turned aside my questions with outrageous replies, had pretended to misunderstand or simply refused to speak. This time, no. This time she told the truth. A blow as direct and hard as mine.

"How . . . how did he die?"

Sara lowered herself to the floor next to me. Close, but not touching. "The official report calls it an accident," she said.

An accident. War spawned accidents by the thousands. But something about Sara's tone pricked a hole in my grief.

"What do you mean?" I said. "Tell me what happened."

The incident started with the weekly trip to Decatur, she told me. Captain Martínez had set off at four P.M. on Thursday in a company jeep, accompanied by a second medical officer, Captain Mayhew, and Corporal Ayers, the company supply clerk.

"Ayers took the wheel," Sara said. "They had just crossed Route 159 and were headed for U.S. 55 when she lost control of their vehicle and the jeep crashed into a ditch. They were not discovered for several hours after the accident, when they failed to report as expected in Decatur. Captain Mayhew died immediately of a broken neck. Corporal Ayers remains in a coma as of this morning. Her condition is guarded. Captain Martínez survived the crash with a broken femur and a concussion, but died Sunday morning from complications. The report came to me today, just after you left for work."

I pressed my forehead to the wooden floor. Saúl dead. And Mayhew, too—a man with so little imagination that he had often driven me into a fury, but who was nonetheless dedicated to his patients. Corporal Ayers. That snotty little girl. She used to talk racist trash with her friends when she thought no one else could overhear. I grieved for her, too. I didn't want to, but I did.

"How did he die?" I asked in a whisper. "The real reason."

"Heart failure, according to the official report. A blood clot which the original scans did not detect. As I said, complications."

My gut cramped harder. Saúl had died because of me. The blood clot was merely the weapon. Someone, some set of people, had murdered Saúl. And for no more reason than I had sent him that damnable email Wednesday night.

I must have spoken that last out loud, because Sara said, "You can't prove any connection between the two. Correlation is not cause."

"Shut up," I snapped back. "I know that."

A soft exhalation—of frustration? of sympathy?—was her only answer. I crouched on the polished marble floor of our vestibule, rocking back and forth. Ten, fifteen minutes passed. Sara waited with me. Patient. Silent. She had that gift, knowing how to offer her presence without burdening a person with unwanted talk.

Eventually she reached over and laid a hand on my shoulder. "Come. I'll help you to bed."

"No. I'm fine."

"You are not fine, and we both know it. Oh, my love, my furious love. You would not be Janet Watson if you did not rage against the world. But you can do that just as easily from your bedroom as you can here."

She circled one arm around me. I tried to push her away, tried to tell her that I was nobody's love, least of all hers. Sara refused to give way. "No more fighting me," she told me as she helped me to stand. "I shall put you to bed. I shall brew a cup of tea. No drugs, this time. Unless you want them?"

"No drugs," I said. "No tea."

"Then you shall have none. Later, I might insist you take a hot shower. And possibly a glass of strong spirits. Later still, I shall cook you a meal and stand over you while you eat."

As she spoke, she guided me down the hallway to my bedroom. I didn't resist until I crossed the threshold and stumbled to a halt, overcome by a bout of shivering.

Sara withdrew a step and waited.

It was easier to close my eyes. To listen to the thrum of blood through my veins. To hear the ticking of hot water through the baseboard pipes, which beat in time with my pulse. My throat had twisted into a knot. I wanted to wrap myself in a tight hug, but I couldn't, not with only one arm. I almost regretted my mad act of ripping off my device. Almost, but not entirely.

"I know better," I said at last. "I know the dead will not cease to be dead because I am warm and alive and comfortable in my bed. I have watched too many soldiers die to believe that."

"I never said you did."

"No. You—" My breath caught on the word, a dry, ragged

noise, as though I had forgotten the art of respiration. "You didn't say that."

"But you believe me capable of thinking such a thing."

A longer silence followed. The baseboard ticking faded into silence, leaving only my steady breathing as I counted up and up to a hundred, then down and down to the number zero. I had reached zero for the second time and paused, as the therapist recommended, when Sara spoke.

"I lied."

Now the room went utterly still, as though the air itself had vanished and we were in the soundless void of space.

"I lied," she said again. "Or rather, I was inaccurate—deliberately so. Which counts as a different kind of lie. You see, when an agent is resting, they are rehabilitating their identity. Their mission is complete, for the most part, but they continue to visit the old haunts, chat with the usual contacts, to dispel any suspicions. In my case, I was a liaison to an organization that specialized in money laundering."

You should not tell me this, I thought. *Your people will not like it.*

I didn't bother to tell her that. Sara Holmes already knew what oaths she had violated.

After a moment, she went on. "I can't and won't tell you the specifics of that case. It's not just a matter of security clearance. Knowing the details puts you in danger—more danger. What I can say—"

"Stop," I said. "Don't get me tangled up in your god-damned mission, Sara Holmes."

She laughed softly. "Too late for that. Listen. The science of mechanics tells us that for every action, there must be an equal and opposite reaction. International politics is far more complicated, the consequences multiplied a hundredfold. Just so with this almost straightforward mission of mine. There are repercussions everywhere—among our enemies, among those with more ambiguous ties. We cannot close our books until all those ripples and reactions have played themselves out. Which brings us to the matter of our friends."

"Jacob," I said.

Sara nodded, an almost imperceptible movement on the edge of my vision. "Jacob is my friend. And yet I curse his curiosity that led him to investigate your whereabouts this weekend. He came to visit on Saturday, do you know, and spoke to the groundskeeper. There were rumors at work about your attack, about how I mistreated you."

"That was your fault," I said. "You made everyone think we're lovers."

"I did. It was . . . it *should* have been a suitable cover if other elements had not intruded. I created that fantasy because I needed to protect my friends and colleagues. My mistake was not protecting yours. I am now attempting to do just that."

Oh, yes. A dozen clues shifted into place.

"Is that why you set up that pretty fight outside?" I asked.

Another nod. We had not yet faced each other, Sara and I, but I had become preternaturally aware of her every movement, of her every shift and change of emotion. Odd how she had seemed so opaque to me at first.

"I want him angry," she said. "Honestly and unmistakably furious. I want him to tell everyone that you and I are complete shits. He could never pretend, our Jacob, but his righteous anger is most convincing. My hope is that anyone watching will believe him ignorant and innocent of any connection, and will therefore leave him alone. Which brings me to my next point. Tomorrow you must go to Bellaume—"

"No!" My paralysis broke, and I skittered over to the nearest wall. Only then could I face Sara and her demands. "No, Sara, I cannot—"

"You must," Sara told me. Her face was obscured by the shadows in my bedroom, but as she lifted her chin, I caught the glitter of tears on her cheeks as well. "If you love your friends, you must go to the VA tomorrow. You must keep your appointment with Bellaume. Collect your belongings. Above all, you cannot let anyone see that I told you about your friend Saúl Martínez. Do you understand?"

A chill washed over me. Oh, yes, I understood. Our enemy had a name and a face, shadowed as yet. We would have to lure them into the sunlight.

"Who are they?" I asked. "Do you know?"

"No. Not with any certainty. There are a dozen lines of probability from the events of last Wednesday. Each one of those has another dozen possible outcomes, which leads us to a dozen different candidates. My chief has elected to pursue the most obvious course—that Wednesday night was a coincidence, and that the simplest and most obvious explanations are the correct ones. I disagree. However, I cannot promise anything."

"Except the truth," I said. "Promise you will always tell me the truth."

"Always," she replied.

♀

Hello, Tuesday. Hello, seven thirty A.M.

Twenty hours are not enough to transform me into an undercover spy, but Sara tells me that competence is overrated. Plausible is our goal.

So. At seven thirty A.M. I present myself at the reception desk for mental health services in the VA Medical Center. Our shadow enemy has stripped away my job, and with it, my authorization to traverse the interior stairwells and elevators, but they have not yet taken away my honorable status and its benefits.

"Captain Janet Watson," I say. "I have an appointment with Faith Bellaume."

The receptionist taps her electronic pen over the screen with an expert air. Pauses and frowns. I can guess what she reads on that screen, so carefully tilted away from public view. **Terminated with cause. Handle with caution.** Those warnings, along with any notations from Faith Bellaume, would put anyone on their guard.

Sara has warned me about this moment. I attach a pleasant smile to my face and wait while she taps and reads, reads and taps the screen again. Eventually the woman glances up with an unconvincing smile of her own.

"Ms. Bellaume is waiting for you. Please go inside."

A young woman escorts me to the next waiting room. I have just enough time to consider how much I wish to say, how much I cannot mention, before Faith herself appears.

"Janet," she says. "I am glad to see you today. How have you been?"

I swallow against the sudden thickness in my throat. It's the old tensions all over again. The sweet, soft formula of Southern courtesy, those meaningless phrases calculated to ease a visitor—or a patient—past any difficulties. Luckily those same patterns gave me the proper answer.

"As well as I can be," I say. "I'm glad to be here."

She brings me into one of the now-familiar sets of therapy rooms, and we settle into our accustomed places, both in overstuffed chairs covered in pastel painted fabric. There is a pitcher of ice water on the table between us and two cups. Both the cups and the pitcher were plastic. A signal that they trust me not to bash my therapist over the head, but also they do not trust me with breakable objects.

Bellaume pours me a cup and waits for me to drink.

"You lost your job," she says.

I take a second sip of the water. It's cold and sharp against my tongue. It spurs me into the necessary anger. "I did not *lose* my job. Those bastards took it."

Good, Sara would tell me. *Very good. You are angry, as you should be.*

The angry black woman. A trope, a symbol, a hero. A threat.

Meanwhile, Faith Bellaume, another black woman, faces me. She has her own obstacles, her own history with this nation. She says, "You are angry. You have cause. We can examine that in our next session, if you like. For today, I want to talk about Angela."

My stomach gives a sudden lurch. I bend over and press my palms against my face. *Do not fight your distress*, Sara warned me. *It is both your weapon and your weakness.*

I weep, and while I weep, I hold the image of Jacob in my mind. Jacob who loves me as a friend and who, for no reason I can fathom, loves Sara Holmes as well. I must keep him safe. Keeping him safe also guards Faith and all the others I have touched with my prickly unlovable self.

But Angela, too, is alive and in danger.

"I can't," I say. "Not today."

Faith watches me. "Perhaps not today," she agrees. "But you will need to face what happened with her."

"Next week," I promise.

Faith is nothing if not patient. "Next week," she says. "I shall hold you to that. But what about today? What shall we talk about today?"

During the long hours of yesterday afternoon, Sara and I have worked this out between us. It must be a subject that will distract Faith Bellaume, and yet it must be the truth as well. She is a trained observer, as Sara noted, and therefore more dangerous than many a casual witness. I do not distrust her, but I understand that others might question her about this session. The absolute truth, Sara tells me, is not always our friend.

I lock my fingers together, the metal and the flesh, and let them twist a few moments before I answer.

"I want . . . to talk about Alton."

It was noon before I returned to 2809 Q Street.

There was the session itself. The recovery. Oh, god, the recovery. I spent an hour in the recovery room, drinking cup after cup of cold lemon water. Bellaume's assistant was patient with me, silently appearing at intervals to refill the water carafe or to bring a fresh box of tissues. Once I had regained control, she came back one last time to confirm my next appointment. *Yes, Thursday*, I told her. *No, I don't want a different time slot. I'm fine. Thank you for asking.*

Onward to the front desk, where I dropped off two sets of scrubs and collected my personal items. There were only a few—my coffee mug, a bottle of Advil, a brightly painted carving that Hicks had brought back from her vacation in Mexico. Someone had wrapped them all carefully in old newsprint and packed them into a small cardboard box. Thompson, most likely, though Antonelli was my second bet.

I did not return to the apartment at once. As Sara had suggested, I spent an hour at the diner on U Street, drinking bitter coffee while I read a printout from a Help Wanted newsfeed I'd bought from a vending machine. After that, I took a circuitous route back to Georgetown, with a stop here and stop there to collect newsfeed printouts or books or candies. Sara's chief believed there was no connection between me, Belinda Díaz, and Sara's official mission, but she had promised Sara a surveillance team to keep watch over me for the next week.

For my protection? Or the protection of their own secrets?

I had wanted to ask Sara, but I found I did not care to hear the answer.

If I had any shadows, they had a damp and tedious morning, tracking me from the VA Medical Center, through the streets of the inner city, and into the National Gallery of Art, where I sat for two hours, damp and shivering and staring at Dali's *Last Supper* like a mad person. Luckily for us the city and the museum were routinely filled by the mad.

Eventually, at last, I returned to 2809 Q Street.

I thumbed the security panel of our building. A few moments later, Sara took off my rain-soaked jacket and led me into the kitchen, where she handed me a mug of hot tea. "Put down that box, my love. You were utterly convincing but stupid, or perhaps you were convincing because you were stupid. Like many other agents I have known."

I yielded the box to Sara, accepted the mug, and collapsed onto the nearest stool. It was easier to follow her directions at the moment. Perhaps later I would argue. About her willingness to issue orders. About that uncalled-for endearment that was no endearment at all.

"I have a meal ready," Sara continued. "We eat, then talk." She touched me—a light, impersonal touch—above my device. "How was it?"

I shivered. How to describe the morning? How I had used the truth of Alton to hide our lies. Yes, we had agreed on every detail of my interview with Faith Bellaume—details intended to protect Bellaume as much as ourselves—but the aftermath of those lies had left me shaken.

Sara nodded, a brief acknowledgment of my distress. "I have been looking. Quietly. I will show you after we eat."

I drank my tea while Sara laid out dishes and cutlery and glasses of fine red wine. We ate in silence, with only the pattering of rain, and the hiss of fire, to accompany our meal. Once I had finished, Sara cleared away our dishes.

"Come with me," she said.

There are moments when a lover reveals herself. Angela did, that day she lost a patient after a long and difficult procedure. I'd found her drunk and weeping in the bathroom, holding a scalpel to her wrist, and I saw, for the first time, that she had not yet achieved that immunity to death and suffering a surgeon needs.

Whatever the rest of the world thought, Sara Holmes was not my lover, nor did I mistake her words for an invitation to passion. We had come to a moment of trust, and if the world did not understand, I did. So when she took hold of my hand and drew me into her bedroom, I did not resist.

The room had changed very little since that first day. At the same time, it had been transformed. The floors remained bare. The only furniture besides the enormous bed and piano were a desk and its stool. But now a cascade of golden lace spilled over the piano's closed lid, like a waterfall of sunlight on this dreary day. And now the many bare walls were covered with a host of paintings—one bold and dark, with a luminous face at its center, others watercolors of women, of mountains wrapped in mist, of tigers on the hunt, all decorated in gold leaf and painted with delicacy and power.

Sara clucked her tongue over the lack of chairs. "Sit on the bed," she told me. "We can make do with that."

She produced a wafer-thin device from the desk and tossed it onto the bed. Then she ran her fingertips over a recessed panel by the door. I felt a crackle of tension in the air, then a smothering quiet enveloped the room. I could still hear the traffic from Q Street, but muffled, as though someone had dropped a blanket over number 2809.

Right. So. More secrets uncovered that I was happier not to know.

I maneuvered myself onto the bed and picked up the device—it was one of the newest tablets. Very expensive. Very sleek. It had no power cords, nor any obvious input slots. The tech feeds said these things ran on special batteries, which could recharge from ambient power sources in the city. I ran a finger over the black screen. It sent a ripple of electricity over my skin, then went dead.

"You need the right password," Holmes said.

She settled onto the bed next to me. I twitched away and she laughed, but this time I did not take the laugh amiss. Sara pressed her index finger against a mesh pad next to the keyboard. The screen hummed and clicked. "Welcome, benevolent overlord," it said. "How may I serve you?"

The voice was low and mellifluent, that of a senior male senator with patronage to spare.

"Is that your idea of a joke?" I asked.

"A very poor one," she agreed. "Let me show you what I've discovered so far."

She tapped the keypad, and the screen resolved into a map of the world, which rotated around and shrank to a different viewpoint.

Next to the map was a list in bullet points, in a style I had come to recognize as Sara's. Belinda Díaz's four visits to the VA Medical Center, marked by date, time, doctor's name, medical technician's name, were embellished with an increasing number of question marks. The date of her death went into finer detail: when she collapsed, the exact time of death according to the EMT's report, the approximate time I launched each search, the exact hour and minute I emailed Saúl, and the moment of that abortive attack.

"Nothing conclusive," she said. "But look at this."

Sara tapped again. A new screen appeared, and I blinked in surprise.

"They instigated the paperwork for your dismissal Friday afternoon."

"But you said—"

"That my chief had dismissed any connection? She did. And so this conversation is both private and unofficial, Captain Watson."

I felt a flutter underneath my ribs. "You said they're watching us."

She hesitated only a moment. "Yes. They keep a watch *outside* this building, and around the neighborhood. Which, by the way, is how I knew you were in danger last week. While there are recording devices in this bedroom, I am the only one who can activate them. Unless, of course, they have lied to me. Not impossible."

My reply was a muttered curse. Sara responded by leaning close. "Listen to me," she said softly. "Trust me, even though I've given you no reason to. Any recordings under duress do my chief no good, at least not for the mission at hand. So as long as I carry out my duties, we are safe."

"Define *safe*," I said.

It was a matter of expectations, she explained. Of hiding in plain sight. Her chief expected Sara to continue *resting* between missions. As long as Sara carried out her official duties—of maintaining her cover persona and reporting on the ripples and reactions of her mission, as she called it—she could interleave our investigation with the official one. Her chief was not oblivious. She would have Sara's activities monitored. The same held true for their adversary.

"I must provide my own people with interesting tidbits," Sara said. "I want them to believe I am investigating certain matters connected to my official case. I want them drowning in details so they won't delve into my search algorithms. And you will do much the same for our adversary."

She let her hand drop between us. I felt a shiver of sensation from my ghost arm. I said, "But your people can read the same files you can. They can draw the same conclusions."

"If they do, that's all for the good."

Maybe, could be, as Jacob liked to say.

"We cannot hide from observation, because hiding attracts attention," Sara said. "So I disguise my research in various ways. I use deliberately imprecise parameters. Carefully constructed searches that bury the important details in a flood of extraneous data. You in turn will show yourself to the world. You will go about the city on errands and present our adversaries with the opportunity to eavesdrop on your electronic conversations. Truth and lies. What matters is creating a plausible pattern to our activities."

"So what do they know?" I said. "Our adversaries, I mean."

Sara shook her head, and her locs slithered over her shoulders. "*They* is such an ambiguous word. I don't have enough data for even a guess. Our data says this much, however. The VA filed the preliminary paperwork against you at three twenty-five P.M. Friday afternoon. They, whoever *they* are, acted well before our trip to Florida. They are very, very worried about you, Captain Watson."

"I knew that last Wednesday," I said.

Wednesday, less than a week ago. More than a lifetime.

"Yes, and that gives us our next two data points. They were worried before *we* gave them an obvious reason, which tells me their goal was to separate *you* from your access to both Captain Martínez and the VA database. Saúl Martínez dies so you cannot discuss Belinda Díaz's case, with its possible connections to pharmaceutical companies. You lose your job so you cannot make any more troublesome searches in the VA system. The thoroughness alone convinces me."

"But not your chief."

"No. Which means . . ." Her gaze swept up to pin me with those same dark eyes that I remembered from our first meeting. Holmes allowed herself a fleeting smile as if she remembered that moment as well. "Which means you and I must tread carefully," she said. "I cannot guarantee your safety. My chief has only promised surveillance for the next week, more to protect the agency's concerns than yours. If you wish to retire from the field, we can arrange a different narrative."

"You mean, convince our adversary that I'm harmless?"

She nodded.

"Is that possible?"

"I don't know. There are too many probabilities at work. Perhaps the mystery is a simpler matter, and coincidence explains the rest. Perhaps . . ." She smiled. "Perhaps we've imagined a conspiracy where none exists."

"You don't believe that," I said. "And neither do I."

"No, I don't. So what do you say, Dr. Watson? Shall we solve this mystery together?"

"Of course," I said softly. "I was only waiting for you to ask."

15

OCTOBER 22. *There are days when the words for this journal come oh so easily. They slip off my brain and onto the paper like honey off a white-hot spoon. Today is not such a day. Sara tells me I write in my journal to shed my troublesome thoughts. She might be right. I should introduce her to Faith Bellaume and let them dissect me. On second thought, no, I'm not ready for tag-team therapy.*

On third thought, honey on paper only makes a mess.

Mess. Good word for this week, for this day. Oh god, I am about to weep again

---

I struck out that line so quick, the ink spattered over the page, like a constellation of black stars against a white sky. Across the room, Sara watched but said nothing. She had wanted to lock up my journal, take away my pens and ink. But no sooner had she uttered those sanctimonious words *security issue* than she stopped, held her breath a long moment, then softly said, "Just . . . be careful what you write."

Because they watch.

For a moment, I considered striking out the entire paragraph, but that would only provoke their already lively suspicions. My journal should have been private, but Sara's agents had searched our apartment once already. They might do so again, before we could gather enough proof to act.

I dipped my pen in the inkwell and tapped away the excess while I considered an innocuous ending to that sentence. So. Why did I weep?

---

because what else can I do? I have no job, no friends in DC now that Jacob avoids me. I once thought RN Thompson could be one, but we're separated by my separation from the VA Medical Center. *cue forced laughter* Whatever. I need to find work and a cheaper room to rent. I no longer believe that mere persistence will wring a glorious new device from the government, and I refuse to take Sara Holmes's charity.

I set my pen down and blew upon the wet ink to speed its drying. There was much, much more I wanted to write. More thoughts I wanted to shed. But I was weary with this careful journaling, everything written with the idea strangers would read my words.

Sara had rolled over and now lay facedown on my bed, her locs unrestrained and tumbled about. One arm cradled her head, the other angled around so that fingertips touched lace-covered fingertips. She appeared to be asleep, but I knew she was listening to the news streams pouring through her earbuds. She shivered, then exhaled softly. Her fingertips beat a soft, almost random, tattoo against each other. It was like watching the pulse and flicker of brain waves, writ large. How long had she lived with wires inserted into her skull, with her brain connected to the universe? How much had that changed Sara Holmes?

I tapped my pen over its inkwell. Sara immediately disconnected from her news streams—I could almost pinpoint the moment—and drew herself upright in one fluid motion. "Ready for the next part?"

"Ready enough." I wiped the pen nib and screwed the cap onto the inkwell.

Sara did not remind me that I did not need to follow through with our plans. We had talked for hours, from early evening to well past midnight, drinking expensive red wine as we worked out the fiction of our next few days. If I did nothing, I would likely escape any danger. Likely. As in, *You will likely survive this operation. Unless infection sets in. Unless the cancer is more aggressive than we predicted.* I did not want to do nothing.

"I'm ready," I repeated.

"I knew it," she replied.

She vanished down the corridor while I locked away my journal and changed from pajamas into baggy trousers and my old U-Howard hoodie. We had worked out the details of my appearance the night before. A general impression of neglect was both plausible and reassuring, so though I had tended to my stump, I had not showered and my hair was a nest of fairy knots and tangles.

I packed my duffel bag for the morning. That too was carefully planned. The three paperbacks to be traded at the used-book store. Several empty Diet Coke bottles for the recycling refund. My tablet, carefully hacked by Sara herself so that my Wi-Fi shut down after thirty seconds.

Sara waited for me in the kitchen, where she had prepared an enormous pot of coffee and a plate of freshly baked croissants. The air was laden with the scent of yeast and flour. Sara herself was like a dark witch, casting spells of appetite and delectableness.

"Do you treat all your operatives like this?" I asked.

"When I can." She filled two mugs with coffee. To one she added cream. "One lump of sugar, or two?" she asked.

"Guess."

She smiled and pushed the mug with cream across the table.

"You remember what to do," she said.

Not a question. Not a reminder. A statement.

"It's all possibilities and supposition," she added, unnecessarily.

That was Sara, worrying in advance for the agent she sent into the field of danger. All of a sudden, I had the clearest image of her doing the same for others over the years. A carefully prepared meal of favorite dishes. A warm hand laid on the agent's shoulder—but lightly because she did not want to upset the equilibrium of terror and determination. Was this how my mother had felt, sending her children off to university, to marriage, to war?

I swallowed my coffee and felt my throat loosen from its knot. My appetite woke up, and I ate two of those delectable croissants and drank a second mug of coffee. It was already eleven o'clock.

"I should go," I said.

"Yes, but don't hurry," she said. "And don't come back right away."

I nodded. Let the adversary observe me angry, frustrated, but unafraid of any mysterious assassins. Let Sara's people observe me doing nothing in particular. The paperbacks and bottles were part of that strategy, but Sara had urged me to follow my own instincts, as well.

My first stop of the day was Aida's Electronics on Florida and Third. There I dropped off my tablet and haggled over the cost of its repair with the skinny girl running the maintenance shop. We spent fifteen minutes discussing firewalls and viruses, with a bonus lecture to me about proper backup procedures. Finally the girl agreed that if they couldn't repair the tablet within one hour, they would attempt to extract my files onto a thumb drive. A $50 minimum charge for troubleshooting. Another $100 for data recovery with thumb drive included. Sign here, please.

I signed and paid the $50 deposit via debit card. Step one established: tablet inoperable. Step two: spend a couple hours at the VA headquarters using their workstations to provide an open trail for my activities. I set off on foot from the electronics store.

Saúl is dead. You can't make any more searches. We can't rely on that alone to convince our adversaries that you are harmless. So we add new layers to our story. Misdirection and lies blended with the truth. The word is counterfactual. *An alternate now. And we make it easy for our friends-the-adversaries to discover this new narrative.*

From Aida's, it was a short walk to the Metro Red Line, which brought me directly to Judiciary Square and the VA headquarters. Sara's matter-of-fact voice guided me from point to point. *Turn this direction. Pause at this street corner. Remember the empty bottles now. You have the change? Good. Walk another block. Once you sight the Metro station, you will see a grocery shop. Walk a few yards past, then duck back and buy a bar of chocolate.*

Sara had constructed a plan for my every movement, my every emotion, between 2809 Q Street and the VA. Over and over, she had repeated the assurance that I was safe. Our adversaries were people who acted in secret, in the unlit streets or the lonely back roads of Illinois. Avoid the abandoned stables, the church at midnight, she told me. Above all, do not respond to messages from the mysterious gentleman who asks you to accompany him to his rooms.

No matter what Sara said, I felt the skin between my shoulder blades itch with every step. Once or twice I stopped, pretending to read the election posters. They stole my breath, they did. Foley yammering for peace at all costs, while his running mate, Joe Stevens, offered muttered commentary about a return to traditional values. I knew exactly how to read that dog whistle. Traditional values = women in the kitchen offering up dinner and children. Meanwhile, all those angry men whined and argued and spoke oh so persuasively for a return of the nice polite women, gays, and minorities. Donnovan's posters were so very low-key, as though he didn't wish to offend the white working class, never mind the black working class. And the ones from the third parties, that alliance that Alida Sanches had built, seemed . . . hesitant at best.

By the time I reached the front desk of the VA headquarters, my teeth ached from grinding. I paused in the entryway, huddled inside my hoodie, while I searched and searched for quiet within. That too fit our narrative. That too fit the character of so many who passed through these doors.

Eventually I decided I was human enough to face the next step. I wiped away the tears from my face and clasped the small portion of quiet I needed to approach the front desk and explain what I wanted. I was a veteran, I told the woman. I was out of work. My tablet was in the shop and I knew the VA had a job search center here.

Yes, of course, the woman told me. An escort would direct me to the common room and show me how to access the system. Within fifteen minutes, I had a cup of hot coffee and a desk in the same VA services room I remembered from August. I listened to the same familiar tutorial on how to access the VA services and the restrictions of the internet portal. I almost expected to see the same tech from tekSolutionsEtc dissecting one of the laptops.

Goals. Remember your goals. No longer was I Janet Watson, a surgeon momentarily deflected from the upward trajectory of my career. I was a disabled veteran, willing to take any job to survive.

The VA portal demanded my military ID and password. I provided them.

A new screen slowly rendered itself onto the twenty-four–by–thirty-two rectangle that included links to the usual VA services and to my viewportal to the internet. A few clicks brought me to my personal email account. I scrolled down through a dozen spam messages until I came to one.

Dear Janet, Saúl here. I'm so glad you want to talk . . .

Ohgodohgodohgod. I clamped my mouth shut against a sob. I noticed, as though from a distance, that I was trembling. One of the other vets glanced around. I collected myself long enough to smile and shake my head. *Nothing wrong here. No.* Because of course I could not know about Saúl's death.

The other vet shrugged. I slid my mouse over the desktop, clicking at random, until I was certain their attention had shifted from me back to their own screen. My lips felt numb and I was still shivering deep inside. It was only the thought of Saúl himself, of Belinda Díaz and her companions, that kept me from breaking down and weeping.

Eventually I recovered myself enough to continue reading.

. . . I worried about you, of course. You are invincible but I know invincible comes with a sell-by date. Not for loyalty or honor, but simply the void that Wile E. Coyote discovers when he's run fast and far beyond the edge of the cliff. So how am I? Let's see how much of this message gets past the govern-

ment Yossarians. I am well. The company not as much, but you can imagine the relevant details. I suspect the other side feels much the same. We all want to come home, alive and safe. It's the details of home and safe that we seem to disagree upon.

I'm heading off to Decatur today for the usual run. I'll text you Saturday morning with the best time to call. —Saúl

The time stamp on the email read 10.16 07:47.

Hours before I woke to find myself a prisoner. Longer still before he set off for Decatur. I clicked to see the message headers. The delivery chain showed a few short hops from Decatur's local servers to the central military one, then a much longer delay—nearly three days—before the servers shunted the message onward. That . . . was not implausible. The military censors often took a day or two to review outgoing messages. It was an artifact of the second Iraq occupation, when GOP congressmen inserted extra monitoring regulations.

Now for the hard part.

I drew a deep breath and clicked the reply button.

Dear Saúl, I love you. As a friend. As a companion in arms. Stupid, I know. They told us that first day, do not fall in love with your duty or your colleagues. You will die of disappointment. Fuck them. I love you. Janet.

The words came out in a rush, typed without halt or hesitation. The moment I stopped typing I shut the window and clicked *Discard*. My stomach had twisted into a knot, and I had to breathe through my nose until my gut stopped heaving against my ribs.

All around me was the warmth and quiet of this late October day, the muted *tap, tap* of keys and the click of mouse buttons, the almost inaudible noise of midday traffic from the streets outside. No one glanced in my direction or tried to kill me. For that, I was thankful.

I took a deep breath and held it, willing my pulse to slow

down, my nerves to collect themselves. *Right. Back to the fiction.* I clicked *Reply* a second time. This time, the words came out in spits and spurts. This time, I did not have Sara Holmes to guide my answer.

Dear Saúl, Sorry I missed your email before. You were in Decatur, I was in San Juan. Yes, San Juan. I know. All I can say is that someone else's drama got really old, really fast. But enough about her, let's talk about me. I came to DC to demand a new device. No luck so far. I had that job but lost it. The market for one-armed surgeons isn't nearly as good as it used to be. I'm thinking I should leave DC for parts less expensive. Maybe north to Vermont. Let me know how you are. Love, Janet

Before I could lose courage, I clicked *Send*.

There was a faint whoosh, as if my email were a winged creature, shooting through electronic skies. I stared a moment longer at the screen, then shut down my browser and rested my head on my hands.

Like a voice whispering in my ear, I heard Sara telling me, *You need not make yourself a paragon of cheerfulness. You have lost your job and quarreled with a friend. You are permitted to show yourself discouraged.*

Right. Thank you. I knew that.

I sighed and rubbed my knuckles against my forehead. Outside the skies were muddy gray. Inside, the air felt sharp and dense, like lightning before it struck. It took me ten or fifteen minutes before I could continue the script Sara and I had worked out. It was simpler, if not easier.

I opened up the VA job search portal and updated my résumé, judiciously edited to avoid any reference to "involuntary separation." Next, I applied to six positions in DC listed as temporary or contract only. After that, I added a custom search filter for medical jobs in Vermont, Michigan, and California.

Techs, GPs, physician assistants. Anything for a paying job. And as a final touch, I submitted the necessary forms to receive a copy of my employee file and the reasons for my discharge.

Current time, twelve forty-five P.M. Too early to return to the apartment.

I spent another half hour meandering through the services offered by the VA for returning vets. When I had exhausted all the variations Sara and I had prepared for, I logged off and headed up Sixteenth Street to the U Street corridor.

I bought a falafel sandwich and a large coffee from the next street vendor I met. More wandering brought me to the Mall, now fading into a late autumn brown and gray. I plumped myself onto a bench and arranged my sandwich and coffee next to me. A half-dozen or so office workers on their lunch break surrounded me. One family with the children tumbling over the grass. No one bothered me. I was dressed like the homeless, in my baggy trousers and my hoodie, but I had a substantial meal laid out, and by now I had recovered from the shock of Saúl's email. I no longer twitched, and my rage I carried deep inside.

I'd picked a spot by the World War II Memorial. The Reflecting Pool was a silvery rectangle to my right, with Lincoln's cold pale face gazing over it. Away to my left was the Washington Monument. A couple years back, my mother wrote how some protester had painted Washington's face black. A stupid, stupid person, she had said. Not that she disagreed with the protester, but because she knew the cost of showing anger.

I finished off my sandwich and coffee and bought a second cup that I carried west toward the Lincoln Memorial. This, this was my personal pilgrimage, the magnet of my discontent. Mr. Liberty for the black people of the United States, and oh, we should be so grateful.

Grateful is a bitter word, my father once said.

I tilted my head up at Lincoln. Stared at him while I drank my extra-strong coffee. Maybe he had done all that he could. He had paid with his life, after all. And yet, I could not rid myself of the anger that others had risked as much only to be forgotten by history.

My duffel bag beeped faintly. I ignored the first round of signals, but when the second began, I sighed, tucked the coffee cup between my feet, and dug out Sara's message device.

Okay? it said. The clock blinked two thirty, which was later than I had guessed.

"I'm okay," I said quietly. "Coming back soon."

It was closer to three thirty by the time I had negotiated the locks into apartment 2B of 2809 Q Street. Sara met me at the apartment door and led me into the kitchen, where a mug of chicken-and-peppercorn soup waited for me. I levered myself onto the stool and bent over the mug, breathing in the clouds of spices until I no longer shivered. Sara waited patiently while I drank down the soup, then held out the mug for a second helping.

"Saúl answered my email," I said. "In case you didn't know."

Her only reaction was a swift, assessing glance. "I didn't. Which is an important data point."

Right. Yes. So glad to provide my grief for your analysis.

She handed me the filled mug. I stirred the liquid with my spoon. As with every dish Sara prepared, the soup was a perfection of flavors and texture and color. Even the ceramic mug and wide silver spoon whispered of expensive craftsmanship. *Because she comes from a rich family. She's never lived on a dirt farm or scrubbed toilets in payment for a cottage on the beach.*

Unfair, that. But I wasn't feeling all that fair after my visit with Mr. Lincoln.

"I wrote back," I said, still staring at my soup. "You didn't tell me what to say, but I knew. I—"

I dropped my head onto my hands. I had no more tears except ghost tears. Like my arm that no longer existed but never entirely vanished from perception. Sara made no move to comfort me. She waited, silent and invisible, while I grieved—for Saúl, for Belinda Díaz, for any number of companions who had died in these wars. At least with Saúl, I would get one last message: User Account Not Found. A form of closure, courtesy of the internet.

At last I raised my head, wiped a hand over my face. "This is good soup."

Sara accepted the change in subject. "I thought you might like it. And I have my own contribution of news. Your final employee report." She pushed a thick brown accordion folder over the counter.

"I applied for this already."

"I know. We'll compare this version with the one they send you."

Oh. Right.

I upended the contents of the folder and spread the papers over the counter. Here were my résumé and application, the various forms I had signed when they first hired me, and those I had initialed for each step during training.

A few sheets included commentary from the doctors, nurses, and senior med techs. *Meticulous. Conscientious. Shows an understanding of proper medical procedures.*

Interesting. The doctors had rated me far higher than I expected. Respect for my degree? Honest opinion? A mixture of both? The reviews from the med techs were mixed, but I recognized the ones Antonelli had provided. *Rises to the challenge, even when there isn't one.* Then, in the neat script I recognized as Thompson's handwriting, *Reliable. At times displays an arrogance of intellect.*

"She likes you," Sara observed. "So does that Antonelli."

I snorted and turned over the next sheet. Here started the official transcript of my employment. *Job title: Junior Medical Technician. Status: Part-time personnel.* I skimmed down the list of excused absences and tardy arrivals. Then followed a chart labeled *Metrics,* with my percentage of cases completed at or under the regulation time limit. One hundred percent green was the goal, according to our orientation. Mine was 75 percent. Borderline, if I believed the chart's legend.

Then I came to a page labeled *Reasons for Termination:*

Subject frequently tardy without proper notification. Regulations require medical technicians to be on site fifteen minutes prior to start of shift.

Subject regularly exceeds recommended consultation time.

Subject at times has not displayed a team-player mentality. She argues with senior personnel and has at times abused her access to VA resources to bypass recommended treatment protocol.

Subject often uses prohibited language . . .

That made me pause. Sure, I had said *damn* and *shit* and even the occasional *fuck this.* We all had, even RN Thompson, even Drs. Patel and Anderson. Not to the patients, of course . . .

Oh. Now my skin went stiff with a cold that no soup could vanquish. I turned over the page to see a paragraph rendered in large font and boldface:

Complaints recorded against the subject by patients:
Incident. 8:00 P.M. October 15. Complaint filed

11:00 A.M. October 17. Subject used inappropriate language to patient.

Incident. 1:00 P.M. October 17. Complaint filed 2:10 P.M. October 17. Inappropriate language with violent overtone. Recommend immediate termination.

Lies. Neatly packaged and delivered via regulations designed to protect our patients. I felt a twinge of genuine violence for anyone who appropriated those safeguards for their own murderous ends.

"Those reports are false," I said, handing the file back. My mouth twisted into a cold and angry smile. "I wish I knew who filed them. I'd show them what inappropriate language sounds like."

Sara's smile was equally cold. "So would I. But our best revenge is . . . revenge. So. Let us ignore the false reports. Let us focus on their intended effect. Which comes back to you and your troubling inquiry into Belinda Díaz's medical records. One inquiry probably did not trip their alarm, but you weren't satisfied with those first results. No, you launched a second, far more comprehensive search that romped through the VA medical system and Capitol Diagnostics as well. A few hours later, you sent an email to your friend Captain Martínez, where you explicitly mentioned Belinda Díaz and that you were puzzled by her death. One or both of these actions sent our friends into sudden panic."

"But—"

Sara held up a finger. "Hush. Let me finish. We cannot tell yet which event provoked the attack, only that it happened. However, you yourself are nothing more than a surgeon in the army, recently discharged, with no influence. No, they were not watching you. What I find much more plausible is that someone has planted a trigger, designed to alert our adversaries whenever anyone showed any interest in the surviving members of the Red Squirrels. That, together with their ability to plant false reports, tells us they have burrowed deep into the VA's computer system, and also into Capitol Diagnostics. Possibly and probably any other system connected to the VA as well."

Yes, oh yes. But I held my breath, waiting for the rest of Sara's hypothesis.

Sara smiled, as though she guessed my thoughts. "Eat your soup, and I shall continue. But soft, soft, *doucement, mon amie.* Taste the soup before it dies from the cold."

Knowing she would not go on otherwise, I dipped my spoon into the thickening broth and listened as she continued to detail the supposed plots of our enemies.

"So. You conduct this search," she said. "It failed, but the mere act sets off alarms for our adversaries. They think to themselves, *This woman is a lowly medical technician. If she dies, no one will notice.* So they hire a thug to murder you. An extreme answer to their problem, but easily accomplished. The difficulty is finding a competent thug these days. They ought to have sent for me. I know several."

I laughed, as I knew she expected. It wasn't a happy laugh.

Sara acknowledged that with a brief nod. "They are worried about you," she went on. "Our adversaries know nothing about me, or at least not my true identity. Our trip to Florida proves that. Let us hope they continue to be baffled by that point. Anyway, our friends fret over you the next day, but you remain at home. Injured, they hope."

"Locked in my prison," I muttered.

"Hush, my love. Do not interrupt. I am hunting criminals."

I am not your goddamned love.

But by now I understood she meant nothing by that careless endearment, so I hushed. I listened.

"You were safe the following day only because you vanished and I took measures. That same day, Captain Martínez's jeep crashes for no particular reason. Two people die and a third remains in critical condition, unable to tell anyone what happened. What do you say? Coincidence or opportunity?"

"Opportunity," I said. "Though how they could arrange such a thing, I don't know."

Sara, however, nodded. "Let us proceed with that assumption. I propose that our enemies discovered your email to Captain Martínez. Perhaps they feared you suspected more than you admitted in that email. Perhaps they wished to prevent you from sharing those suspicions. It's even possible he held certain clues that were innocuous on their own but dangerous when combined with yours. Therefore they arrange for that tragedy on the road to Decatur, which tells us they are adversaries with a great deal of money and unsavory connections. Also, a secret they will protect by whatever means they believe necessary.

"But you, you survive. You return to work, to the VA Medical Center, where you are free to cause more strife and worry. So they have you fired and discredited. And they include that very generous offer of a week's pay, an offer tied to those odious forms you signed. No lawsuit. No further investigation. No more trouble from Janet Watson. All these contingencies very neatly fit together. We only need to know why.

"One thing I am certain of," she said. "This has nothing to do with the New Confederacy. If they had infiltrated the VA computer system, they would not stop at a few murders. They would wreak havoc with electronic funds, they would sow disorder and confusion. They would win their war."

"Then who?"

She shook her head. "The first question is why. That might tell us how. And that will lead us to who. And *who* can be a dangerous question to ask. The New Confederacy might be innocent of this particular crime, but the crime is most definitely connected with the war. Ask yourself if there was something in the events of last June that our beloved president does not wish known."

October 22. _____

Make that October 23. It's almost four A.M.

Over twelve hours since I came back to apartment 2B. Sara went out from six P.M. to one A.M. Running errands, she said. More business for the FBI and those loose ends connected to her money-laundering case. She wore outrageous, expensive clothes and a perfume distilled from unadulterated pheromones.

Before she left, she handed me a stack of her self-destructing paper. "Write if you must. And if you must, use this."

And because she is Sara, she also left me a cook pot filled with a savory stew of chicken and white beans and fiery peppers, along with instructions on how to prepare the pasta.

I am in the parlor now. I am sick of my bedroom, sick of this apartment, but I don't need Sara's warning about tempting our adversary with trips outside. Sara herself has returned and has retreated to her bedroom where she plays endless variations on the piano. I don't recognize the composer. My untutored ear says it's medieval, but there were no pianos in medieval times. I can imagine, however, rows of monks chanting to this music, their voices overlapping in a complicated winding of tones. Music is to Sara as writing is to me.

But let's get back to the investigation.

Until Sara said it, I had not even considered the political side. Typical surgeon, focuses on the immediate symptoms. How to cut away the disease, to repair the broken body. No thought about the family or the rest of the outer world, or at least not while I'm operating.

So let's talk politics. Election Day is twelve days from today. The mainstream newsfeeds are useless. The independent feeds and political squirts claim that Donnovan and Foley are tied in the polls. Half the nation supports Foley and his call for compromise—Texas, Florida, Georgia, and a number of the Plains States. The other half, the ones who support Donnovan, point to our recent victories in Jonesboro and Little Rock as proof the Democrats and their Progressive allies can lead us to victory, if not unity.

All I know is that Saul is dead and we have no proof, only speculation.

(Dear god, we have a mountain of guesses and speculation.)

Leaving aside our guesses, here is what we know so far . . .

Saúl: The driver that day was Corporal Ayers. For all her nastiness, she was good at her job. No record of drug or alcohol abuse. No recorded conflict between her and the two surgeons, which might explain a momentary lapse of attention. Ayers had driven that same route a hundred times. She probably knew every rut and pothole.

I will give the investigators credit. They examined the jeep and the accident scene thoroughly. The vehicle had undergone routine maintenance two weeks before the incident. No chance of tampering, unless our adversaries had access to the motor pool and the list of vehicles assigned for Thursday. Local weather reports stated heavy rainfall on Tuesday, but no precipitation after that. The investigators noted a few patches of mud, but nothing to explain the jeep's sudden swerve off the road. A sniper bullet aimed at the front passenger tire could have led to the same results, but no spent casings were found, and the investigators therefore did not include such speculations in their report.

In other words, no proof. No explanation. Nothing.

DEAD END

The Red Squirrels: Belinda Díaz's squad. Eight died on the mission, including the staff sergeant. Of the seven survivors, four died later, two are in prison on assault charges, and one died of a drug overdose. Geller's body was cremated. Díaz's body was returned to her family in West Virginia and has been committed to the ground. The same is true for Walker and Molina, both now buried in a cemetery reserved for those without immediate family. Sara could request an autopsy, but she would need just cause. Otherwise, her chief will not support her request.

DEAD END

Badger Squad: Six died on mission. Staff sergeant court-martialed and currently serving her sentence in military prison. Charge: desertion in the face of combat. Her defense was that their orders did not include taking the outpost. She further stated that she had signaled to the other sergeant for a retreat, but the other squad had already charged forward. She has filed for an appeal.

NOT QUITE A DEAD END BUT DAMNED HARD TO INTERVIEW SOMEONE IN MILITARY PRISON WITHOUT ALERTING THE ENEMY. ALSO, SEE ABOVE ABOUT JUST CAUSE AND ALL THAT.

16

A cramp seized my hand. I dropped my pen and massaged my right palm against my metal fist. A very awkward, ill-formed fist, since my fingers froze halfway. How many more days or weeks until this device refused to answer to my commands?

Outside, the night sky was like an expanse of black silk with pale gems strewn across it. The rust-colored moon high above the city. A scattering of lights along the horizon. Pennies and pearls, they were. One luminous stroke that marked the Washington Monument.

In her bedroom, Sara continued to play her variations, but softer now and slower. Give her another hour and I might knock on her bedroom door, but not yet.

The cramp in my hand eased. I picked up my pen once more but paused. What was there left to write?

Nothing, I thought. Nothing that would not lead to that damnable phrase *Dead end.*

I blew out a breath and touched my finger to the corner of one sheet. A spark of electricity bit my fingertip. The paper shivered, like a living thing, then evaporated into dust. Out of perversity, I did the same to six more sheets, until I had a heap of paper residue on the parlor table.

Twelve dead soldiers, I thought as I swept the dust into the waste bin. *One dead surgeon. No, make that two dead surgeons and one company clerk in critical condition. It could be a coincidence. Soldiers die in war. Soldiers survive battle, only to come home carrying wounds that kill them later.*

What about Sara's theory that our own government was connected to this case? The only connection I could draw was to the election. Even so, that made no sense. Why not eliminate them under the cover of battle? Or later? The military hospital itself could provide a dozen different means to kill. A contaminated needle. An accidental overdose. Why wait until the survivors had left the service?

I let myself fall into the world of *what if.* What if our mystery had nothing to do with our elections or the federal government? What if . . . the outpost contained biological weapons, ones that left no ordinary traces? Gunfire might have set off an explosion, broken through the storage containers. One accident leading to another, leading to soldiers' dying from a myriad of inexplicable causes.

Except they had not all died from medical causes. Heart failure, yes. An embolism, yes. But Molina and Walker had died from too many bullets. Besides, how did the New Confederacy track down these veterans? Unless these biological weapons came from a supplier outside the New Confederacy, perhaps a supplier from the Federal side who wanted to keep the connection a secret.

A possibility that took me back to square one. We could not prove the existence of biological weapons without an autopsy. No autopsies without a reason, no reason without an autopsy.

I retrieved my pen and a fresh sheet of Sara's paper.

Dear Escher, I wrote. *I hate you.*

I pressed my thumb in the upper right corner to destroy the paper. Thirty pages were left of that enormous stack Sara had given me. Perhaps she guessed my propensity for destruction.

What if was doing me no good. Time to play *if only.*

I took another sheet and wrote:

If only we knew what the Red Squirrels saw. We don't. We can't. Even if we could interview them today, here in the secrecy of this apartment—which I am certain is secret and safe because Jenna Hudson is undoubtedly connected to the same organization Holmes reports to and why didn't I realize that before . . . But I digress. We could ask them until the cows come home about what they saw on June 3, but they might not know. If it wasn't painted with signs reading "Hello, Dangerous Shit," how could they?

More ink. A brief pause to flex my hand.

Backing up. We know the Red Squirrels died and the Badgers lived. An oversimplification, but we'll let that stand for now. If only we knew why the one staff sergeant ordered a retreat and the other one ordered an assault. We know

---

I paused and stared at the page. We knew very little, I thought. We had a list of who lived and who died that day in June. Nothing more.

If only we could talk to these soldiers in the moments before the attack. If only we could sit in the hospital tent, next to the survivors, listening to them as Saúl Martínez once listened to me as I babbled in a fever haze.

I closed my eyes and called up an image of Private Belinda Díaz. I recalled her emaciated face, skin drawn tight over her bones, that day of our last encounter. How she begged for help against the black dog of depression, her voice rough with tears.

Dr. Anderson gave me those pills, but they don't do shit. They used to, back in Tennessee, but now? One isn't enough. I tried two and that went better. I could breathe. I could . . . I could almost sleep a whole night. But I got scared because Dr. Turner said that wasn't safe. The doctor back in Tennessee said the same thing. She said—

I flung down my pen. Abruptly the piano went silent. I was already on my feet when Sara appeared at the entry to the parlor. The brilliant light from the hallway cast her into a sharp shadow, but I could plainly see the tension in her stance.

"I have an idea," I said. "About the survivors and what they remembered . . ." I gripped my left arm above the device. It ached, down my shoulder to the stump and into the ghost arm itself. I badly wanted a painkiller.

Sara reached my side in a few steps and clasped my left hand within hers. "Keep talking," she told me. "Before you lose that lovely spark of inspiration."

Her fingers intertwined with mine, her palm of flesh pressed against my metal one. Her touch was like a breath of electricity. The fog cleared from my brain.

"It's your idea, really," I said. "That our soldiers witnessed something during their mission. And I thought—" I felt that "lovely spark of inspiration," as Sara called it, slipping into doubt, and spoke faster. "I thought they might not understand what they saw, but soldiers talk after a mission—especially the wounded. If we could find a nurse, an orderly—anyone who might have attended them. Díaz mentioned a doctor in Tennessee the last time I saw her. She said something about pills to help with her PTSD. The doctor might know more about that mission on June third. Or if not her, there might be others who talked to the survivors in the squad."

Sara nodded slowly. "That is a possibility. Come. I'll make tea and tell you my idea, which has several points in common with yours."

In the kitchen, I settled on a stool in the dining nook, while Sara busied herself with the tea. She filled the kettle with fresh cold water and set it to boil. From one cabinet, she retrieved her favorite glass pot, then measured out several spoonfuls of leaves into its basket. All her movements were precise, contained. I waited, my pulse beating faster, for her to speak.

She measured out another spoonful, then laid the spoon to one side. Gently. Carefully. "There were more deaths. Several more."

Her words, so quiet and soft, were like a punch to my gut. "Who? And how—"

"Staff Sergeant Miller committed suicide last night."

Oh. Oh, god. Yes. The sergeant convicted of desertion. I felt another blow, as if I'd been struck under my ribs. The guards were trained to notice the ones who might suicide. They were supposed to safeguard them . . .

"Who else?" I demanded. "Who the fuck else died while you and I tippy-toed around?"

Sara flung the tea canister to one side and punched the teapot. Glass and ceramic shattered over the floor. When she rounded on me, I skittered back, but not in time. She grasped my wrist and pulled me close. "Too many and not enough to convince the lords of security. And yes, I am furious. Yes, I care. Are you *happy* now?"

Her eyes were bright with an anger that matched mine. Her breath grazed my cheeks. This, this was not the breath of a lover, but of a dragon.

Our gazes matched and locked. Sara nodded. She was trembling too. "Yes, there are others," she said softly. "Our two friends in military prison died in a riot last week. But those are not the only ones who trouble me. You know about Jonesboro, Little Rock. Our victories after the so-called Shame of Alton. Well, there were other deaths, and none of them as glorious."

The kettle whistled. Sara snapped off the burner and began to rummage through the cabinets. "Hush," she told me when I made an impatient noise. "We shall have our tea in my bedroom. Not for your sake, but mine. Please. I have . . . documents to show you."

Documents. I let my breath trickle out. Another understatement, no doubt, but I had come to expect that from Sara Holmes.

Sara gathered the fragments of the teapot and deposited them in the trash. Her movements were slow and methodical as she prepared a second pot with fresh tea and boiling water. A new tray with another pair of cups, since the first had also fallen victim to her fury. Once everything was ready, she ushered me down the corridor to her bedroom.

Oh.

I stopped on the threshold at the sight of this bedroom, now utterly transformed over the past thirty-six hours. All those exquisite paintings? Gone. In their place were a dozen or more digital screens, most of them densely covered with text, the rest with maps showing various regions of the United States. DC. Florida. Michigan. The largest screen showed the Midwest and near western states, with a dark gray mass that represented the New Confederacy. The center, over Oklahoma, was like a thundercloud, and dotted lines showed how the mass had expanded over the years. A silver nimbus covered more territory within the Federal grounds, and I wondered if that indicated more ground that would fall to the enemy.

"How interesting," I said faintly. "What do your other visitors think about these?"

"They don't." Sara tapped a few keys on her slate. The screens vanished. The paintings and watercolors blinked into view. Without thinking, I leaned close to the dark storm cloud of an oil painting. The brushstrokes were just as vivid as I remembered. I reached out to touch them . . .

The screens crackled and sprang back into view.

"Please do not touch," Sara said.

"I won't," I breathed. My fingertips prickled, as though from an electric shock. I rubbed them over my T-shirt, trying to rid myself of the sensation. The paintings were genuine, and set in translucent frames with a black strip embedded into the material. When I leaned close, I could see the original through the haze of outer electronic image. I wondered what else hid in plain sight in this room.

Sara motioned for me to sit on the bed. She had poured out tea for us both and handed me a cup. I cradled the mug and let the heat flood through me.

"Won't your people notice this research?" I asked.

"Of course they will, but not immediately. What I've done is set off hundreds of bots, most with requests for data about different cases—official ones—and wrapped our own unofficial research inside them. Do not ask the whys and wherefores. Let me only say that certain *overlapping* parameters between our missions make this possible. So I download the results, cut all external connections, and filter them locally. However, I cannot guarantee that someone might not get curious. Until then, here is what I've discovered."

She tapped a sequence on her tablet and new images appeared on the screen. One showed casualties during the previous winter. Very few in January and February, as I recalled. We were all, Federal troops and rebels alike, sunk into frozen mud, crusted over with ice and sleet. Rum and whiskey had been in short supply, and our patience even shorter. Sara flicked her fingers across the tablet again. Pinpoints of light glanced off her lace gloves, and a secondary window opened over the first, showing a statement from President Sanches issued in March, about the necessity for a driving offense and a decisive end to the war.

"There were difficulties with funding," Sara said. "Followed by the usual delays introduced by Texas and Arizona. However, Sanches managed to ram through the necessary legislation by making numerous promises to her allies, and even a few of the conservative opposition parties, in the House and Senate. Two weeks after that came Alton."

Alton appeared as a series of troop movements, calculated after the fact. Half the screens flickered and regrouped into color-coded maps. The other half showed aerial images taken from drones. Through them I watched, as though from a vantage point in the skies, as the New Confederacy overran a complacent border and left blood and fire in its wake.

My vision blurred into red and gray. I could hear the drumbeat that signaled the approach of helicopters, and I was trembling.

Sara laid a hand on my shoulder. I flinched away and she sighed. "Alton," she repeated. "A bloody mess that left both armies immobilized for a period. Our government went into overdrive to counteract the PR disaster. The New Confederacy also suffered setbacks when the news came out about their treatment of our wounded. Oh, there was a reconnaissance mission here, a few tentative drives there. None with casualties outside the standard deviation. But then we come to the end of May."

She tapped more virtual keys on her tablet, pointed to the next screen. The aerial drone shots vanished, replaced by new maps that marked confrontations ranging from skirmishes to organized battle. Green dots represented victories, Sara told me. Red meant defeat. Nearly half the dots were gray, meaning an undecided outcome.

"And June," she said.

The screens shifted. Green dots outnumbered the red and gray.

A steady advancement of our Federal troops—that much was clear.

"What about the deaths?" I repeated.

"All in good time. Here are a few other statistics. All the squads connected to these victories came from the First Infantry Division. More important, they all came from the Dragon Brigade. Nearly two hundred had died in combat or shortly afterward. Several dozen more received medical discharges directly related to those missions. And here are the ones who died later."

She gestured toward the largest screen. I saw a series of bright yellow bars. Death rates. Deaths ranked by date. The highest totals were centered around the skirmishes Sara had named, but others came later—weeks or months later.

"I have their medical reports," she said. "Unadulterated, as far as I can tell."

She had handed over her tablet, with the relevant files already loaded and set to maximize. I managed not to drop it, though my hands were shaking. Sara's hands trembled as well—a detail I would no doubt find important later. For now . . .

The list of dead and injured came from seven different missions. Two hundred and twelve casualties. Twenty-seven died later from their injuries. All very straightforward, at least on the surface. The reports for those who died later were less so. A handful had died of heart failure or stroke, including Díaz. Twice that number had died from drug overdoses. There were two suicides. Geller's was the only recorded embolism.

"I did some research," Sara said. "Geller was Jewish. Specifically, she listed her religion as Reform Judaism, though her parents follow Orthodox teachings. It's not *impossible* that a Reform Jew would have requested cremation. But her parents would never have allowed it, and indeed, the hospital received a complaint from them about the matter. Even so, the evidence so far is circumstantial. What we need are eyewitness accounts, or failing those, accounts directly related to these events. Which brings us to your idea."

She entered a new set of commands. One by one, the maps vanished, to be replaced by lists of service personnel, which scrolled from one screen to the next. Here and there, the names went gray; others changed from ordinary black text to brighter blue or green. Sara typed faster, humming to herself. *Appassionata* again. The pulsing of the electronic screens seemed to echo the music.

"Yes. There we have it."

Sara hit a key. All the screens except one went dark.

"Look," she said.

The screen held one very short list—just five names.

"These are medical personnel formerly assigned to the Dragon Brigade, and who left the service after June. Not very many, you see." She tapped again, and the lines of plain black text became a pattern of colors. "We have one nurse, one physical therapist, two medical technicians, and a doctor."

"Can you find these people?" I asked.

"Ah. That is the interesting point."

She tapped her tablet's screen. The screen on the wall blinked and the short list became five separate tiles, each of them filled with text.

"Our nurse and physical therapist returned to their home states and their original employment. One medical technician has enrolled in a training school for computers. The other is currently unemployed, which I find curious. But our doctor . . . has disappeared."

Her name was Katherine Anne Calloway. Age fifty-seven. Most recent civilian address was Bethlehem, Pennsylvania. Back in August, she was a senior medical officer in Tennessee. Duties included supervising a staff of nurses and medical technicians, performing medical exams for mid- to senior-level officers. Oversight of standard inoculations for both officers and enlisted.

Sara tapped her screen again. The other tiles vanished, and Calloway's expanded to fill the screen. Calloway's image occupied one low-res square off to one side. Pale blond hair streaked with gray. Equally pale eyes that dominated her narrow face.

"No current spouse, no children," Holmes said. "An ex-husband who absconded with all their savings to Canada, which is when he became the ex-husband. That is the same year she volunteered for the army. But here is what intrigues me."

A series of text windows sorted themselves like so many cards in a deck. One leaped into the foreground and I skimmed through a summary of our doctor's background. Graduated from Columbia University. Completed her residency there as well. She had the usual number of offers for someone with a top-tier education but chose to enter research instead. She held a series of positions at different universities, followed by a long stint at a commercial pharmaceutical company, which ended at the same time as her divorce. When I read the name of that company, I jumped.

Livvy Pharmaceuticals. The same company that provided so many drugs to the VA Medical Center. I was certain LP#2024016 had not killed Díaz, at least not directly, but was there another connection? Livvy had other contracts for the military, and LP#2024016 was not the only drug they supplied. Saúl had mentioned a VIP from a pharmaceutical company in our very last conversation. Was this our clue?

"When did she disappear?" I asked. "And how?"

"Very recently, to answer your first question. She applied for retirement from the service in August. September ninth, she closed out her bank account, canceled her credit cards, and left a message for her landlord that she had been called out of town for a family emergency. As for the other, that will require more research."

Sara brushed her hand over her tablet. The screen on the wall blanked out, leaving the room in darkness.

"Is she the one we want?" I asked.

"I believe she is. But to find her, I need to be more direct."

I interpreted that to mean her activities would definitely attract notice. "Let's say you are more direct. How much time before your people come for us? And do we have enough evidence to convince your chief?"

"So many questions, dear Captain. No, we do not yet have enough evidence. We might, once we speak with our doctor, but I cannot guarantee my chief will agree on the necessity of that. We have half an hour, perhaps less."

I sucked in a breath. "Well, then. We'd best hurry."

Sara nodded. "Go, pack a few clothes."

And be ready to run, I thought.

17

Our doctor's new name was Katrina Bachman. Her new address was Newark, New Jersey.

Sara delivered the news just as I finished packing. "We'll leave in five minutes," she said. "We can get to Newark by noon if we take the back roads. Sooner by highway, though they might set a watch on the Jersey Turnpike." She scanned the contents of my duffel bag and plucked out several T-shirts. "Forget these. You'll need something warmer. Scruffier. Do you have anything from a thrift shop?"

I rummaged through a drawer for a sweatshirt. Sara scattered the T-shirts over the floor, and when I protested, she said, "Artistic license. We want a certain air of haste and disarray. We want them to underestimate us."

"That only matters if we get away," I said. "And how *do* we get away from DC without anyone noticing? Where do we get a car?"

"You shall have your answers, my love. Leave that here." She pointed to my journal. "Also, your cell and text device. Do not argue. I have my reasons, as you know. Let me fetch things of my own. We should be safe and in custody by to-morrow, but one likes to be prepared."

"Custody?" I said. "Sara, what—"

But she had vanished into her own bedroom. Mutter-ing curses, I unpacked my journal and pens. Of course we would leave these behind. We had carefully arranged for me to write nothing about our investigations, after all, and its contents might prove another distraction. Why I had to leave behind my cell and text device was less clear, but I did as she asked—no, as she commanded, but the commands no longer rankled. Sara had clearly planned for this moment. Scratch that, she had planned for a dozen different moments, each with its own branching set of outcomes.

Question was, could those other agents figure out her plans and counterplans before we got to our doctor? And what about our adversary? What about Livvy Pharmaceuticals?

I won't think about that. Not yet.

I grabbed my fleece jacket from the closet, slung my duf-fel bag over my shoulder. My left arm buzzed with excite-ment, with terror, flesh and metal alike. It was exactly like that morning in April when I heard the first explosions, the first rattle of gunfire.

Sara met me outside the kitchen. She wore a baggy leather jacket and knit cap, both dark brown and mottled with black. The jacket bulged with pockets. She had her satchel over one arm and her cell pressed against one ear. "Meet us at the cor-ner of Twenty-Ninth and P," she was saying. "Oh, and a dis-traction on Q Street would be lovely. Yes, yes, Micha, I know it's short notice. Call it a challenge to your ingenuity."

She dropped the phone into the trash bin. "Ready, Dr. Watson?"

"Ready."

"Good. Wait here, please."

Sara unlocked the front door and tapped the alarm sequence onto the security panel. But instead of motioning for me to follow, she herded me swiftly back to her bedroom, shushing my attempts to question her. Only twenty minutes had passed since Sara had ordered me to pack. The moon hung low over the horizon; the monuments had lost their illumination. Sara had switched on the overhead lamp and dialed the dimmer to its lowest setting. The room had a desolate, untidy appearance with its rumpled bed and the floor littered with dirty cups and an empty wine bottle.

"The answer to your first question," Sara said. "How do we leave unobserved? Thus, my love."

She slid the door to the middle closet open and pushed aside the dozens of dresses and coats inside. A waterfall of silk, all the colors dark and muted in the faint glow from overhead, but here and there the light caught and glittered off metallic threads. Clothes for whatever role she had played for her mission? Or merely an excess of costumes from someone who wore as many personalities as she could?

Sara ran her fingers along the interior of the doorframe. "I haven't had to use this exit before," she said. "I must trust that Jenna followed directions."

She pressed some unseen button or device. I heard a hiss, then the back wall yawned open.

"You're kidding," I said.

She gave me that familiar slanting smile. "I would never josh you, Dr. Watson. And close that mouth before you catch a fly."

Sara fetched a black cylinder from another pocket—a miniature flashlight—and switched it on. The beam illuminated a rough plaster wall and a narrow wooden staircase zigzagging downward. "You first," she said, handing me the flashlight. "Wait for me at the bottom."

I hurried as fast as I could down the stairs. From above came the rattle of hangers, then another hiss as the door slid shut. Sara's descent was as swift and noiseless as mine was not.

"How much time?" I asked when she caught up to me.

"Twenty, thirty minutes."

"You said—"

"Margin of error. Keep going."

I muttered a curse at Sara, who laughed softly. But keep going I did, one hand of metal brushing the wall to steady myself, one hand of flesh clutching the flashlight, whose bright narrow beam jumped and bounced off the walls with every step. The rough plaster changed over to concrete blocks, then to dirt partially covered by wooden planks.

The stairs ended in a cramped and dusty chamber. The air here felt chilled and raw, thick with the scent of damp earth. I swung the flashlight around and caught a glimpse of empty spider webs. A narrow passage led off into the dark straight ahead, another to the right.

Sara grabbed the flashlight from my hand. "This way," she said.

We headed single-file down the right-hand passage. The walls were lined with brick, but the ground was packed dirt. Here and there moss grew in the cracks. Other places the mortar had crumbled. I thought this might be how a dungeon looked, or a castle from antiquity.

"When did you have this built?" I asked.

"Three, four months ago. Convincing, isn't it?"

At the next intersection, Holmes swung left. We were padding along faster now. Was that the echo of metal against stone I heard behind me? I kept glancing over my shoulder even though I could see nothing beyond the dim circle from the flashlight. I nearly ran into Sara when she abruptly stopped.

"Hush," she said, though I had not spoken.

She ran her hands over the bricks, counting softly to her-self.

"Ah."

Sara laid both hands against the brick and leaned into the wall. A click sounded overhead. I jumped back to avoid a metal ladder that unfolded from the new gap in the ceiling. "Last-minute caution," Sara said, handing me the flashlight. "I go first. If all is clear, I shall hoot twice like a screech owl. That's a *joke*. Stop scowling. If we cannot laugh at death, we cannot truly live. But I do want to survey our exit."

She dropped her satchel on the ground. Her gun had reap-peared from another of her myriad pockets, then she swung up the ladder and into the darkness. I waited anxiously, shift-ing from foot to foot, until she leaned down through the opening. "All clear. Hand me that bag, then follow."

The exit was in a storage shed crowded with rakes and shovels and half-empty bags of mulch. One grimy window overlooked an immaculate lawn, which led up to a brick building, both silvered by moonlight. "Let me guess," I mur-mured. "Hudson Realty owns this property as well."

"Excellent deduction, my dear Watson."

She restored the ladder to its slot and slid the metal cover back over the exit. Together we scattered mulch and dirt over the floor. Sara glanced at her watch. Made some silent calcula-tion, and nodded. "Now for our next delicate maneuver. Did I mention this exit might be watched?"

I was no longer surprised by what Sara had or had not mentioned. "If we get caught, it's because of your chatter."

Sara laughed softly. "My apologies. So. We shall be serious. Turn off the flashlight. Did you bring your gloves? Tschah. I should have reminded you. Very well, roll down your sleeves and keep your left hand in your pocket. Metal catches light, you know. Good. Now, we have a dozen yards or so between this shed and the street where Micha awaits with the car. We shall not run, because that would attract attention, but neither shall we dally. We glide, like swans over a lake, our eyes cast discreetly toward the ground so that any chance light does not reflect from them. Keep a firm grip on your bag. Ready? Let us leap into opportunity."

We did not exactly leap. Sara eased the shed door open and glanced around the corner, so exactly like spies in the movies that I almost laughed. *This is not funny. This is dangerous, what we're doing.* But oh, this lovely flood of energy, this sense of everything right and proper, such as I had not felt since long before Alton. A bubbling excitement that reminded me of that day I stepped into the operating theater for my first solo round of surgery.

Sara touched my arm, my right arm, and nodded. *Outside,* she mouthed.

One by one, we emerged from our sheltering shed. Sara pointed toward a wooden fence and its gate. The gate opened onto a lawn populated by oak and dogwood trees. Beyond that the trees gave way to a brief verge of grass and then the street.

We passed underneath the trees and between two houses. The streets were empty, except for one car parked at the curb. Once more Sara signaled for us to pause. "Do not panic," she whispered in my ear. "We shall proceed to the sidewalk, indifferent, unhurried. Get into the rear seat. Micha will be driving at first."

We held hands for the last distance, and though mine was metal, I swore I could feel the beat of her pulse in counterpoint to my own—to my real pulse and not the ghost of memory.

The car was an ancient gray Saab, its rusted bumpers decorated with stickers from the Montreal International Jazz Festival. Sara bundled me inside first and tossed her bag after me. She had barely pulled the door shut when the car eased away from the curb. In the late dawn, our driver was little more than a shadow within darker shadows. I could just make out a bulky coat, a profusion of box braids, and the gleam of a bracelet as our driver spun the steering wheel for a left onto Twenty-Ninth Street.

"Micha," Sara said in an undertone. "Thank you for your ingenuity."

"Anything to make my Friday morning livelier," Micha replied. Her voice was soft and rough, like Sara's, but with a breathless quality. "You do know Grandmama will count this as a favor—a very great favor. She will insist on repayment with interest."

"Of course she will," Sara said. "I expected no less. Tell her I shall pay my respects the moment it's safe."

Micha nodded and turned left onto O Street. Four minutes later we pulled into the taxi lane for the Hotel Palomar. Micha exited the driver's seat and handed Sara the keys. "Be careful."

"I will." Sara pressed something into Micha's hands as she kissed the other woman on the cheek. "Thank you. Tell Grandmama she needs a sedative."

Micha laughed and danced off into the shadows, her thick braids swinging from side to side. Sara slid into the driver's seat. I took my place next to her.

"Next stop," she said, "Newark, New Jersey."

Dawn streaked the skies as we crossed into Maryland on State Route 5. The last time I had ventured into the outskirts of DC, I had been a med student at Howard University, visiting my parents in Suitland, going out with friends from high school and discovering we had all of us changed beyond recognition.

I had the same strange sense of vertigo now. I recognized

a bowling alley, the building that had housed the first incarnation of Nick's Market, the church hall where my sister, Grace, and I attended youth fellowship. Grace had continued her membership. I had dropped out after I started to wonder about my own identity. Sara negotiated the madhouse that was Old and New Branch Avenue and sent us hurtling south past the tumbledown house where Mary Surratt once lived, where John Wilkes Booth had planned for Lincoln to die.

"Tell me," I said. "What more do I need to know?"

"A great deal," Sara told me. "Humor me just a half hour more, then we can talk."

Beyond Clinton, Maryland, we came to a series of new housing developments, then the road narrowed and we were in the countryside. Sara took the twists and turns as though she had grown up in this neighborhood. We coasted to a stoplight in Brandywine, turned left onto 301 North.

"Now?" I asked.

Sara glanced in the passenger-side mirror, made a minute adjustment to our speed. "Now, yes. Do you prefer to ask questions first or later?"

Oh, a complicated discussion. Color me not surprised, Agent Holmes.

"Questions later," I said. "First you talk."

She nodded. "Very wise. Well, as you know, our mysterious Dr. Calloway spent several years with Livvy Pharmaceuticals. You know about their contracts with the VA Medical Center. Perhaps you did not know they are the highest profit center for Adler Industries, with dozens of patents directly connected to drugs for treating our ever-growing numbers of veterans.

"Connections," she repeated in a musing tone. "That is the heart of my work. Never mind the drama, the secret passageways, the guns and glamour. Pinpointing the link between

A and B is what I do best. So. Dr. Calloway worked for Livvy Pharmaceuticals. Livvy in turn is one of three research companies owned by Adler Industries. AI's history intrigues me on several points, including certain details about its founder, but the essential is this: Adler Industries won several major multiyear contracts to deliver medical supplies to the U.S. military. It also owns several laboratories in the DC area, including one called Capitol Diagnostics. It *also* owns a computer service company called tekSolutionsEtc."

Oh. Oh, yes. I remembered those names.

Capitol Diagnostics handled *all* the standard lab tests from the VA Medical Center. Two other labs had lost the bid. The third had been acquired by Capitol's parent company and dismantled. tekSolutionsEtc serviced the workstations in the VA veterans' center. If I remembered correctly, they had also taken over the contract for the VA Medical Center as well.

I relayed this information to Holmes, who seemed unsurprised.

"Adler has a certain reputation," she said. "Or rather, its CEO, Nadine Adler, does. She's ambitious, thorough, and demanding. If Capitol Diagnostics loses even one test result, she knows. And if she knows . . ."

But Sara did not continue that tantalizing thought. Perhaps that spurt of honesty had exhausted her. Perhaps she did not want to reason ahead of our data.

And what data did we have? A dozen clues pointing to one Katherine Calloway, now known as Katrina Bachman, as our best source of information. A few more data points concerning Adler Industries. Troubling ones, but nothing definite. Pharmaceuticals would explain several aspects of our case, but we still had no motive, no hard details about what happened to our soldiers.

We need to know why, that will tell us who.

I hunkered down into my seat and stared out the window, pondering *why*. Crimson stained the horizon. Pale sunlight rolled over the bare fields, which were covered in mist. My stump ached from several days of neglect. When I massaged my upper arm, I felt pinpricks of electricity deep inside. Next to me, Sara drove steadily, competently, as though the sleepless night had not occurred.

"I have a question," I said at last. "Who is Micha?"

Her mouth quirked in a brief Sara smile. "Family."

"Is she safe? I mean, what if—"

"Micha is safe. She has various protectors. Our family. Allies. However, I doubt she will need them. I suspect that Micha arranged for two, possibly three, other cars, identical to this one, to drive in contradictory directions from 2809 Q Street and its neighborhood. No doubt a fourth was parked around the corner from the Palomar for her use. Micha is a meticulous woman."

"Your family has . . . interesting talents."

"That is one way to describe them."

Sara's mouth had tucked into an unhappy smile, and I remembered what Jacob had told me, those many weeks ago. *She comes from a rich family . . . Times they remember her. Times she remembers them.*

And where was Jacob now? Was *he* safe?

I rubbed my knuckles over my eyes. My earlier exhilaration had faded. A headache lurked behind my skull, and I felt that old familiar queasiness from my on-call days at the hospital, from other days in the field when the casualties came fresh from the border and we worked ten and twelve and fourteen hours without a break.

Sara laid a hand on my shoulder, then clasped my metal hand in hers. "I haven't forgotten our friends. My family will see to that."

Grandmama will insist on repayment.

"How much will you owe them?" I asked.

"More than I like," Sara said. "Less than I ought to."

Onward, through the rusty brown of tobacco fields and subsistence crops that made up Maryland's agriculture economy these days. Sara continued to handle the car as though she were an automaton, unaffected by sleepless nights and high anxiety. I dozed as much as I could, but I had lost the knack of my residency days, when any sleep came deep and easy. What I noticed, when I noticed it, was that more and more strip malls and apartment complexes interrupted the fields, but the businesses had died off in the last ten years, the apartment dwellers heading north or south, and leaving behind islands of asphalt and concrete, which the weeds were gradually overtaking.

Route 3 joined us, then split away to the north. We continued east on 301 to the coast. I caught the scent of brine in the air. All my imagination, because we were too far from the coast, but as Faith Bellaume would say, imagination is a powerful god.

The long night overtook me not long after that. I dropped into sleep, only half aware when we crossed over the narrow neck of the Chesapeake to Kent Island, then to the Eastern Shore. But when the car stopped completely, I jerked awake with a smothered cry.

"We're safe," Sara said at once. "Time for breakfast and a few errands."

The errands came first. Sara told me to wait in the car while she visited a drugstore. We had parked on the street, right outside a coffee shop. Small-town Maryland it was, with its rows of local stores, brick and plaster alternating with each other, and all of them with checked or striped awnings. The bank across the street said CENTREVILLE SAVINGS AND LOAN. An elderly couple passed by, walking a pair of poodles. A couple kids rode past on bicycles, heading to school and already late. Such an ordinary town, and such an ordinary day.

Sara returned in fifteen minutes with a bag tucked under one arm. "Now for breakfast," she said. "More important, coffee."

In the coffee shop, she dispatched the waitress with orders for two omelets, extra hash browns, and a pot of their strongest, hottest coffee. Then she spread the results of her errands on the table.

One prepaid cell phone. Three highway maps, for Maryland, Pennsylvania, and New York. A city map for NYC and another for Pittsburgh. "Distractions," she said to my questioning glance. "We'll stop one more time in New Jersey for local maps."

It was then I realized she no longer wore her lace gloves or earbuds. The word *untraceable* came to mind, but then I had immediate doubts.

"Can they track us through your implants?" I asked.

She shook her head. "Those only function with the rest of my toys. Now, let us plan our sightseeing tour."

☿

We rolled into Newark around twelve thirty. Our destination was a walk-in clinic on Bloomfield Avenue, where Katrina Bachman worked. Sara had apparently memorized our maps, because she did not bother to consult them as we coasted down the street, scanning the almost illegible signage on the buildings and street corners. There were no electronic billboards here, no high-tech plasma displays advertising the latest luxury item or political candidate. Here the mottled brick and concrete structures carried paper banners or the occasional metal plaque. DISCOUNT WINE & SPIRITS. RODRIGUEZ MINI-MART. E&G SERVICES. Or more frequently, THIS SPACE FOR RENT.

"Ah, there she blows," Sara murmured.

She nodded to our left, toward a three-story clapboard structure, its windows masked by yellow shades. The paint was fresh, the color a muddy shade of gray. A metal signpost advertised MEDICAL SERVICES, 8 A.M.–8 P.M.

Sara rolled past the clinic to the next stoplight.

"Now what?" I asked. "We can't bully our way inside and demand she talk to us."

"No, we can't. *You* can."

Before I could protest, she made an abrupt left onto Fourth Street and sped past a line of stores barricaded behind metal security gates, landing us next to an expired parking meter. "Get out," she said. "You can walk to the clinic from here. My sources tell me Dr. Bachman has the primary shift this afternoon."

I briefly considered punching her with my metal fist, but there was the gun to consider, not to mention innocent pedestrians.

"And what do I say to her? 'Hi, I'm from the government and I'm here to help'?"

Sara snorted. "That would be my line. No, pretend you are a patient. Convince her to talk about Alton and Jonesboro and all the rest. We can use your testimony to persuade my chief about a formal investigation, and once we do, we can take our doctor into protection and I shall question her myself."

"But—"

"Janet, you are the doctor. You are the veteran. I can pretend a great many things, but not that." And when I hesitated, she laid a hand on my shoulder. "We know she's frightened. She won't talk to someone like me. Now go. I'll drive around and wait for you across the street."

I blew out a breath. Sara was right, goddamn it. "I shall do my best."

"I know. I trust you for that."

Oh. Well, in that case.

I exited the car, taking care not to stumble over the broken sidewalk. Sara pulled away from the curb and turned into a side street.

It was colder, here in New Jersey. Cold and bleak, in spite of the sunny day, or perhaps my impression was colored by the deserted streets, with their tumbleweeds of garbage and the graffiti splashed over the concrete and brick. I was right about the cold, however. By the time I reached the clinic, I was shivering in my fleece-lined jacket.

The door rattled with bells as I opened it. Inside was a ten-by-ten waiting room with a linoleum floor and water-stained plaster walls. A young woman with purple nail polish and a collection of studs along her lower lip occupied the tiny receptionist cubicle. "Write your name, your insurance ID, and the time of day," she told me.

Sara's caution had infected me. I scribbled Jacky Wilson for the name, followed by an equally made-up ID. The time was 12:42 P.M.

I took a seat among the other patients—several elderly men and women, one younger woman with two small children and a baby, a teenage boy who coughed every few minutes. Over the next hour, a nurse came to the door at intervals. One by one the other patients took their turn following her into the back rooms.

Eventually the nurse reappeared. "Jacky Wilson? Ms. Jacky Wilson?"

She repeated the name a third time before I jerked to attention. The girl behind the reception desk smothered a laugh. I made a pretense of yawning—not that I had to try very hard—and followed the nurse through a pastel-colored hallway and into an examination room. There I waited another twenty minutes, my bare heels kicking against the metal exam table, until the door opened once more.

Katherine Calloway.

I knew her at once, even though the image from Sara's documents showed a younger, less haunted woman. She had aged these past five years and looked much older than fifty-seven. Her fine hair—now completely gray—was drawn back into a severe ponytail. Her skin was paper white, with a scattering of pale red freckles, and folded over and around her jaws. And her eyes . . . I had seen those same eyes in my patients rescued from the front lines. The eyes of someone exhausted beyond endurance.

"We seem to have a problem," she said, studying the clipboard in her hand. "The health ID you gave us doesn't match your name. However, we can still treat you, as long as you're an American citizen or the child of one."

She glanced up with an expression faintly quizzical, but clearly expecting me to give some rational answer.

I drew a deep breath. Here came the test. *Oh, Sara, Sara, I hope you were right about this one. I hope you were right about me.*

"The ID doesn't match because I lied."

We both jumped when I said that. Hurriedly, before she could back out of the room, I added, "I lied because you did, Dr. Calloway."

Calloway's cheeks flushed, bright red patches against her

pale skin. "You . . . That is a strange accusation, Ms. Wilson. Have you held these absurd convictions very long?"

"No," I said softly. "Not until Alton, Illinois."

The color vanished from her face. She stared at me, her eyes no longer dead, but wide and bright with terror. "Who are you really?" she whispered. "Do you want money? I don't have much but—"

"I don't want money," I said at once. Dear god, why wasn't Sara here instead of me? She would know what to say to this woman. "I'm a doctor just like you. Mobile Medical Unit #2076 in Illinois. At least I was up until April. I . . . I need to talk to you about one of your former patients. Belinda Díaz. Do you remember her?"

Calloway acknowledged the name with a flinch. "I might."

"She died," I said.

Another flinch, less obvious than the first. So. Was this a surprise? Or merely guilt? I remembered Sara's last words to me. "Maybe you were frightened," I said. "I know how that feels. But maybe you know how it feels to lose a patient and forever wonder why."

That got me no response, not even a twitch. But I could sense her nerves, how she might bolt at any moment.

"I am—I *was* a doctor," I went on. "A surgeon in the army. I met Private Díaz later in Washington, DC. She came to the VA Medical Center, where I worked. She told me about her plans for her future. All those plans ended October fifteenth. A blood clot leading to heart failure, they told me, but I don't believe that. It's too simple an explanation. I was hoping you could tell me more about her, about her last mission—"

"No."

Calloway's voice cut through my babbling.

"No," she said again. "Not here. Not now." Her gaze flicked over to my device. "You lost your arm in Alton?"

I nodded. No need to mention my subsequent discharge and the loss of my career. It would be obvious enough to her.

She scribbled on her prescription pad and thrust the sheet at me. "I can talk to you later. After my shift. Let's say eight thirty."

♀

The address was a sports bar located on the same street, a mile from the clinic.

"She wouldn't talk," I told Sara, who waited for me across the street. "I can't tell if she was afraid someone might overhear, or she just wanted to get rid of me."

"Possibly a little of both," Sara said.

She had bought a pack of clove cigarettes from a nearby smoke shop. Now she drew on her cigarette and released a trickle of smoke into the cold October air. "So, here's our new plan. You meet the doctor alone and let her talk as much or little as she wants. I'll get as close as I can and record her testimony. Once she leaves, I take her into custody and go to my chief for a full investigation. Let's go, before someone at the clinic sees you loitering here with me."

She reached out a hand. I jerked mine out of reach. "Go where?" I demanded. "Sara, you were right. She's terrified. And she mentioned my arm. What if she tries to run away *again*?"

Sara answered each of my questions in turn, as if I were an utterly reasonable creature. "Of course she's terrified. That is another important data point, which I can explain later. For now, we shall retire to a motel for some badly needed sleep. Meanwhile, I have arranged for certain friends to keep watch."

I translated *friends* to *family*. *More debt* was my first thought, followed by a growing uneasiness with Sara's seemingly endless family and their connections. But Sara gave me no time to argue. She herded me to the Saab, now parked around the block. We drove to a nearby motel, where she paid cash for one room and two sets of keys. Then she locked me inside with orders to sleep.

Sleep. As if I could order my body around like that. I spent the next hour fidgeting on the bed until Sara reappeared with a bag of Italian grinders and an extra-large bottle of Diet Coke. We ate. We drank. She set the room's ancient alarm clock for six P.M. Then she took the other bed and dropped immediately to sleep. I lay on my back to stare at the ceiling, convinced I would spend the next five hours awake, when I too followed her down that rabbit hole.

Sara woke me with a touch. I started up, caught my breath. The alarm clock showed seven fifteen. Our room was dark, with just a faint illumination from the bathroom. I caught the scent of soap on Sara's damp skin. She smiled at me.

"You needed the sleep, my love," she said. "But not to worry. We have time enough to shower and eat and transform ourselves into respectable people, the kind our doctor might be convinced to trust."

"Calloway?" My voice was thick from sleep.

"At the clinic still," Sara told me. "My friends will keep watch until we arrive. We shall follow the doctor to our rendezvous."

She had procured hot coffee and a stack of grilled cheese sandwiches. I choked down my share, then scrubbed myself clean in the motel's less-than-adequate shower. Sara brought our bags in from the Saab, and I took the time to disinfect my stump and replace the sweat-stained cotton sock with a clean one.

I still wasn't sure what Calloway could tell us. Yes, she had worked for Livvy, and yes, Livvy and Adler Industries had connections to the VA Medical Center, but I had no idea how that connected to Belinda Díaz and the New Civil War.

Don't worry about that, Sara had told me. *Just let her talk. The connections are my job. Remember?*

We arrived back at the clinic ten minutes before eight. The clinic windows showed a pale yellow glow behind their shades. There were few cars parked on either side; fewer still drove past. Sara exited the Saab and ducked into an alley. Consulting with our mysterious watcher, I guessed.

I sank back into my seat and tilted my head up, staring at the mottled gray of the car's ceiling. Sara had made it sound so straightforward.

Talk. Sure, yeah. And what do I say to Katherine Calloway this time? Do I ask her leading questions? Do I buy her shots of whiskey until we're both weeping over the patients we've lost?

The thudding of running footsteps snatched me from my thoughts. "Change of plans," Sara said breathlessly as she slid back into the driver's seat. "Our doctor left her post early, but my friend reports she did show up as promised at our meeting place."

The address for the sports bar was also Bloomfield Avenue, a half-dozen blocks away. We pulled into the parking lot ten minutes later and maneuvered around until we found an open spot near the trash bins. The evening was cold, the air brittle with a hint of an early snow. A spattering of stars interrupted the blue-black expanse overhead.

Sara glanced around and made a signal. I caught sight of a figure underneath a lamppost across the street. "Why can't you have your friends take the doctor into custody?" I said. "Why all this sneaking around?"

"Because that would be kidnapping, and our government

disapproves of that. Unless the kidnapper has an official reason. Which we do not. Yet. Besides, I want our doctor to speak willingly. We learn more of the truth that way."

The bar was as crowded as the parking lot, and much noisier. A soundtrack echoed from the ceiling, and there were video screens embedded into the walls. Most of the customers were young and white, most with studs like the girl at the medical clinic. I felt my senses go to high alert. Sara and I did not fit in here. Nor did Calloway.

Sara was scanning the floor, looking for our doctor and shaking her head.

"She's not here," I said. I had to shout to make myself heard.

"We check the bar," Sara shouted back. "Then the restrooms."

We wrestled through the crowds to the bar. Sara caught the bartender's attention and shouted an order for two Budweisers. She slapped down two bills in exchange for the glasses and motioned for me to follow her around the bar. Still no sign of Calloway. Then Sara made a dive for an empty stool that was nearly invisible in the crush. She plucked a coaster off the half-empty glass on the counter—that standard signal that someone would be coming back for their drink.

Sara slammed her beer onto the counter and leaned close to me. "She was here," she said into my ear. "Not five minutes ago. Come on."

The women's room was empty. The men's room as well. Sara was snarling, but then her lips pulled back into a grin. "That way."

That way led down a short hallway to a service entrance. We found ourselves in an alley between the bar and a parking garage. At one end, a wooden fence blocked the alley. In the other direction, the bordering street was just visible beyond several trash bins and a mountain of wooden crates.

Sara took her anonymous cell from her pocket. "What's the word?" she whispered into it. "Good enough. We can discuss the terms later. Keep watch out by the street. If you hear any noise, you know what to do."

To me, she said, "Our doctor went into the garage a moment ago."

We hurried through the nearest door. The echo of footsteps sounded from above. Sara pointed to a brightly lit stairwell to our left. "Follow her. Get her to talk. I'll come around by the ramp."

I nodded once and ran for the stairs. As I rounded the first turn, a heavy door slammed shut, the crash reverberating down the stairwell. She had exited on the second floor, then. My metal arm felt heavy and cold. The rest of me was alight with a strange electricity. I reached my goal, flung the door open, in time to see my quarry pelting toward the opposite end.

"Katherine!" I called out. "Katherine Calloway."

She stumbled and swung around. "You."

I hesitated, then took a few steps toward her.

"Yes, me. You said you would talk to me."

"Maybe I changed my mind."

She was edging away from me. I dared one step, but no more. Her body was strung tight, and she clutched her car keys in a fist. *Soft, soft and slow,* I told myself. "You said we could talk." One more step. "You said—"

"Stop. Right there." Her voice broke on a sob. "Yes, I said that. I . . . I know about Alton. That's the reason. But then I saw *her* and—"

Footsteps rang from the opposite end of the garage. It was

Sara. Her hands were empty and held out to either side. Calloway spun around with a cry. "No!"

I darted toward her. She cursed and aimed a punch at my face. Then Sara was there and had captured her wrists. The car keys went skittering away. Calloway struggled and kicked. Sara merely twisted her captive's arms around and held her securely. "No more tantrums," she said. "My name is Holmes. I'm with the FBI. We have a few questions for you, Dr. Calloway."

Calloway hissed. "You lied to me. You tricked me."

"No and yes," I said. "I *did* serve at Alton. I was there in April when the rebels overran us." I lifted my device and, with an effort, forced the fingers into a fist. "It's because of Alton that I'm not a surgeon anymore. So I got myself a job as a med tech at the VA in DC. Private Díaz came to us for treatment. She died, Calloway."

"So did the rest of the Red Squirrels," Sara said softly. "And others since then. You can help us."

Calloway shook her head. She was crying. "It wasn't my fault," she whispered.

"Perhaps not," Sara said. "We'd like to find out who is to blame."

Another shake of the head.

"A name?" Sara suggested. "I can promise you immunity for evidence leading to prosecution. It's a way to help the dead."

But the dead were apparently none of Calloway's concern. She clamped her lips shut and glared at me, since she couldn't glare at Sara. Her ponytail had come undone, and her thin hair straggled over her face.

"Very well," Sara said. "The dead do not matter. Let's talk about Livvy Pharmaceuticals."

That produced a frantic struggle. "You already know,"

Calloway choked out. "You don't need me to say anything. Just let me go. Please. Oh god, please."

"Livvy," Sara repeated. "A pharmaceutical company that belongs to Adler Industries. That strikes another chord, I see. It should. You worked at Livvy for six years in its research division. Your name is associated with several drug patents, and you were likely due for another promotion when you entered the service. Oh, yes, I would say you know a great deal about both Livvy and Adler, including their connection with the events of June third. Specifically, the events concerning the Red Squirrels. Tell us for my friend's sake. You meant to earlier."

Calloway shuddered. "I did. I saw her device and . . ." She gulped down a breath. "Promise you will give me immunity. Promise."

"I promise." Sara's voice was cool and remote.

"Okay, then. I . . . I was the senior medical officer for our brigade. First Infantry Division, Fourth Combat Brigade. The one President Sanches reactivated. I had oversight for our standard health practices for officers and enlisted. Vaccinations. Annual examinations. It was a good assignment. I didn't ask for anything more."

"But others did ask more from you. Who were they? Your commander?"

Sara's voice was soft and understanding. Even so, Calloway dithered. "No, not her. It was Vandermay, our lieutenant colonel. She—I don't know what she told our commander, or if she ever said anything."

Sara gave a breathy sigh. I had not dared to move at all these last five minutes.

"Who else knew?"

"No one else, I swear. Vandermay ordered me to her office. Early May, it was. She said we were in trouble. Not us, but the army." Calloway's words poured out in an almost incomprehensible flood. How the war had continued for too many years. How the U.S. was crumbling into a second-rate country. How with that attack on Alton, the Confederate troops had robbed our people of courage, and if we didn't take victory, then victory would never be ours.

"But she had a plan," Calloway said. "How to stop the rebels and grab those victories. She didn't want to say more until I agreed. It was only later I found out the plan wasn't hers. It was Nadine Adler who gave her the idea."

Oh, and oh. Now my enemy has a name. Now she has a face.

Calloway sucked down a breath. "I recognized her right away from my job at Livvy. She used to visit the lab once a month. I heard she did the same for all the companies she owned. 'Make it personal' was her motto. If we had a breakthrough, she knew it before the end of the day and we all got raises. If we screwed up, she knew that too, and someone got fired . . ."

Another gulp, another pause before she continued. "Adler paid a visit to Vandermay in May. I was there too. We told the commander this was part of Adler's new policy for their government contracts. She wanted to meet with senior medical officers in the field, take down their concerns. Make it personal, you know. What really happened was she brought us a new drug. Code name SX#99. That meant an experimental drug in Livvy."

"And what did this drug do?" Holmes asked.

"It made . . . super soldiers."

Impossible.

Except I knew it was possible. No matter what the preachers told us, I knew what all doctors knew—we were bags of chemicals and nothing more. The right combination could make us spew our dinner. Another could recalibrate our emotions, for good or bad. We could turn ourselves into sheep or monsters.

Calloway had not stopped that soft and ceaseless whisper. "It hadn't passed FDA trials. Next month, she claimed. I knew right away it never would. I'd already seen reports about the side effects. But Vandermay ordered me to conduct our own trials. So . . . I did. Three soldiers. I told my people these were a new flu vaccine. Oh, God, forgive me. And the first round seemed to have no effect. So the second time we scheduled two injections. Same excuse, different squad. The Red Squirrels. The other squad was our control. You know what happened there."

"Not exactly," I said. "Why don't you tell us, Dr. Calloway? What did SX#99 do to your patients?"

She was weeping now. Great gobs of genuine tears. I almost felt pity. I would have, except for the small matter of those veterans who had died under her care.

"Tell me what happened," I repeated in a softer voice. "How did SX#99 make these men and women into super soldiers?"

Calloway shook her head, as if she didn't want to answer. Sara gave her a shake. "Answer the nice doctor, or you won't get any immunity."

Her lips pulled back to show an edged smile. That broke through Calloway's haze of terror. "Hormone boosters," she said. "It tripled the body's testosterone and adrenaline production. It added a megadose of pain inhibitors. All of it temporary. At least it was supposed to be temporary."

But it wasn't. I already knew that.

"Side effects?" I asked.

Another hesitation. This time I wanted to shake her myself.

"A few," she said reluctantly. "The hormone boosters didn't

evaporate as expected. Our patients showed signs of hyper-tension. Edema. Behavioral disorders. By then, my lieutenant colonel had ordered two more missions. Big ones."

Jonesboro and Little Rock.

"I told her about the side effects," Calloway said. "Van-dermay told me those were aberrations. *Expected* aberrations. The same words Adler used back at Livvy. By that time, Adler had shipped us their new drugs to counteract the side effects, and those did help, but not enough. When I asked about government trials for the new drugs, Vandermay or-dered me to follow through with our third mission. It would be the last one, she promised me. If I didn't make trouble, she could guarantee me an honorable discharge. I . . . I said yes."

She fell silent. *No need to confess more,* I thought. We could piece the rest together from the names and dates she'd given us. One drug to create the super soldier that Vandermay and the Federal Army wanted. Another to counteract its unfore-seen side effects. Adler had made its profits twice over. And Calloway knew all that, even as she pretended otherwise.

Sara, evidently, was not quite satisfied. "That explains a great deal, doctor," she said. "What about Nadine Adler's connections with the New Confederacy?"

Calloway gasped. "What? I don't know anything about that."

Sara was unimpressed. "You do. Or you guessed. Adler supplied the New Confederacy with those same drugs, didn't she? She's the reason behind Alton. She sold SX#99 to both sides, to keep the war and her profits alive. That's the real reason you're so frightened."

Calloway shook her head. "I have no proof—"

She broke off when Holmes flung her to the ground the same moment a loud crack echoed through the garage. I dropped to the concrete, my brain yammering, *Incoming, in-*

coming. Another crack sounded; a burst of sparks and concrete exploded from the wall next to us.

"Adler." Calloway sobbed. "I saw her in the bar."

Sara was cursing softly. "Let me take care of our new friend. Janet, you must get our witness away from here." She gestured toward the line of cars. "That will give you some protection. I can do the rest."

She released Calloway and rolled over into a crouch, gun in hand.

I can't do this. I can't.

It was April all over again, but this time I knew I was not invincible. This time I knew I would die.

Sara threw herself into the open. She fired off two shots before she landed and rolled again. I saw her dive behind a car opposite us. She mouthed the word *go.*

I grabbed Calloway's wrist. "Come on."

"No, no, no—"

Her terror broke mine. "Yes, yes, yes. Unless you want to die."

There were five cars between us and the stairs. I had not counted them before, but the number jumped into my mind. I dug my fingers into Calloway's wrist and dragged her with me to the next car. Another bullet ricocheted from the concrete. We buried our heads in our arms. Across the way, Sara let off another round of shots.

Next car. No bullets this time, but also no reason to get cocky. My doctor had given up arguing. She only whimpered when I adjusted my grip. *Damn you to hell,* I thought. *You never cared about your soldiers. You wept because you were terrified for yourself.*

Two more cars. Two more rounds of bullets. Did this count as noise to Sara's watchers?

One more car, then a longer distance to the door. We

gained our first goal. It was then Calloway dropped limp to the ground. "Let her kill me. I don't care anymore. Fuck you. Fuck all of you."

"Fuck *you*," I said savagely. "*I* care."

I dragged her toward the stairwell, grabbed the handle. But my left hand would not close. I had to let go of Calloway to open the door. I had it propped open with one foot and was hauling this useless woman to safety when the bullet punched through me.

18

After that, the world fractured into pieces. I remember a buzzing chorus of voices. Sara shouting orders. More gunfire. Running footsteps, then Sara and Katherine Calloway, arguing over me. And oh, oh, oh, the agony, the weight against my chest that made every breath a struggle. I tried to warn them about the rebels, or Adler, to tell them to keep watch, but my lips and tongue refused to obey me.

"She's coming around."

"Better if she didn't. You have no idea—"

"I have every idea. Stop the bleeding, damn it."

My vision flickered from there to yesterday.

I crouch next to three bodies. Two corporals, a sergeant, their uniforms caked with black mud, their faces covered in blood, their limbs now frozen in odd contortions, as if they had all been caught in mid-convulsion when they died. They had outlived an IED attack, surgery, and the madness of the attack on Alton, only to bleed out in this muddy ditch. I am nearly ready to lie down and surrender myself, but I have six more patients who depend on me.

"Janet, Janet, my love. Hush. Keep still. We've called for reinforcements."

I twisted around to see Sara's face, but agony was a dragon, ripping me with its claws. I choked on a mouthful of vomit. Calloway swore. Together she and Sara raised me onto my knees. Calloway pounded between my shoulders until I heaved and coughed and cleared my throat. I sucked down a breath, tasted the salt on my cheeks, the sour residue, the blood and grit from where my mouth hit the pavement.

"Don't," I whispered. "Don't ever call me your love. Don't lie to me."

Sara's hand brushed over my cheek. "I would never lie to you. You are my love. Not as you once loved your Angela. But there are other ways, my friend."

The meaning of her words slowly seeped through my molasses thoughts. "My friend," I tried to say, but all I could manage was inarticulate noises.

And then the miracle happens. I hear the thump, thump, thump *of a helicopter. SPC Jefferson is stabbing her finger to the east. Ours, yes, ours. I rouse the other patients and we creep toward salvation. One, two, three scramble through the open doors, when gunfire breaks out. One of the soldiers stumbles. I drag her to her feet. Hand her over to Jefferson. That's when I hear the rebel yell. That's when the bullet shatters my arm.*

A third voice joined the argument over my body. A stranger, a young man with a New Jersey accent I could barely understand. He and Calloway exchanged a rapid-fire dialogue thick with medical terms. Penetrating wound to the left lumbar region. Possible perforation. There was talk about the ambulance, the necessity for a blood transfusion, and how to raise my core temperature. Sara broke into their conversation with arguments of her own. Something about national security.

It was then I heard the distant *thump, thump, thump* from a helicopter. I felt a cool imprint of lips against my cheek. Felt a stab in my right arm. Cold flooded my veins, and I was falling, falling, falling into darkness at last.

$$\text{\textcircled{?}}$$

It was just like any other downtime in the unit. Saúl sat cross-legged on his bunk, smoking a cheap cigar. I lay on my back and waved my hand to blow the smoke away. In between was a bottle of Jim Beam Black Label and two glasses.

Why did you die, Saúl?

He took a drag from the cigar.

No reason at all. What else did you expect, Captain Watson? That we would dance through this war, invincible?

But of course I had expected that. I had always wanted the impossible, as my mother would say. I wanted the best university, the best job, the best life, and never mind any obstacles in the way. My mother and father had warned me, tried to school my expectations, even as they taught me to aim for the skies.

Goddamn skies, I said.

Saúl laughed.

$$\text{\textcircled{?}}$$

Later, some interminable stretch of time later, I emerged from the darkness to the brilliant glare of indoors, to stark white walls and a circle of masked faces peering at me. Sara had vanished. So had my device, leaving behind a strange void. My mouth felt sticky and dry, and when I tried to speak, to give them my own diagnosis, I could only make a croaking noise, which they ignored.

The strangers bundled me from one location to the next. When I struggled, they fastened padded cuffs around my wrist and ankles. There were more stabs from needles, more shameful episodes involving catheters and probing, as if I were merely an object to be inspected and repaired. I wanted Sara. I wanted a friend to hold my hand and whisper reassurances in my ear. I never got them.

As from a distance, I registered what had to be standard prep for surgery. I tried to explain that I understood the procedures. That the bullet was not like the one from Alton. Of course no one paid attention to me. I had never paid attention to my own patients. I vowed that the next time I operated on someone, anyone, I would tell my patient what to expect.

If there would ever be a next time.

ℭ

There were more dreams, interspersed with other, more lucid interludes. Once or twice I thought I saw a familiar face. Jacob, several times. Faith Bellaume. Roberta Thompson. Imaginary visions. Wishful ones.

Eventually I woke and remained awake.

Sunlight poured through the window, pale and inadequate. Late afternoon, then. The presence of the window itself meant I had been transferred from surgery to a convalescent ward. My right arm was immobilized, with IV drips installed. Nutrients and hydration, I guessed. The dull throb in my right hand would be the needle for the pain medication.

My ribs ached, too, but that could have been from bruising or even dislocated pain. My gut felt entirely numb, which I suspected meant more severe injuries.

I was shot. I guess that qualifies as severe.

"Captain Watson. You're awake."

I suppressed the urge for snark. I was too tired. I hurt too much. "Where am I?"

My visitor came into view. She was a young white woman, her brown hair slicked back, with one tattoo on her upper arm that came into view when she reached to take my pulse. "You are at the VA hospital, Captain. Do you remember what brought you here?"

An enemy of the state was my first thought. But I simply shook my head.

My nurse operated the controls to tilt my bed at an angle, then offered me a cup of water, which I drank. Clear, fresh, blessedly cold, and free of medication. Her name badge said she was Ellen Kirby, RN. She was glad to see me awake. She had not served in the war, whichever war you chose, but she had a brother stationed in Kentucky and a sister overseas with the Coast Guard. Her manner was pleasant and professional, calculated to set me at ease. I found myself liking her.

"And," she added, this time with less assurance, "you have a visitor."

"Oh." My voice came out as a harsh exhalation. "Who is it?"

But Kirby had vanished. In her place stood a figure dressed in drab and anonymous gray. A woman, I realized belatedly, her blond hair pulled back over a narrow skull. She held a thin tablet in one hand, and she wore a set of earbuds and implants. No lace gloves, but I noticed a wide silver bracelet that glittered with indicator lights.

"Captain Watson, I'm Special Agent Davidsson. I have several questions for you."

She flipped open an ID. It looked official, as far as I could tell, with its badge and photo and a quantity of text in fine print. *As if you knew what a genuine ID looked like,* said Sara's mocking voice in memory.

"Where am I?" I said. "They told me the VA hospital. They didn't mention which one."

Davidsson tucked her ID in her breast pocket. I caught a glimpse of a gun holster underneath. "We thought you knew," she said. "You're in Washington, DC. They brought you directly here by Lifestar. We thought that best, under the circumstances."

"I can imagine," I whispered. "What kinds of questions?"

"Just a standard interview, to confirm your role in recent events." She granted me a thin smile. "I trust you will cooperate."

I nodded, reluctantly. It wasn't as though I could sucker-punch this woman and make a daring escape through the hospital corridors.

Agent Davidsson tapped her fingers over her tablet screen and recited her name, mine, and the date. October 29, it was. Yet another clue how much time had passed. She asked me to recite my name, former rank, and military ID. Then she rattled off what had to be a standard formula about this interview taking place under the regulations governing matters of national security. I understood that I would not be granted a lawyer, nor would I discuss the questions or my answers with anyone without proper security clearance.

"State your name and the words *I understand and agree*."

I did not understand, nor did I agree. "What if I refuse?"

"Then our interview changes its nature."

Her fingers hovered over her tablet. I had no doubt she could summon reinforcements with a single tap. Reinforcements who would transport me to a different kind of hospital, with more guards and fewer windows.

"Fine," I rasped. "I understand and I agree."

Davidsson smiled. "Thank you. Let us proceed."

She told me that it was understood I had not fully recovered, so our interview would take place over several days. She began with an overview of my activities starting on August 20. The reason for my appointment at VA headquarters, more specifically why I came to DC and not one of the regional branches. She did not question me about my decision to remain in DC, but she did inquire about every mundane detail associated with that decision. The name and address of the hostel. The number of jobs I applied for. The various shops I frequented during that interval, from the hole-in-the-wall deli to the used-book store. I was reminded of Sara's comment about sending out a hundred bots to confuse our watchers about her true intent.

"What about Alton?" I said at last. "Don't you want to know those details?"

Davidsson shrugged. "That is not the purpose of this interview."

"It should be. All this . . ." I attempted to wave my arm. "This is all about Alton and Jonesboro and all the rest."

My mention of Jonesboro provoked the barest flicker of those eyebrows. "We are not ignorant of our own affairs," she said. "But those questions are for later."

Right. I shut down after that. Let them lock me away in one of those invisible prisons. I no longer cared. When Davidsson tried to insist, I slammed my head against my pillow. Slammed it again and again until my vital signs jumped and RN Kirby burst into the room. Kirby grabbed hold of my head with both hands. I tried to fight her, but then what little strength I had vanished. I collapsed against my pillow, weeping.

♀

Davidsson had vanished, but I knew she would return. Meanwhile, the nurses kept me sedated, and an anonymous doctor made hourly visits to adjust my pain medication. I overheard enough to catch another handful of clues. The bullet had penetrated my left lumbar region. The ache I felt was the result of a rib deliberately broken to help them operate. The bullet had not shattered, but there was damage to the kidney.

"Why am I alive?" I asked the nurse on night shift. RN CHO, said her name tag.

"That sounds like a philosophical question," she said.

"That sounds like an evasion," I replied.

She laughed but did not answer my question. Just as well. I wasn't sure I wanted to know the real answer.

Agent Davidsson returned the following afternoon.

"Tell me about your encounter with Agent Holmes."

"Tell me about Jonesboro," I said. I was still fuzzy from the sedatives and my words came out slurred.

Davidsson made a pointed gesture toward her tablet.

I sighed. Such an eloquent threat. But effective. "Fine. I met her August thirtieth, in the National Gallery of Art. Dalí's *Last Supper,* if that makes a difference. She wanted a partner to share the rent. I wanted out of that damned hostel. My friend Jacob Bell—"

I stopped. Wished I could snatch Jacob's name back. But of course they already knew about Jacob from our military records and my journal.

"He introduced us," I said.

"A fortunate coincidence."

"I'm not so sure." I made an abortive gesture to take in the hospital room and the IVs still plugged into my body. Davidsson's mouth tilted into the barest of smiles, which vanished almost immediately.

"Tell me more about that introduction," she said. "How soon did that take place after your first encounter with Bell?"

We continued with more questions about that day, that week. Davidsson was especially interested in Sara's recommendation that I take the job at the VA Medical Center, and our arrangements for rent at 2809 Q Street. I wondered if Davidsson had read my journal, then realized of course she had. She knew about those eight days when I nearly succumbed to drugs and despair. She had read my rants about the VA Medical Center, my rage and grief about my lost arm that evening when I vowed to take back my life.

I am naked, undone. My heart lies open like a bloody jewel.

Fragments of a poem Angela had loved to recite. I remembered how I told her the poet needed a good dose of reality, or they wouldn't write such nonsense. Angela had shrugged and said occasional extravagance was good for the soul. I wondered what she would say about Sara, who was nothing but extravagant—the way she spoke, her sprawling script across the page, the glittering lace gloves she wore.

Davidsson had asked me another question, which I had missed. I shook my head. "Where is Sara? Is she safe?"

No answer.

"What about Jacob? What about Calloway?"

Still no answer.

"It *is* about Jonesboro. And Alton. Calloway told us that much. You know it."

"We are not here to dissect what I know. Now, I would like to hear more about your financial arrangements with Sara Holmes."

"Fuck those arrangements. Let me tell you about Belinda Díaz, about Geller, Molina, and Walker. Let me tell you about Saúl Martínez."

On and on I rambled, telling her everything I knew or suspected. Davidsson simply listened without any trace of compassion or concern. Eventually I ran out of words and strength and sank back into my pillow, eyes shut and my heart fluttering strangely in my chest.

♀

Four more sessions, each much shorter and less dramatic. Davidsson never declared our interview finished, but after two days passed and she did not make an appearance, I gathered she had either collected enough evidence or she was tired of my rants.

Truth be told, I was tired of my rants.

"How am I doing?" I asked Kirby the next morning.

"Better than you ought to." She had brought me a breakfast tray with oatmeal and stewed fruit that looked as though someone has resurrected the products from the late 1950s. My first solid meal since I could remember. "No peritonitis. No bullet fragments wandering around ready to make trouble. We're keeping an eye on your kidney function, of course."

"Of course."

There were other nurses on the day shift, but Kirby was my favorite. Ever since she realized I would not argue about medical treatment, she'd answered all my questions. So, when she insisted I eat this miserable gray goop that passed for nutrients, I didn't resist. Much.

"All done?" she said at last.

"Done enough, sunshine."

Kirby laughed. "They told me you were a right tartar."

"Who are 'they'? And do you even know what that word means?"

She laughed again and exited with the tray. I cursed softly and steadily. It wasn't as though I could do more. Simply eating had drained me. The surgeon part of me calculated how much longer I needed to recover. At least three, four more weeks, until they discharged me, based on what Kirby told me. Several more weeks until I could call myself whole.

And meanwhile?

But *meanwhile* was too vague a term.

I was dozing when the door clicked open an hour or two

later. I started, then saw one of the regular janitors. He gave me a perfunctory smile as he emptied out the trash can into one bin, the medical waste into another. He replaced the plastic liners, made a note on his log. Then with a few swift steps, he stood next to my bed. "They said you might like these," he said softly as he deposited a sheaf of paper, clipped together and folded in half lengthwise, underneath my right hand.

I waited through a count of ten after he left before I dared to examine this gift.

The paper was thick and rough, with a faint gray cast, like the stuff used by cheap newsfeed printers. The outer sheet was blank, but the rest were covered with dense lines of print, the ink faintly smeared, as though these pages had been plucked only a few moments ago from the machine. I took a moment to bring my pulse and breathing under control before I unfolded the printout.

Washington Post. Morning Edition, November 5.

The headlines were almost enough to send my vitals into overdrive. Donnovan the next president. Stock exchange ricocheting from bull to bear. A positive response from Europe, a more ambiguous one from Africa, South America, and Asia. Yeah, well, I could understand that with Donnovan's record.

A part of me, the illogical angry part, wished Donnovan had lost. Not to Jeb Foley, that miserable toad, but to someone worthy of the title. Sanches had done her best, given the legacy of Bush and Trump, and those who followed that same creed. Her best was damned good. And yet, here we were, with yet another white man to rule over us.

The headlines talked about the continuing difficulties for the professional sports industry, the wrangling between Congress and the president over military funding. The pages were creased and rumpled, as if handled by several careless people, and I nearly missed the first clue.

November 4. Lieutenant Colonel Regina Wells Vandermay has received a Meritorious Service Medal for her tireless service in Afghanistan, Syria, and the Crimea, and most recently in the Fourth Combat Brigade of the First Infantry Division, including several key actions in Jonesboro and Little Rock. She received the medal from Major General Patricia Bennett in a ceremony at Fort Campbell in Tennessee. Vandermay will retire from active service in December this same year, but will continue to serve her country in an advisory position.

I wanted to punch my bed. Damn that Vandermay. She was as guilty as Nadine Adler. She had agreed to experiment on her own soldiers—not once, but half a dozen times. She had taken credit for their impossible victories. She had covered up the aftermath. The government might not see things my way, however. Vandermay's crimes had led directly to those victories in Jonesboro and Little Rock. Perhaps they'd had nothing to do with those crimes, but they sure liked to take credit for what went right. Perhaps they considered her early retirement punishment enough.

Or a bribe for her to keep silent.

Oh, Sara. Is that what you wanted? Justice served as long as it was convenient?

Sara Holmes was not here. But I suspected she was the agent behind this mysterious gift. Were there any more clues? I scanned through several articles about returning veterans, funding difficulties with the VA, a pious speech from Jeb Foley about the ravages of an unnecessary war . . .

And there I found my second clue. Underneath Foley's useless blathering, the paper was double-creased, making the shape of an arrow, for anyone of a suspicious mind. I followed that arrow and turned the page . . .

Adler Industries in Turmoil, read the headline.

The paragraphs that followed were hardly less sensational. Nadine Adler, former CEO of Adler Industries, had vanished from the country twelve days ago, only hours after a warrant was issued for her arrest. The details of that warrant remained obscure, but various news squirts listed rumors about misuse of corporate funds and possible corruption charges concerning various government contracts. Rose Adler, older sister to Nadine Adler and a board member of Adler Industries, had come out of her self-imposed retirement to assume the CEO position until the board of directors could vote on a replacement. Even then, the company faced a series of crippling fines and the loss of their military contracts.

Nothing about FBI involvement, however.

Nothing about Agent Sara Holmes.

I lay back against my pillow and stared at the ceiling above. The stark white paint. The loops of cables and tubes off to one side that snaked down to connections along the floor, ready for any doctor or nurse to save my life, barring cases of national security.

So. My enemy had a face at last. Several. Nadine Adler, who had used her research companies to construct the drugs that drove soldiers onward past reason, and later killed them. Lieutenant Colonel Vandermay, who used those drugs to further her own career. Maybe Sanches and Donnovan weren't explicitly involved, but neither had questioned these impossible victories. Neither had investigated what lay behind Alton, Illinois.

Neither had cared about Private Belinda Díaz and her comrades.

Only Sara had cared, in her own strange way.

And she isn't here.

I remembered back when Alida Sanches had won her first

election. *We had us some dark days back in 2017,* my mother had said. *All those mainstream newspapers talking about white people this, and white people that, and woe, their lives were so hard. As if only white people needed jobs, as if only white people could be Americans. But we got past those dark days. The sun did rise again. Maybe it wasn't as bright as we liked, but there it was.*

So maybe the sun wasn't as bright as I liked, but at least we had a sun. And maybe, someday soon, if we didn't give up, we'd get us a bright bold sun shining down on every citizen of the country.

There was a pattern of dots imprinted on each page. I pressed my thumb on the topmost one. Once the paper had shivered to miniature black flakes, I pressed the next and the next, until they all turned into dust.

November 11. _____

I have my journal. My real journal. And my favorite
pen. Only one bottle of ink, though. I shall have to
ration my words, unless the single bottle is a signal that
my stay won't last much longer. Or my mysterious
benefactor chooses to gift me with another.

Mysterious, yes. Because the journal and pen
materialized overnight, wrapped in crumbling
newspapers dated 2013 and tied with a silk cord. Kirby
claimed the package was in my room when she arrived
on shift. Cho, the senior night nurse, said she didn't
know anything about any packages. I bet they were both
telling the truth. I bet I know who retrieved my pens
and journal from the apartment and infiltrated the
hospital as easily as she once infiltrated my trust.

If I write her name three times, will she magically
appear?

19

DECEMBER 1. *RN Frances Cho brought me the news during the eleven P.M. rounds that I would get my walking papers today. She made a show of checking my blood pressure and oxygen levels—a totally unnecessary chore, and I told her as much—while the trainee she had in tow turned off lights and lowered the volume of the TV. They tried to take away my pen and journal. I told them to stuff it. Frances smiled and said she would miss me. Dammit, I'll miss her, too.*

Frances was right. By eight A.M., the nurses had restored my long-absent device. At nine A.M., the patient services administrator appeared with a binder of paperwork and an electronic slate. His badge read M. K. WHITTAKER. He looked seventeen, or perhaps that was me feeling aged beyond my ordinary years.

"You've been cleared for discharge," he told me.

Whittaker led me through all the signatures and the releases. There were fewer than I expected, and more than I thought necessary. The binder was mine to keep, he told me, and contained photocopies of everything.

My next visitor was RN Kirby, who checked over the electronic clipboard at the foot of my bed before she set a familiar duffel bag on the chair. She had a new tattoo over one wrist and her hair was edged in purple. Just barely within regulation. I was going to miss her, too.

Kirby smiled at me. "A friend left you a change of clothes. Just press the button there when you're ready."

Before she had shut the door, I had the bag unzipped and its contents poured onto my hospital bed.

It was a mass of dark gray wool, shot through with gold and crimson thread. Like the skies at sunrise. I separated one item from its fellows—a jacket cut long and loose, with sleeves that belled out. The second item was matching trousers. I sorted through the rest and found a black silk tunic and everything else I would need, from skin outward. There was even a small jar of oil for my hair.

One last gift, I thought. *She's saying good-bye.*

Underneath everything I found a wine-colored down coat with a hood. And yes, there were black wool gloves in the pockets. It was the same coat she had lent to me on our mission from Florida to Michigan.

This was most certainly a good-bye.

I had the sudden urge to stuff this gift into the trash bin. I had a second, equally strong urge to bury my face in the cloth. Both of them inappropriate and sure to bring Kirby running. Instead, I breathed slowly and carefully until my pulse no longer thundered in my skull. Then, with great care, I dressed in that exquisite suit, which of course fit me as though Sara had measured my body herself. I rubbed the oil into my scalp and hair, working any tangles free. Then I packed my journal into the duffel bag and rang the bell.

It was at the exit where I had my next surprise.

Jacob Bell waited for me outside. He was dressed in a military surplus jacket, patched with mismatched fabric, and a black knit cap pulled low over his forehead. His arms were crossed tightly, and he was scowling.

"You don't want to be here," I said.

"No, I don't."

The next moment we were hugging each other fiercely.

"God, I missed you," I said. "Jacob—"

"Shut up. I know, Captain. I . . . Never mind what I know."

I started to laugh, couldn't stop. Jacob held me tighter. He was weeping, too, but deep inside where no one could see it. *Oh, Jacob, we hurt you, Sara and I. We had no choice, but that doesn't make it better. It doesn't make it okay.*

"I'm going away," he said. "I have a cousin up in Maine. He runs a news squirt, or maybe it's as respectable as a feed these days, with local news, politics, and such. He says he's getting enough contributions to hire some staff, and he wants me to write about the war. It won't pay much, but I still have my pension."

"Doesn't sound like you, not at all." I drew back and wiped the tears from my eyes. I was losing everyone, everything, and I didn't like it.

Jacob touched my arm lightly. "Hey, Captain. It'll be fine. I have me a new job, nothing much, but enough to tide me over while I go to college. Maybe medical school after that." He almost smiled at my surprise. "Yes, me. I want to help the rest of us, Captain. The ones who come home empty and raging. The ones like you and me."

We hugged each other again.

"You are my friend," I said. "I didn't do right by you."

"You were angry, is all. Been there myself, as you know."

I nodded. Hugged him tighter.

"I have something for you."

He gently detached my grip from his jacket and pressed an envelope into my hands. "From Sara," he said. "She takes care of her people."

$\wp$

The envelope contained two fifty-dollar bills, scented with clove, and a square of parchment with one line of print: *10 A.M., Georgetown University Hospital.* Underneath, Sara had written, *For you, my love.*

And this time, I did not mind.

$\wp$

It was already 9:35. I flagged down a cab and demanded the driver take the fastest route to Georgetown University Hospital. When the man balked, I shoved one crumpled fifty into his face. "Drive, damn you. Or I shall loose the hounds of hell into your life."

Later I wasn't sure which had terrified him the most—my clearly manic self or the threat of hounds. Whatever. He barely waited for me to click the seat belt before he flung himself into the DC morning traffic.

Nine fifty-five. Destination achieved.

"Dr. Watson." The receptionist greeted me with a smile. She fed me an expensive cup of coffee and had a minion escort me into a private waiting room. Within ten minutes, a precisely timed interval that allowed me to savor the coffee, another minion brought me up a private elevator to a level marked EXECUTIVE OFFICES.

I remembered this floor, these sun-filled spaces. I had interviewed here three years ago, shortly before I volunteered for the army. There was the spacious interview room where I had chatted with the chief of surgery, with its wide windows that overlooked Shaw Field and the Potomac beyond.

There were several significant changes, however. Both the chief of surgery and the CMO were present. And when I exchanged those perfunctory greetings, I thought I detected a hint of nervousness, as though our roles had reversed themselves over the past few years.

We worked our way through the usual pattern of exchanges. The stock gratitude offered a veteran for her service. The regret for my injuries, as though they themselves shared any blame in the matter. Two months ago, I might have raged at them, told them to fuck off with their artificial sympathy, but the month with Faith Bellaume had helped me gain distance and perspective. If these two powerful women resorted to platitudes, it was because they feared to offend.

Intent might not be magical, but it counts for something. Words my mother said when I came home from school furious because some well-meaning teacher had called me articulate.

And so I returned their platitudes with ones of my own. I complimented them on their reputation and that of Georgetown. I spoke of colleagues in the service who talked about the good the hospital did. And when we had exhausted these, the conversation turned at last to the reason for their invitation.

"We want you," the chief of surgery said.

She'd used that same inflection three years before.

"Let me be more specific," the CMO said. "We have need of surgeons like you, Dr. Watson. Your track record throughout medical school and your residency were exceptional, which is why we made you an offer three years ago. You've done much more, so much more, since then. Your experience . . ." And I swear she was about to say *in the trenches* but quickly reconsidered. "Your experience in the service brings invaluable insight, and not just for veterans. We need that insight."

"We need *you*," the chief of surgery said.

I glanced from one woman to the other. Waited.

The CMO smiled. "Do you need us to be more explicit, Dr. Watson? Or is that indecision I see?"

"Not indecision, but uncertainty." I drew my left sleeve back over my device and held it up. Its metal plating had turned dull, and even though I held it still, it twitched and shivered in the thin December sunlight.

"A surgeon needs two hands," I said matter-of-factly. "Two good hands."

"You shall have two," the CMO said. "Let me explain the terms."

The terms were straightforward. The position offered was that of senior surgeon, two full pay grades above the offer I had rejected three years ago. Along with the position came the guarantee of a new prosthetic arm—one of the advanced models that could be custom-fitted and programmed for my work.

"You will need training," the chief of surgery told me. "Four months at the minimum. Until then, you would have an advisory position with the hospital, with commensurate pay."

Commensurate pay turned out to be 60 percent of my future salary, not counting a generous signing bonus, plus extras for mentoring junior staff.

It was everything I wanted. It was clearly a bribe for my silence about recent events on the front and in Newark, New Jersey.

I closed my eyes a moment, pointed my thoughts toward the future and not these past two months. Sara had bid me farewell. She would no doubt be assigned to another city, another partner. This new job meant I could keep the apartment for myself, or one like it.

Damn you, Sara Holmes. Do you think you can bribe me so easily?

But Sara had understood from that first moment how much I valued beauty and quiet. Gifts . . . gifts were temporary, but even if this one proved temporary, I could not resist.

"I accept," I said.

The CMO nodded briskly. "Excellent. There are a few formalities to go through. My assistant has the necessary paperwork . . ."

Another hour and I was free.

The fifty dollars was more than enough to buy me a ride back to 2809 Q Street. I preferred to walk the half hour along the banks of the Potomac and up Thirty-First. So much had changed in these past seven weeks. The election posters and signboards had vanished, replaced by advertisements for Christmas. Our new Democratic Progressive president was victorious. True, he faced a wall of Republicans and Conservative Party members in the House, but the third-party progressive factions continued to give him their conditional support. Even if he didn't have a mandate, he had a clear victory.

Somewhere, hidden away in the White House, Alida Sanches planned her retirement years. Somewhere else, the New Confederacy plotted to win their war. They had not yet surrendered. They might never.

I came at last to Q Street and number 2809. The flower boxes were empty, cleared of their dead stalks. The oak and apple trees had long ago shed their leaves, and the faint breeze that whirled about me carried the scent of snow.

Do I belong here? I asked myself.

Yes felt more like a challenge than the truth. And yet I needed, loved, a good challenge. Or I thought I had, those three months ago.

I climbed the steps to the front door and pressed my thumb against the security pad. Immediately the lock unclicked, so quickly I could almost imagine its apologies for the delays of last September.

The entryway had not changed. There were still the pots of ferns and English ivy, tended by Hudson Realty's meticulous staff. The marble tiles still gleamed, and the corridors were still hushed.

I rode the elevator up to the second floor and unlocked the door to apartment 2B.

It was not until I had shut the door behind me that my self-possession deserted me. I let my bag drop, tilted my head back against the heavy wooden door.

Holmes had arranged that Georgetown offer, damn her. The salary, the promise of a new device, the ability to resume the life I had before the war. (Almost. Not quite. But let's not be picky.) The salary would account for my presence here. And my presence would offer a transition for Agent Holmes from one identity to another. And Jacob, Jacob she had sent off to his own new career. All safe. All wrapped up into a tidy bundle.

I expelled a breath, as if I could expel my anger, and continued into the parlor.

Nothing had changed in the past six and a half weeks. No, that was not correct, and the exceptions proved unsettling. The kitchen was immaculate, floors mopped and counters wiped clean. But I could see a few broken bits from the teapot Sara had swept to one side. Someone had clearly watered her herb garden, but the herbs themselves had overgrown their pots. I rubbed my fingers over the sage leaves and breathed in their fresh sharp scent. Small comfort, but I was used to taking small comfort.

Would she come back for these? Or had she discarded them as she had me?

I pushed myself away from the herbs and continued along the corridor, noting the bathroom with its shampoos and oils and soaps, the other signs of Sara's former presence here, then turned toward the bedrooms.

It only took a glance through Sara's open door to see what had changed, what had not. The piano remained in its glorious sunlit nook. The paintings with their secret screens had vanished. Someone had cleared away the wine bottles, the cups, and the accumulated dust. I could not make any sense of what had changed, what had not. But my belly trembled as I passed on toward my own bedroom.

Less than nothing had changed here. My clothes were still scattered over the floor, just as Sara had left them. My books were still on the shelves, with a copy of *Kindred* on the bedside table, where I had attempted to pass the hours that last evening. A film of dust covered my desk, without even a handprint or two.

But someone did come here, I thought. *Someone who robbed me of my journal and my pens and ink.*

I heard the faint tread of shoes behind me and spun around.

Sara Holmes stood in the doorway, arms crossed and with a faintly challenging air. Right. I could get behind that kind of attitude. I crossed my own arms and waited for her to speak.

Her mouth tilted into a smile. "Hello, my love. I see you found your way back."

My pulse ticked upward at the phrase *my love*. I wanted to protest, but I thought I understood her better. At least I hoped so. "I did. I found your gifts. Thank you. But what about—"

"I had nothing to do with Georgetown. No, that's a lie. I did, but only because I badgered my chief into granting you the kind of arm you deserved. You, *you* earned that yourself, back in April. And you earned it a second time over, at the VA

Medical Center. The rest is me, and our country, doing what we failed to do before."

Oh. Oh and thank you and why do I still want to bash her over the head?

"What about your next mission?" I demanded. "What about that?"

My words came out harsh, but something in my expression must have warned her otherwise, because she grinned. "Oh, that? Well, I did tell them I had unfinished business here. Not to mention a colleague in need of cover. Was I right?" she asked, her voice going soft and rough. "Do I have unfinished business here?"

The breath stilled in my chest. I nodded, more stiffly than I liked. "You do, actually. You promised me one more question, among other things. But this time, I want an honest answer."

Sara Holmes regarded me with a brilliant smile. "And perhaps you shall get one. Let's make a reservation for dinner, and we can discuss how honest I should be."

ACKNOWLEDGMENTS

There are many people who helped me turn this idea into a story, and the story into this book. I am so damned lucky to have such friends, mentors, and co-conspirators. Guys, guys, thank you so much.

Shout-outs and gratitude to . . .

Stephanie Burgis, who read the first draft chapter by chapter and cheered me on.

My wise and sharp-eyed readers Delia Sherman, Jessica Reisman, Hyeonjin Park, Darlene Marshall, Paul Weimer, Jeremy Brett, Alice Loweecy, Cat Hellisen, Nerine Dorman, Paul Magnan, and Fade Manley.

Tempest Bradford and Nisi Shawl, for their workshop Writing the Other.

My amazing editor, Amber Oliver, and the rest of the team at Harper Voyager, for all their hard work to turn my manuscript into a finished book.

Michelle Cahill, for telling me I was awesome.

And finally, my husband and son for giving me the love, the space, and the encouragement to write, not to mention reminding me when to eat. I could not do any of this without you.

ABOUT THE AUTHOR

Claire O'Dell grew up in the suburbs of Washington, DC, in the years of the Vietnam War and the Watergate scandal. She attended high school just a few miles from the house where Mary Surratt once lived and where John Wilkes Booth conspired to kill Lincoln. All this might explain why she spent so much time in the history and political science departments at college. Claire currently lives in Manchester, Connecticut, with her family and two idiosyncratic cats.